ALSO BY EMILY HARDING

How Freaking Romantic

BOOKS BY EMILY HARDING AND AUDREY BELLEZZA

Anne of Avenue A

Elizabeth of East Hampton

Emma of 83rd Street

THANK YOU FOR REMEMBERING

A NOVEL

EMILY HARDING

GALLERY BOOKS
New York Amsterdam/Antwerp London
Toronto Sydney/Melbourne New Delhi

Gallery Books
An Imprint of Simon & Schuster, LLC
1230 Avenue of the Americas
New York, NY 10020

This book is a work of fiction. Any references to historical events, real people, or real places are used fictitiously. Other names, characters, places, and events are products of the author's imagination, and any resemblance to actual events or places or persons, living or dead, is entirely coincidental.

The authorized representative in the EEA is Simon & Schuster Nederland B.V., Herculesplein 96, 3584 AA Utrecht, Netherlands. info@simonandschuster.nl

First Gallery Books trade paperback edition September 2026

GALLERY BOOKS and colophon are registered trademarks of Simon & Schuster, LLC

Simon & Schuster strongly believes in freedom of expression and stands against censorship in all its forms. For more information, visit BooksBelong.com.

Interior design by Julia Jacintho

Manufactured in the United States of America

10 9 8 7 6 5 4 3 2 1

Library of Congress Control Number: 2026936437

ISBN 978-1-6682-2520-2
ISBN 978-1-6682-2521-9 (ebook)

PRAISE FOR *HOW FREAKING ROMANTIC*

"A perfect balm for the love-shy heart."

—*Library Journal* (starred review)

"Flawless. Harding is set to be a rom-com powerhouse."

—Lauren Layne, *New York Times* bestselling author of *Made in Manhattan*

"The setup! The snark! The spice! Emily Harding had me at 'storming the office of her best friend's ex-husband's divorce lawyer' and kept me cackling all the way through. This book is an absolute delight."

—Colleen Oakley, *USA Today* bestselling author of *The Mostly True Story of Tanner & Louise*

"With razor-sharp wit and perfect prose, Emily Harding has crafted a romance that had me laughing one minute and crying the next. Harding's characters are heartbreakingly real, and Bea is the exact kind of heroine I love to root for. *How Freaking Romantic* is sexy and smart and completely captivating!"

—Falon Ballard, *USA Today* bestselling author of *Change of Heart*

"[A] witty debut. The zippy plot and endearing love story will leave readers wanting more."

—*Publishers Weekly*

"Inject this cynical angry woman into my veins! *How Freaking Romantic* is truly for the ragey girls among us, and I loved every second of it. Emily Harding writes the scrappiest, wittiest, most heartfelt characters to root for, and we're all the luckier for it."

—Ali Rosen, bestselling author of *Recipe for Second Chances*

"With biting wit, a tender and truthful take on modern adulthood, and a romance that threatens to burn up the pages, *How Freaking Romantic* is one of my favorite reads this year. This book made me an Emily Harding fan for life."

—Sarah T. Dubb, author of *Birding with Benefits*

"The verdict is in: Emily Harding's *How Freaking Romantic* delivers with snarky banter and steamy sexual tension. This book takes enemies-to-lovers to law school and schools us all—on the complexity of evolving friendships, on dropping our defenses in the name of love, and on what to do when that new co-professor is hot as hell. (Give in! That's what!)"

—Nora Dahlia, author of *Pick-Up*

"The humorous chemistry and enemies-to-lovers trope between Beatrice and Nathan makes the story a fun read from a promising author."

—Booklist

"Emily Harding has a forever fan in me! I fell in love with her heroine Beatrice from the very first page. Watching her relationship with Nathan bloom is the perfect antidote for anyone who ever wondered if they are too loud, too quirky, or just too much. With Bea and Nathan's exceptionally original, oh-so-swoon-worthy love story, readers will be reminded that even when life is complicated, the best type of romance should be simple. I simply loved this book."

—Becky Chalsen, author of *Kismet*

For Audrey,
who is actually magic

CHAPTER 1

I don't know what time it is when I wake up in the hospital, only that Goldie Hawn is standing at the foot of my bed.

Wait. That can't be right.

"Andrew?" Goldie calls out. "Are you going to bring me my lemon, or do I have to squeeze it from my hat?"

I try to fully open my eyes, turn my head, but my body is too heavy. It's like a dozen weighted blankets have been strategically placed over each limb. All I can do is lie there as the blurry lines of the room come into focus. Gray walls, gray blanket, gray pajamas. A washed-out world where everything is muted except the glowing television mounted across from my hospital bed playing the '80s movie *Overboard*.

Huh.

I don't know why I'm in a hospital bed. Right now, it doesn't even seem like the most pressing concern. I'm much too focused on how dry my mouth is, like I swallowed a handful of sand and cotton, and why my pajamas are so ridiculously itchy. Oh God, are they polyester? Did someone give me polyester pajamas?

My grandmother is going to be so disappointed in me, I think. That was one of her rules for life: Never wear synthetic materials; they disrupt your divine energy. But that concern is quickly usurped by a new thought: *Do hospital pajamas count as disruptive?* Then another: *I should ask her*. And then another: *Wait . . . I can't ask her. She's dead.*

That's right. My grandmother died two years ago. And honestly, the fact I didn't immediately recall this should be more worrying than the polyester. But my brain is too foggy to hold firmly on to any one thought, especially when my half-open eyes find the television again. It's an old unit and the colors are dull, but I don't care. Right now, the hospital bed and the polyester and my grandmother take a back seat to Goldie Hawn as she glides across the television screen in a stunning red swimsuit, her blond hair swept up in a high bun. She's that perfect shade of blond, really—buttery without being too yellow, bright without being too platinum. The color I've been chasing for years.

I'm so riveted by the movie I almost miss the sound of someone sighing nearby, low and gravelly. The sound thrums through my body, finally dragging my attention away from the movie. I try to loll my head to the side to see where it came from, but the motion takes effort, like I'm operating my body underwater. When I finally manage it, I'm rewarded with the view of a man. A doctor. At least, I think he's a doctor. Why else would he be standing a few feet away from my bed, glasses perched on his nose and his brow furrowed as he studies the nearby beeping machine? Except he's not wearing a white coat like doctors do on TV. Instead, he has on a thick navy sweater that's fraying along the neckline, and there's about a week's worth of stubble along his jaw. His dark hair is too long for a doctor, too, like he's missed about a year's worth of haircuts. Shouldn't he be wearing a hairnet? Or am I thinking of food workers?

Regardless, this question isn't nearly as pressing as the one currently sitting at the forefront of my mind.

"Excuse me," I croak, only slightly aware that my voice sounds like I spent the night gargling shards of glass.

He stills, then turns enough to look at me over the rim of his tortoiseshell glasses, a serious brow and serious eyes and a mouth that should be serious, too, except his lips are so full, it almost looks like he's pouting.

"Do you think Goldie Hawn uses purple shampoo?" I ask.

His expression skews with confusion and something else, something I can't pinpoint. "I'm sorry?"

Oh, his voice is lovely. Deep and rumbly in a way that I love. But there's also a slight tinge to it. Not annoyance, exactly . . . maybe concern? I don't know. I would ask him, but I can't because Kurt Russell is on-screen now, and the only thing I can focus on is the circumference of Kurt's biceps. Have I always found sleeveless T-shirts on men sexy?

"Do you need something?" Doctor Sweater asks, his deep voice breaking through my blurry consciousness.

What were we talking about? Oh, that's right. Goldie's hair. I flop my head to the side again, ready to swing my own long blond locks over my shoulder to explain the importance of a good toner.

But when I finally manage to lift my hand up to my head, ready to comb my fingers through the tangles and knots that inevitably extend down past my shoulders, there's . . . nothing. Just a blunt straight edge at my chin where the rest of my hair should be. I try to find it again. And again. Then I run both hands through what I can only imagine is a blunt bob, clumsily grasping at the ends as if pulling at them will somehow make the missing eight inches reappear.

"Where's my hair?" I ask, eyes wide, my brain finally connecting all the disparate dots around me. If my hair is gone, and I'm wearing polyester in a hospital bed with an IV line connected to my wrist, then something must be very, very wrong. "What's going on? Why am I in the hospital? Am I dying?" Then I see something out of the corner of my eye, a piece of hair sticking out from my forehead. "Are these bangs? Do I have *bangs*?"

The beeping machine begins to sound manic, but before Doctor Sweater can answer, the door to the room opens and a nurse appears, her expression calm as her gaze slides from the machine to me.

"Good afternoon," she says, stopping beside my bed. "I'm Brenda. Glad to see you're finally awake. How are you feeling?"

"Someone cut my hair," I say, hoping Brenda will grasp the severity of the situation.

"It looks really cute." Then she offers me the smile of someone who knows they're placating you and doesn't care if it's obvious that they're placating you.

Another nurse enters and I loll my head to the side to watch as she starts to fuss with the mess of tubes and wires on the other side of my bed. A moment later, the beeping machine falls silent and I turn back to Brenda to see that she's busy pushing buttons on its front panel. I also notice that Doctor Sweater is gone.

"Where's the doctor?" I ask.

"He'll be by in a few minutes. Right now, I just need to check your vitals and make sure—"

"What about Matt?"

She doesn't take her gaze away from the machine as she asks, "Who?"

"Matt Amos. My boyfriend." I'm trying to keep my voice steady but it's starting to waver the way it always does when I'm panicked. "Has anyone called him?"

"If you give me his number, I can have one of the nurses contact him. Visiting hours end at nine, so if he can get here in the next few hours—"

I try to shake my head but fail miserably. "He can't. He's not here. I mean, I know he's not *here* here. But he's not even here in LA. He left for Boston two weeks ago."

The nurse toying with my IV pauses before sharing a confused look with Brenda.

"Boston is three hours ahead of us, right?" I ask. "I always mess that up. But it doesn't matter, you can still call him, even if it's early. He won't mind."

I don't know why I add that, because of course he will mind. Over our two years together, I've learned there's nothing Matt minds more than being woken up early, especially if he's been stuck working late the night before. But I'm making an executive decision. I may not have any idea what's happening right now, but I'm sure whatever it is trumps Matt's sleep schedule.

"Okay," Brenda responds carefully. "Why don't you give me his number, and I'll give him a call myself."

I recite Matt's phone number, and Brenda notes it on the nearby computer.

"Is there anyone else we need to call, Margaret?" she asks. "Any family?"

No, I almost say. *There's only me.*

Instead I reply, "It's Marnie."

"Sorry?"

"I go by Marnie."

Brenda offers an overly sympathetic smile. "Okay, Marnie. Just hold tight and the doctor will be here soon."

By the time *Overboard* cuts to commercial, there are more nurses scurrying around my bed like they each have their own important task, though I have no idea what they're doing. Then the door to the room swings open again and a middle-aged man enters. Unlike Doctor Sweater, he looks the part with a white coat over his blue scrubs. He has a classic doctor haircut, too, gray hair that's thin and meticulously combed back, and a pair of wire reading glasses perched on his nose.

"Hello, Ms. Stephens," he says flatly, his attention on the tablet in his hands. "I'm Dr. Buterman, one of the critical care neurologists here at Mass General. How are you feeling today?"

"Okay?" I answer, only slightly aware that it comes out like a question. My foggy brain is too busy trying to place the hospital. Mass General . . . is that in Ventura? Or Burbank?

"Do you remember why you're here?" he asks.

No. I don't even know where here *is. Or why no one has turned off the television yet.*

When I don't reply, Dr. Buterman notes something on his tablet before he continues. "You were brought to the ER yesterday evening after you were found unconscious and unresponsive. The initial CT scan showed a cerebral contusion on your medial temporal lobe, causing an acute subdural hematoma . . ."

Dr. Buterman keeps talking, a steady drone of words and medical jargon I didn't even know existed. Syllables and letters strung together like they're significant. I try to follow along, or at least look like I am, but I can't keep up the ruse. Everything becomes a jumble in my mind, so when he's done, all I can say is: "I don't know what any of that means."

He sighs as he gives me a look over the rim of his glasses. And I hate how, out of everything I've been confronted by in the past few minutes, that look is the only thing that's familiar. Another person who sees a blonde from Malibu and assumes every stereotype is true.

I'm not dumb, I want to say. *I'm just terrified and confused and so so itchy.*

But I can't admit that because even though my mind still feels muddled, I know enough to not be difficult. Not even a brain injury can derail thirty years of people-pleasing tendencies.

"Sorry," I say. "It's just . . . could you explain that again in layman's terms?"

"You hit your head and your brain started bleeding," he says bluntly.

My eyes widen. "My brain is *bleeding*?"

"Not anymore. It *was* bleeding. On the right side there, but we kept you sedated overnight until it stopped." His attention goes back to his tablet. "You're lucky you got to the hospital as soon as you did, or it could have been a lot worse."

My brow furrows as I gaze down at the IV sticking out of my wrist, the various wires coming out of the sleeves of my pajamas. Despite the moonstones and dream catchers and evil eye talismans my grandmother gave me over the years—all of which are sitting in a storage unit somewhere in Malibu—this feels like the very antithesis of luck.

"But how did I hit my head?" I ask. "Did I fall? Was it at home?"

"I'd love to tell you, but like I said, you've been sedated, so we couldn't ask you. What I can say is that you hit your head twice. The first time was likely a few hours before you passed out. That injury caused the intracranial hemorrhage. You probably didn't even realize it was serious, just thought it was a headache, but the blood built up around your brain for the next few hours until you passed out and hit it the second time." He finally looks back up to me. "Do you recall anything about the initial fall?"

At this point, I think it's obvious to both of us that the answer is no, but as the seconds pass, I realize Dr. Buterman expects me to say *something*.

"Maybe I fell off the stepladder when I was cleaning out the closet?" I offer, hoping it rings true.

Dr. Buterman's brow quirks up. "Excuse me?"

"The closet in my bedroom," I explain. "My boyfriend and I are moving to Boston and I'm in the middle of packing up our apartment in Silver Lake. He got this offer from a cybersecurity firm there—which is great, but it meant he had to start right away—so we decided that he should head out first while I stay behind to pack up the apartment before I fly out to meet him. It sounded like a good idea at the time, but I didn't realize we had so much *stuff*. We've only lived together for a year, so I don't even know how that's possible. The bedroom closet alone has taken me forever. It's so big, I have to practically climb inside to reach anything, and . . ."

The words fade when I realize the line between Dr. Buterman's eyebrows doesn't disappear. I'm not sure if it's just because of my tendency toward verbal diarrhea, which has seemingly survived a traumatic brain injury, or if I've missed some fundamental component of my diagnosis.

"Let's back up a bit," he says, his tone changing slightly, like I've fully engaged his attention for the first time. "What's the last thing you remember before you woke up here?"

"The last thing I remember?" I repeat.

He nods. "Let's start with yesterday."

The question hits an empty corner in my brain. Yesterday feels like such a bizarre concept. Like "business casual" or "sustainable fashion." Something that should make sense, but if you take a minute to think about it, only gets more confusing.

Objectively, I know what I did yesterday, because every day has looked the same for the past month. After eight long hours at my desk at Probus Recruiting—proofreading job descriptions, screening résumés, and leaving countless voicemails that never seem to be returned—I navigate the 101 back home to Matt's and my apartment in Silver Lake. Then I order takeout and spend the evening packing up our life, box after box piled by the door, ready for the next adventure.

That's what my best friend, Sara, called it: an adventure. Like Matt and I were two intrepid explorers on our way to discover some uncharted territory. That sounds so much better than the truth: My boyfriend was offered a lucrative role at one of the top cybersecurity firms in the country, and I'm tagging along until I figure out what to do with my life.

But when I try to assign those moments to yesterday, recall the finer details—what I had for breakfast, what I wore to work—there's just a big empty space in my mind where all those details should go.

"I . . . I don't know," I admit, my pulse beginning to thunder in my ears.

Dr. Buterman watches my expression carefully, then notes something else on his tablet.

"But this is fine, right?" I continue, trying desperately to smile. "Forgetting a few details is probably normal for this sort of thing? I just need some time to recover. Like Maria Chen! When we were in high school, she fell off her skateboard crossing the Pacific Coast Highway after volleyball practice, and when she came to, she didn't remember where she was. But it only lasted a few minutes and then she was back. I'm sure I just need a few minutes, and then I'll be fine!"

Dr. Buterman hums to himself. "When dealing with injuries in that particular section of the brain, it's not unusual to observe some memory loss. That said, I am concerned about your level of cognitive deficit."

Cognitive deficit. The two words make my stomach drop. I remember going to see my grandmother in the hospital once her health had gotten really bad, and how the doctors used that phrase, as if a medical term could soften something awful.

"And what does that mean?" I ask carefully.

His attention goes back to his tablet. "Well, your brain is healing nicely, but it's clear there are some significant retrograde impairments likely caused by trauma to your hippocampal formation that—"

"Dr. Buterman!" I cut him off, my voice shrill with panic. "Layman's terms. Please."

He looks back up at me, his thin lips making a stark line across his face, like he's getting ready to deliver bad news to someone not aware they're about to receive it. And then I realize . . . oh, that's exactly what's happening right now, isn't it?

"That means you don't have to worry about that move to Boston, Ms. Stephens," Dr. Buterman says. "You already live here."

CHAPTER 2

"And then I told the doctor I can't be in Boston since I haven't actually *moved* to Boston yet. But he said the reason I don't remember the move or where I live or why I cut my hair is probably because the injury to my brain caused some kind of retrograde amnesia. So now I don't know how much of my memory is missing, which sounds impossible. I mean, not *impossible*, obviously, but it's not exactly something you hear about people experiencing on a regular basis, you know? But maybe the reason we don't hear about it is because this type of thing goes away so quickly. Maybe people lose their memories but get them back so often that, in the grand scheme of things, it's not a big deal. That's a possibility, right?"

The radiographer—whose name is Ryan, according to the badge clipped to his scrubs—stares down at where I'm lying in front of him, his eyes wide.

Even my broken brain knows this diatribe has reached peak levels of crazy, but I can't help it. When I was wheeled into the

CT scanning room a few minutes ago, Ryan had seemed so friendly as he helped me get situated on the machine's narrow bed. Then he made the mistake of asking how my day was going.

In my defense, that's probably not the best question to pose to a person who's about to have a brain scan. But in the moment, it didn't feel awkward—it felt like a lifeline. For a fleeting moment, I thought this man who takes pictures of brains for a living might be able to offer some solace. Maybe he sees this type of thing all the time. He might even tell me there really is nothing to worry about.

Instead, he looks like a deer caught in my proverbial headlights.

"Right," he finally replies, then clears his throat. "So . . . have you had a CT scan before?"

According to Dr. Buterman, I have. Two, in fact. But I don't remember them, since I was technically unconscious for both, so I don't know if that counts. I'm also too self-conscious at this point to ask, so I just say, "I don't think so, no."

"Well, it's pretty straightforward," he says, reaching up to press a few buttons above my head. "This bed here is going to feed you into the center of the machine, which will capture some images of your brain for the doctor to review. It'll only take a few minutes, and then you're good to go."

"Okay," I say, staring up at the ceiling panels above. "And what do I do while I'm in there?"

"Nothing," the radiographer says. "Just relax and let the machine do its magic."

My heart does an odd stumble at the word "magic."

But what if I don't believe in magic anymore? I want to ask, but Ryan disappears from sight before I can. A moment later, the long table I'm lying on begins to slide backward. Then the CT machine whirls to life around me, and for the first time in years, I wish all those things my grandmother told me were true.

The world is full of magic, Marnie, her voice whispers in my head as I close my eyes to keep from panicking. *The magic is the universe's way of telling you which way to go. All you have to do is trust it.*

When I was little, I believed her. It was hard not to—everything else had just been so confusing. At six years old, I didn't understand why my parents never came home from their trip to San Diego, or why the strangers who tried to explain it to me—opaque stories about drunk drivers and tragic accidents—always seemed so uncomfortable. But I understood when my grandmother sat me down on the floor of her bungalow in Malibu with a cup of tea and told me about real-life magic. That, despite how awful things seemed, how much I missed my parents, and how unfair losing them was, the universe had a plan for me, a destiny just waiting to reveal itself. Sitting there across from her, with jagged pieces of moonstone and rose quartz lined up on the windowsills and the smell of patchouli and sea salt in the air, it felt impossible that she could be wrong. There had to be some big, universal plan because that's the only way anything made sense. Because a world without that kind of magic was just too bleak and scary.

"You're doing great, Margaret," the radiographer's voice echoes out of a speaker nearby.

It's Marnie, I want to say. But instead, I lie still just like he told me and wait for the magic to work.

~

Overboard has apparently ended and started again from the beginning by the time Brenda wheels me back into my hospital room an hour later.

"Dr. Buterman has scheduled a few more cognitive tests for this afternoon," she says as she helps me get situated. The irony of a movie about traumatic brain injury and severe memory loss airing on a loop seems lost on her. "Nothing too crazy; they just want to get a better understanding of the extent of your memory loss. In the meantime, can I get you anything?"

I pick up the remote control and turn the television off. I don't need Goldie right now. I need something familiar. I need Matt.

"Do you happen to know where my phone is?" I ask, working hard to offer her a smile.

"I'm not sure. It might be with all your personal belongings that were collected at the ER. Do you need to call someone?"

"My boyfriend. Matt Amos," I manage to reply.

"I can ring him from the nurse's station and send the call in here. How does that sound?"

"That would be great, thank you."

"Anything else?"

I want to ask for a cup of tea—chamomile with a touch of honey is my usual go-to during stressful situations—but I don't want to be too demanding. Despite whatever overwhelming fear and panic might be coursing through my body, the last thing I need is for the nurses to not like me.

"No, I'm okay," I reply.

She smiles back and leaves, closing the door behind her so I'm alone for the first time all day.

I stare at the dark television screen for a long moment, and suddenly I want to cry. I can already feel a sob rising in my throat. Which is odd, because I've never been a big crier. Even when my grandmother died, I don't remember crying. Her funeral was full of smiles and laughter, a celebration of a life that was anything but somber. No, the only time I really cried over losing her was a year earlier, when I finally moved her into assisted living and had to sell her old bungalow in Malibu to pay for it. I stopped by one last time to find it hollowed out, crystals and rainbows gone, and I felt hollowed out, too. Suddenly, years' worth of fear and sadness and grief flowed out of me in sobs so overwhelming I thought they might never stop. But they had. By the time the Realtor arrived to pick up the keys, I had somehow swallowed the tears back, covering the red splotches on my skin with some well-placed makeup so she didn't even notice.

I don't think I can swallow back the tears now, though. Everything feels too unfamiliar, too overwhelming. Too *much*. And I have no idea what to do with that.

The phone beside my bed starts to ring. I reach for it, so desperate to grab the receiver that my hand gets tangled in the various tubes and wires hanging off my body before I can finally pick up.

"Hello?" I answer.

"Marnie?" Matt's voice fills the line, soft and familiar.

That's what finally does it. I burst into tears.

"It's okay, Marn," he says soothingly. "Don't cry, it's okay."

But it's not okay, I want to say. *It's so far from okay that I don't know how I'll ever find my way back again.*

Unfortunately, I'm in the middle of that embarrassing part of crying where I can't quite form words around the sobs, so I don't even try.

"Just take a deep breath," he says. "In and out. That's it."

I do, one after another, before I manage to eke out, "They said I hit my head. *Twice*."

"That's what they told me, too."

"The first time caused my brain to start bleeding, but I must not have known it was bleeding, because I didn't pass out until hours later after the pressure built up in my *skull*."

"I know."

"And now I'm in a hospital. In *Boston*."

He lets out a long sigh. "Yeah."

Somewhere in my head I had been holding out hope this was all some elaborate misunderstanding. That my injury had somehow made everyone else confused about my location, not me. But Matt's confirmation destroys it, and I let out another sob.

"I don't even remember what happened!" I cry. "Did I fall at our apartment? Was it when we were moving in? Did I trip over some boxes or something?"

"I don't think that was it," he says.

"Why not?"

Another sigh. Over the past two years, I've become an expert in Matt's catalogue of sighs, how a slight change in the inflection can switch the tone from sympathetic to uneasy. "Because we moved to Boston a while ago, Marnie."

Something heavy falls in the center of my gut. "A while ago" sounds substantial. An amount of time too great to be measured in days or weeks or even months.

"How long ago?"

A moment passes before he replies. "A year."

My brain trips, like a bicycle skipping a gear. We moved to Boston a year ago? But that's impossible. A year ago, Matt and I drove up to Big Sur for Sara and Garrett's wedding. I had moved in with him just a week before and had barely unpacked before we had to leave. Matt was the best man and I was the maid of honor, and we wrote our speeches together on the drive up, detailing the love story of how Sara and Garrett met at a bar in Santa Monica, how they were so full of love they set up their two best friends—me and Matt—in the hope that we'd share that same sort of love, too. How the four of us became our own unit: Matt and Marnie, Sara and Garrett. Then, after we delivered those speeches during their sunset reception, when all the guests took to the dance floor, everyone had asked when it would be our turn, and we'd laughed awkwardly to avoid answering.

Except . . . that wasn't a year ago. There's apparently a missing chunk of time in between, a gaping hole that's not only swallowed up our move to Boston, but everything that's happened since.

"I forgot an entire year?" I ask, my voice going screechy with panic.

"But there's a good chance you'll get it back," Matt adds quickly. "I talked with your nurse earlier, and she said you just need to rest and your brain will heal itself. You might even be able to go home in a few days."

"A few *days*?" I shriek. Who approved that? What was their barometer? Because the more aware I am of just how jumbled my head is, the more I'm convinced I am absolutely not well enough to do anything except sit in this hospital bed and watch Goldie Hawn's entire filmography.

"I know it's a lot, but try not to get upset—"

"I'm not upset. Honestly, I'm not upset," I reply, my voice sounding increasingly upset. "I just don't understand how I can go home when I don't even know where we live. And what about my job? I know Probus transferred me to the Boston office, but I don't know my manager's name there. Do they know I'm in the hospital? What if they fire me? What if I lose my health insurance? Is this hospital bill going to bankrupt us, or—"

"Everything is going to be okay," Matt cuts in. "I'm in Toronto for a conference, but let's meet up for coffee when I'm back so we can talk about everything. Sound good?"

I take a deep breath in, trying to calm down . . . until my broken brain finally processes what he just said.

"Why would we have to meet up for coffee?"

He pauses. "Sorry?"

Something is telling me to stop, turn back, there's danger ahead, but I barrel on. "Why would we have to plan to meet up? We live together."

"Shit," he murmurs to himself, like he's been caught in a lie he's been trying to maintain since he got on the phone. Then there's a long moment as he seems to summon the courage to continue. "We don't live together, Marn."

"What are you talking about?"

Silence. The worst gut-wrenching silence in the history of silences, before he finally says, "We broke up six months ago."

My pulse tumbles as I stare at the blank television screen ahead. This can't be right. How could I spend an entire year in a new city, six months without the man I moved here with, and not remember any of it? "But I came to Boston with you."

"Yes—"

"We signed a lease on an apartment in Beacon Hill."

"I know—"

"Then what happened?" I ask desperately. "Something must have happened, right? Was the apartment awful? Did we have a big fight about something? What?"

"It wasn't one specific thing, Marn," he says. "We just . . . didn't work anymore."

One of Matt's signature nonanswers. They had never really bothered me before, just a form of people-pleasing I recognized. Sometimes I almost found it endearing. But now that I'm on the receiving end, the vagueness feels weak, like the worst kind of appeasement.

I want to call him out on it, force him to list all the details so I can pick them apart, but there's a loud knock on the door. A moment later, Brenda appears again.

"Sorry to interrupt, but I need to bring you downstairs for those cognitive evaluations," she says. Her smile is entirely too bright, considering the situation.

"I have to go downstairs for some cognitive evaluations," I parrot back into the phone, my voice despondent.

"Okay, I'll let you go," Matt says, voice taking on that soft, soothing tone again, except now it sounds almost condescending.

"But call me when you get home. I'm serious about meeting up. I know this is a lot to process, and I'm here for whatever you need. In the meantime, your nurse said the hospital would organize a car service for when you're discharged. You'll feel better when you're home, I promise."

That seems like a pretty bold promise when I don't even know where "home" is. The world outside feels upside down, and every answer I get seems to only spawn a bigger question. Or maybe it's just that my brain is so broken, I can't make sense of it. And if that's the case, how do I even begin to try?

But instead of saying that, of admitting just how terrified and confused I am, I reply, "I hope so."

Because, honestly, I do. Despite my fears and doubts, I *need* to feel better. Because if I don't, then there's a very real possibility that the world is just as bleak and scary as I always feared.

And no amount of my grandmother's moonstone can change that.

CHAPTER 3

Three days later, I'm forced to accept another sobering truth: My haircut is awful.

I stare at it in the mirror of my cramped hospital bathroom, frowning at the blunt cut that ends at my chin, the erratic angle of the bangs. I've never had bangs before, and my body seems to be rejecting them, refusing to accept their appearance so they're physically unable to lie flat against my forehead.

This feels like a tragedy on par with losing a year's worth of memories. My hair had always been the physical feature I was most proud of. My blond locks had fallen halfway down my back for as long as I could remember. And, yes, I had started needing highlights to maintain the color when I reached high school, but it hadn't mattered—my grandmother would still gush about my hair, how it was exactly like my mother's. It was always the one thing about myself that I didn't wish would change. And now it was gone, replaced by the same haircut I gave my Barbies when I was five.

I'm doing my best to use the tap water to force my bangs into submission when I hear a knock on my hospital door.

"Ms. Stephens?" Dr. Buterman's voice calls out.

For a moment I consider staying silent. Maybe if no one knows I'm in here I could buy myself a few more days, maybe even a week, before I'm forced to face whatever is waiting for me out there in the real world.

I close my eyes and try to manifest him leaving, the way my grandmother always told me to. If I just focus hard enough, maybe some innate magic will do the rest.

Then the knock is on the bathroom door. "Ms. Stephens?"

I never really mastered that whole manifesting thing, did I?

"I'll be right there," I call out, hastening my attempts to get my hair in order until I finally give up, forcing a smile onto my face as I emerge. "Hello, Doctor."

Dr. Buterman looks just like he did the first time I met him, and in every subsequent visit to my room. Same scrubs, same white coat, same perfectly combed hair. I'm starting to wonder if he ever goes home, or if he just keeps wandering the halls until he runs out of batteries and someone plugs him back in again.

"Is now a good time?" he asks, eyeing my wet bangs.

"Sure," I say, trying hard to maintain a smile, even though I have no idea what constitutes a good time anymore, let alone if this is one of them.

Dr. Buterman taps on his tablet while I make my way over to the bed.

"I have your latest scans here. Your injury is healing nicely. And your motor function seems to be fully intact, which is good.

We'll keep an eye on it, but for the moment, you don't need physical therapy. I think you're ready to go home."

He looks up and nods, as if the silver lining to not remembering the last year is that I can walk right back into it unencumbered.

"But I still don't remember anything," I say.

"Yes, your memory." His attention returns to the tablet. "We've scheduled you an appointment tomorrow with a neuropsychologist here. They have the results of your cognitive tests and will work out a plan for tackling all that."

All that. Like my lack of memory is a sidenote, a minor inconvenience.

He continues talking, this time about something called pathophysiology and neuronal tissues, until he's interrupted by another knock on the door.

"Hello!" A nurse I don't recognize enters, pushing a wheelchair with a plastic bag full of clothing on its seat. "I've got your ride here when you're ready."

Dr. Buterman clears his throat, already turning toward the door. "All right. Your discharge paperwork has all the recommendations for you to follow over the next few weeks. Reduce your screen time. Abstain from alcohol. Get plenty of sleep. That sort of thing. If you have any questions, give me a call."

Is he serious? All I have are questions, and he just added about a dozen to the list. But he's already out the door before I can ask even one.

"Do you want to change?" the nurse asks. "Your clothes and things from the ER are there on the seat."

It's only then that I fully register that the bag sitting on the seat of the wheelchair is for me. Through the clear plastic I can see a blue sweater, a pair of jeans, something gray that could be a jacket. I don't recognize any of it, but that doesn't matter, because I also see one thing that is familiar: my purple leather tote.

"Is my phone in there?" I ask, wide-eyed.

She just shrugs.

I grab the plastic bag and pull out the tote to empty its contents on the nearby bed. My wallet is there, and when I open it I see my license staring back. Except it's not my California one. This one has MASSACHUSETTS emblazoned across the top. The home address is unfamiliar, too: 41 Sheafe Street, Apt. 3A. The only reason I even know it's mine is because of the picture. Those are my wide, blue eyes, and my big, bright smile. And there, tucked behind my ears, is my gloriously long blond hair.

I scowl down at her. *Bangs? Really?*

She only smiles back, blissfully unaware of what the future holds.

I move on to the other contents of the bag. There's the *Last Toast on the Coast!* key chain I got at Sara's bachelorette party that I remember, but three brass keys are hanging from it that I definitely don't. I don't recognize the two tubes of lip balm, either, or the pair of oversized black sunglasses.

I find my cell phone at the bottom of the bag. The pink-and-red-striped case is the same one I had in California, but when I press the button on the side to light up the screen, the wallpaper is new. The photo is too abstract to make out any details, but it looks like it could be a sunset, close-up and out of focus. Regardless, I don't have time to decipher it now. The battery is at 7 percent, just enough to reveal that I have seventeen missed calls.

I don't know enough people to have seventeen missed calls. I can't even think of a reason why my limited number of contacts would call me seventeen times. Matt already knew I was here, and the only other person I talk to regularly is Sara.

My pulse jumps. Does Sara know I'm here? Did Matt call her? Garrett is his best friend, so it would make sense.

I quickly tap the screen and type in my passcode to find out but am immediately thwarted.

Incorrect Passcode

I try again.

Incorrect Passcode

Oh no. No no no no.

I try again, then again, so close to a breakdown that I don't think to stop until the screen goes black and I'm greeted with a new message.

iPhone Unavailable
try again in 1 minute

Matt used to chide me about having the same passcode our entire relationship, reminding me I should be changing it at least every six months. Apparently, I had picked the worst possible time to start listening.

"Oh my God," I mutter to myself.

The nurse is kneeling beside me, too busy getting the wheelchair footrests situated to notice my anxiety. "Everything okay?"

I hold up the darkened screen. "I can't unlock my phone."

"Oh, I've been there," she says, shaking her head as she stands up. "My five-year-old hid in the bathroom with my phone and tried so many passcodes that the whole thing shut down and I had to take it to a store to get fixed."

I can feel the tears forming in my eyes again as I run my hand through my hair the way I've always done when I'm stressed. It's a habit from childhood, and I don't remember to stop myself until my bangs are back to their original jaunty angles, sticking out in every direction. All my hard work erased without a trace.

The nurse smiles, oblivious, as she stands and comes around the back of the wheelchair to take hold of the handles. "What do you say we get you home?"

~

Ten minutes later, I'm sitting in a wheelchair parked outside the hospital's main entrance, wearing the jeans and a light blue sweater from the plastic bag. I still don't recognize them but they fit perfectly, so I put them on along with a very nice but completely unfamiliar gray wool coat. The blue polyester hospital socks peek out from the pair of red Crocs on my feet that are supposedly mine, too. My tote bag is sitting on my lap, while I clutch my discharge papers in my hand. I can see the nurse who brought me downstairs in the periphery, keeping an eye out for the car that is supposedly taking me home. I can also see my bangs sticking out from my forehead toward the street, like they're reaching for freedom.

So this is rock bottom, I think.

Thankfully, no one else seems to notice. There is a steady stream of visitors and hospital staff coming in and out of the nearby revolving glass doors who are completely oblivious to my plight. I hear snippets of conversations as they pass—test results, weekend plans, someone complaining about parking—but no one comments on the blond woman looking utterly dejected by the curb. Which is probably for the best. I don't think I can muster the smile required to make sure they don't have to worry about me. Even if they probably should.

It's not quite nine o'clock and the morning air is cool enough to send goose bumps over my skin despite the coat. I'm used to brisk mornings—even while I was packing my and Matt's apartment in the middle of July, the Pacific Ocean kept Los Angeles cool enough to need a sweatshirt—but here in Boston, the cold has a different bite, like it's only hinting at its full potential. Maybe because it's autumn. At least, I think it's autumn. There are yellow and orange leaves falling from the nearby tree sprouting up from the sidewalk. I watch them scatter across the pavement as my breath curls in the air in front of me.

Trust the universe, Marnie, my grandmother's voice echoes through my head. *The magic will find you if you just—*

"Ah, here we go!" the nurse exclaims, making me jump.

I look over to see a beige Toyota Corolla with a dent in the passenger door come to a stop in front of us. During the elevator ride down, the nurse had explained that the car they organized to take me home was approved by the hospital. I had assumed that meant some sort of hospital van, or dedicated taxi service. The only thing with any sort of official branding on this car is a Yankee Candle air freshener hanging in the window.

The driver is busy playing with the radio as the nurse helps me up from the wheelchair and into the back seat. The whole time she's reciting information from my discharge paperwork: how to confirm my appointment for tomorrow, who to call if I need to reschedule, where to find my medical records on the patient portal. By the time she closes the door, I feel dazed. All the facts and numbers are an impossible mess in my head.

"41 Sheafe Street?" the driver asks gruffly, looking at me in the rearview mirror.

Was that the address on my license? I had shoved my wallet into my coat pocket before I got in the elevator earlier, along with my keys, so it would be easy enough to pull it out and double-check. Except it doesn't *feel* easy. It feels like everyone is forcing me to face the trauma of the past few days over and over again until I finally buckle and break. So instead, I just stare back at him dumbly while my bangs stick out from my forehead like hands on some insane, oversized clock.

The driver seems to gauge that I'm as clueless as my blond hair would lead him to believe, because he frowns, then throws the car into drive and turns up the radio. It's a sports program with two hosts yelling about last night's Red Sox game against the Guardians. I don't know baseball—I'm not even sure what city the Guardians are from—but I listen because it's nice to know there are two other people out there just as stressed as me.

"AND THEN THEY PULL THEIR STARTER IN THE SIXTH INNING!" one of the radio hosts yells. *"ARE YOU KIDDIN' ME?"*

I stare out my window, trying to focus on the narrow streets as they fly by, each corner we turn. Left, then right, but I can't keep track of the route. It's like someone is scrambling the information in my mind as soon as I receive it.

I've always been so good with directions. Maybe it comes from a lifetime of living near the ocean—you can never get too lost because you always know what direction is west. But now I don't have a reference point, no familiar landmark to guide me. There's just a labyrinthine mess of reddish-brown brick buildings and cracked sidewalks. Bars and convenience stores. Nothing looks familiar at all.

"COME ON, HIS ON-BASE PERCENTAGE IS BELOW THREE HUNDRED!" blares from the radio. *"MY KID GETS TO FIRST MORE THAN HIM!"*

I give up after we pass a third Dunkin' Donuts and bring my attention to the discharge papers in my hand. There are pages and pages of instructions, in font so small I can't even attempt to read it in a moving car, but on the top page I see that the most important information has been highlighted. There's a phone number to call to confirm my neuropsychologist appointment tomorrow, and another one to schedule a car to pick me up and drop me off.

Both incredibly helpful, I have to admit, if only I could actually place a call.

I reach into my bag and feel around until I find my phone. The warning screen is gone, and the hazy sunset wallpaper is back.

Did it forget my previous passcode attempts? Or is it secretly keeping track, waiting for me to mess up again?

It takes another moment to muster the gumption to slide the bar across the screen to unlock it. A prompt appears, asking me to enter my passcode, and I carefully press each number so I don't mess up . . .

iPhone Unavailable
try again in 5 minutes

My heart drops to the floor of the Corolla. How many tries do I get? And what happens when I run out? This is exactly the kind of question I would usually ask Matt—except I can't because my phone won't let me call him. It won't even let me look up his number. My stomach twists as the realization ripples through every other facet of my life. I can't confirm my doctor's appointment tomorrow. I can't call Sara. I can't even contact the hospital with any questions. All because I can't remember six simple digits.

It's the head injury, I tell myself. But at the same time, all my old insecurities come roaring back. Growing up, it was easy to pigeonhole me as the spacey blonde who daydreamed through school, the ditz with the weird grandma. The girl with a thousand different dreams, who thought she could travel the world and do everything. It wasn't until I was older, after my grandmother got sick, that those assumptions took on a new, painful edge. Marnie Stephens, the college student who had to move home to take care of her sick grandmother. The young professional who spent most of her twenties cycling through temp jobs while still hoping the universe was just taking its time.

Marnie Stephens, the thirty-year-old who still has no idea what she wants to do with her life.

Then I'm hit with another devastating realization.

Oh God. I'm thirty-one now, aren't I?

"Here ya go," the cabbie announces, putting the car into park.

I look out the window at the muddy-brown brick building just outside the car door.

This is not the Boston I was promised. The apartment Matt and I had planned to move into was on the top floor of a black-shuttered townhouse in Beacon Hill. There were flower boxes on all the windows and a tall linden tree rising from the brick sidewalk out front. I had daydreamed about watching the foliage change on its branches in the fall and picking what flowers to plant in the window boxes in the spring.

But there are no window boxes here. No tree. The sidewalk is barren except for an empty Dunkin' Donuts cup rolling in the wind. The four-story building in front of me looks almost identical to the rest lining the narrow block except the color of the mortar is mottled, patched in places where it's given up, and the windows are slightly off-kilter in their frames. The front door is painted a rust color that at some point probably matched the brick but is now faded and flaky.

"Are you sure this is it?" I ask.

The driver turns to quirk an eyebrow at me from over his shoulder.

I smile even though I have no idea why. I'm so terrified, I think I might throw up all over his worn beige interior.

"Okay. Well . . . thank you," I say, gathering up my phone and my bag before opening the door.

I step out onto the curb, then turn back to the car, ready to ask the driver to wait until I've figured out which key unlocks the building's entrance, but he's already thrown the Corolla into drive and started forward.

I clutch my bag in my hands and watch as the car rolls down the narrow street—as if maybe, possibly, it will stop and turn around. Maybe the driver will realize he forgot to tell me something, some vital secret the universe needs me to know that will magically make all of this make sense.

But he doesn't turn around. The car just zips left around the corner and disappears.

Totally fine, I think. *If this is where my driver's license says I live, then it must be true.*

I pull out my license again just to make sure, and my heart drops a little when the bold text confirms it: 41 Sheafe Street, Apt. 3A.

It takes me another moment to step toward the front door. The faded rust-colored paint of the door looks almost brown under close inspection. Not exactly the high-gloss red from the pictures of our Beacon Hill building, but if I live here, it must have some redeeming qualities, right?

Please let me be right, I think, swallowing down the panic clawing its way up my throat.

In perhaps my only stroke of luck today, the first key I try turns the lock and I push open the door to step inside. I expect a lobby, or at least some sort of foyer, but there's just a sterile hallway. It smells of cheap lemon cleaner, and there's a line of locked mailboxes along the right side with a fluorescent striplight above.

I've been standing there for a moment, looking for some detail that might be familiar, when a man emerges from the stairwell and shuffles to the mailboxes. He looks like he's just woken up, with mascara smeared under his eyes and a purple velvet bathrobe draped over his shoulders.

Should I say hello? He's my neighbor, after all. Not just on the same street, but in the same building. And if I've lived in this building for six months, then surely I must know people here. He and I could even be friends.

For the first time all day, I feel a bit of hope. After all, in our small neighborhood in Malibu, my grandmother and I knew everyone. When Sara and I were roommates in our two-bedroom apartment in Santa Monica, no one hesitated to say hello when they passed each other in the hall. Even in Matt's giant apartment building downtown, the neighbors still smiled at one another in the elevator. Boston couldn't possibly be *that* different, right?

By the time the man looks up from his mailbox, my smile is so wide it's hurting my cheeks.

"Hi!" I say a little too loudly.

His mouth offers an inverse of mine, a frown that communicates annoyance as much as it does confusion. Then he turns and heads back up the stairs.

Okay. Not friends, then.

And that's fine, I remind myself. I haven't lived here *that* long. Maybe he's never even seen me before. Or maybe I inadvertently took a package meant for him and now he can't forgive me.

I'm so distracted thinking about every possible scenario, I don't realize there isn't an elevator until I step forward to press the button. There's only a door to the stairwell.

I don't know why I'm shocked. There wasn't supposed to be an elevator in our Beacon Hill apartment, either. Matt and I had even joked about what a fantastic workout it would be, climbing three flights of stairs every day. But here, it feels necessary. Sure, this building might not have Beacon Hill's window boxes or cobbled street or crown molding, but at least an elevator would help explain why I chose it.

Apparently not, I think as I start up the stairs.

As I pass the second floor, I hear ABBA's "Waterloo" ringing out from one of the apartments, but the song fades when I get to the third story. There seem to be two apartments on each floor of the building, and apartment 3A is the one on the right. A small welcome sign hangs by the door, and a knot-weaved doormat lies out front, which I quite like.

Then it hits me: Of course I like it. I probably bought it.

I have to try a couple of keys before one slides into the lock. I turn it and carefully push open the door, craning to peek inside.

"Hello?" I call out, half hoping, half dreading a reply from some unknown roommate.

The fluorescent bulb from the hallway illuminates the threshold and the line of coats hanging on the wall. A pair of boots and two pairs of running shoes—one of which I recognize—are on the hardwood floor below them.

It's enough evidence to step forward. It's a small entryway, not much more than a short hall, and beyond it is a long living room with a kitchen taking up the wall on one end and two tall windows overlooking the building across the street on the other. The morning sun hasn't quite hit this side of the building yet, so the light through the gauzy curtains is soft and hazy, falling across a worn vintage rug. Plants crowd the windowsills, and a short bookcase with a small television on top sits opposite a long sofa, its navy blue cotton upholstery slightly faded.

Curiosity quickly eclipses my caution. I don't bother taking off my coat; instead, I just drop my bag on the hardwood floor and continue inside.

There's a set of French doors just past the television, across from the sofa, and I push them open to find a barely made bed, its pink-and-white gingham duvet thrown haphazardly across the sheets and half covering the pillows. *A Marnie special*, Matt used to call it. He'd say the same thing about the stacks of books on the nightstand, the piles of random papers on the small desk in the corner. My old laptop sits there, too, and I'm honestly surprised it survived the move. A few years ago Sara had insisted I buy it—*All professionals need one*, she had said—but I'd never used it much. I tentatively lift its screen, not sure I would even have it charged. It turns out I do. But when I type in the last password I remember, and the computer immediately denies it, I shut it again. There's only so much rejection I can handle in one day.

I can hear the muffled chorus of "Waterloo" playing downstairs as I head back out to the living room and look around again. There's just one other door by the kitchen, and it appears to lead to a small bathroom. Does that mean I live alone?

I've never lived on my own before. At thirty years old—wait, thirty-one—that feels almost embarrassing. Like up until this point, I'd missed some key milestone in life. It wasn't that I avoided it, only that I had so many plans when I was younger, it didn't seem like living alone needed to be added to the list. It would just happen, an inevitable outcome of everything else I wanted to do. Move to New York and pursue photography. Learn to sail and get a job aboard a ship traversing the Atlantic. Paint in Italy, and bake in France. The list went on and on. But it always ended in the same place: Malibu, where my grandmother and I would turn her bungalow into a bed-and-breakfast and share stories of our adventures with whoever came to stay.

Follow your dreams, Marnie, my grandmother always said. *The universe will handle the rest.*

So I had. Or, at least, I tried to. Then she was diagnosed with dementia my freshman year of college. Suddenly, moving out of the dorms and back into our bungalow to take care of her felt like the only option. Four years later, as the medical bills piled up and I was taking on more and more temp work to keep them at bay, accepting a full-time position with Probus Recruiting after graduation hadn't felt like part of any cosmic plan, either, just a necessary evil. And on the bright side, I met Sara in the break room on my second day. We bonded over our shared hatred of inspirational quotes in our colleagues' email signatures, and over the next year, our friendship grew so strong that when I finally had to move my grandmother into assisted living—and sell our bungalow to pay for it—Sara didn't hesitate to offer me the spare room in her apartment. Then, when she got engaged to Garrett, it seemed obvious that I would move in with Matt.

None of it had felt like a compromise. At least, not at the time. Still, I couldn't ignore how much my life had narrowed with each decision, taking all my possible futures with it. The magic behind every one of my dreams felt dimmed, like it had only existed because my grandmother took the time to stoke it. Then, when she died, it was gone completely.

I push back the thought before any tears reemerge, and begin to explore the living room. The low bookcase opposite the sofa is filled to the brim with titles I recognize, including my well-loved hardcover of *Jane Eyre* that I found on Zuma Beach when I was twelve. There's one of my grandmother's crystals, too, a jagged chunk of rose quartz she used to keep by the front door. And there's the 35 mm camera she gave me on my thirteenth birthday. It still has the green-and-white floral strap she embroidered to go with it.

Next to it is a framed picture of the woman herself: my grandmother, Cynthia Aldridge. Wisps of her long white hair falling along her cheeks, the corners of her blue eyes creased, thanks to a small, warm smile. It's one of the last photos I took of her, from when I visited her at her assisted-living facility after work one day. I didn't normally stop by during the week, but I'd had my first date with Matt the night before and wanted to talk to her about it. I needed to. Back in high school, I told her about all my first dates. My crushes, my heartbreaks, everything. She had been my grandmother, my parent, and my best friend, all wrapped up in a five-foot-two, caftan-wearing ball of light.

But when I walked into her room that day, she didn't even know who I was.

I still stayed for a while. I told her about the date, about work, about a thousand other insignificant things. And just before I left, she smiled. So familiar and so beautiful, I had to take a picture.

Looking at it, such a comforting reminder of *home*, is when it truly hits me: This is my apartment. A strange place in a strange city, and I'm here all on my own.

Tears prick my eyes, and this time I'm tempted to just give myself over to it. Collapse into a puddle here in the middle of this unfamiliar but still very pretty rug, and fully embrace my wallowing. Or I could do what I usually do when I'm feeling sorry for myself: make a cup of tea.

The red Crocs scrape across the hardwood as I shuffle to the kitchen. There's a half-eaten piece of toast still sitting on a plate by the sink and a corkboard hanging next to the fridge, crowded with notes and pictures. A grocery list in my handwriting. An envelope with PHOTO-RAMA printed across it and a roll of 35 mm film stuffed inside. A receipt from a bookstore I've never heard of. A piece of red-and-white string that I don't remember at all.

Is this what it's like for people with split personalities? Does one go about their daily life, keeping notes and mementos along the way, only to have another personality emerge who has to start at square one, piecing together their past with what's been left behind?

A kettle sits on the narrow stovetop, and the cabinet above it is full of an eclectic mix of mugs. But when I reach for the box of tea bags beside them, it's empty. In fact, there's not much food on the shelves at all. It's the same in the refrigerator. All that I can find are two tubs of yogurt and some milk, and it's all expired.

I'm so frustrated, I almost miss the blur of motion in my periphery.

Almost.

I turn just enough to look back out to the center of the living room. The faint sound of a car horn echoes from outside, but here in the apartment, everything is quiet and still. I let out a deep breath, and after another minute, I almost convince myself that I've imagined it, that it was another lingering effect of the brain injury. But then I hear a faint noise, see another faint twitch of movement. A small, round furry thing on my Persian rug.

A mouse.

As soon as I make eye contact with him, he runs. To where, I have no idea. All I can do is scream as I stumble backward, fling open the front door, and throw myself into the hallway. It's only after I slam it shut behind me that I notice the man already standing out there. He has a worn leather bag over one shoulder, with a set of keys in one hand and a phone in the other, as if he's just left the apartment across from mine and is about to lock the dead bolt. Except he's paused mid-motion, his attention on me.

I pause, too, suddenly distracted by his dark hair that's a bit too long. The stubble that hides the clean line of his jaw. And that look, the serious line of his brow as he stares at me like he's annoyed. Or maybe that's concern?

I know you, I want to say. But how? Then some rusty gear in my brain lurches into place.

Doctor Sweater.

CHAPTER 4

"Hi," I say, my heart racing so fast I can barely form words. "Hello. Sorry."

He stares back at me, his expression unreadable, and for a moment I wonder if I'm hallucinating.

"Do I know you?" I blurt out.

He frowns. "I'm sorry?"

Oh, it's definitely him. There's that voice again, deep and rumbly. His dark hair is pushed back from his face now, like he recently ran his hand through it, and his sweater has been replaced by a canvas jacket over a dark green hoodie, but his jaw is still hidden behind a thick layer of stubble that barely conceals his full lips.

"You were at the hospital before. I asked you about Goldie Hawn's hair," I say, as if this clears it up.

His expression suggests that it doesn't. His forehead creases, making a hard line over his dark eyes. Had I noticed how dark his eyes were before? Like two chocolate opals staring at me so intensely, my train of thought is momentarily derailed.

"Sorry, this is probably really weird," I say, waving a hand between us. "I mean, if you think I'm acting weird because we know each other and I just fell out of my apartment acting like we don't. But we must know each other since you were at the hospital, so you probably think I'm weird at this point anyway." I laugh, but it fades quickly. A moment of silence passes and I'm questioning my sanity again. "That *was* you at the hospital, right?"

"I'm the one who brought you to the ER."

"Really?" I ask. "Do we know each other?"

He frowns at that. "I came home and found you unconscious in the lobby."

It takes my broken brain a second to realize that by "lobby," he means the small hallway downstairs with the bad lighting.

"Oh my God, thank you," I say. "My doctor said if I hadn't gotten to the hospital as fast as I did, it could have been a lot worse. Which is really saying something, considering that I have absolutely no memory of the past year. I don't remember moving to Boston, or breaking up with my boyfriend, or living here. I don't even remember the passcode to get into my phone. And if that wasn't bad enough, when I went to go make myself some tea, a mouse ran across my kitchen, so, you know, screaming ensued. And bursting out into the hallway to ambush my unsuspecting neighbor."

The line between his eyebrows deepens. It looks a little like the expression I got from the man downstairs in the purple velvet bathrobe, and I realize that even though Doctor Sweater rushed me to the hospital less than a week ago, this might very well be the first conversation we've had. Somehow that makes this all that much more embarrassing.

"Soooo." I say the word like it has five syllables. "Off to work?"

This is probably the most insane thing I could say right now, because of course he's off to work. He's fully dressed and leaving his apartment before ten a.m. on a Monday.

"Obviously, you're off to work. Where else would you be going?" I add with another laugh, like this is some sort of long-standing inside joke between us. "I should probably be going, too. Lots to do today. You know, with the whole memory thing. And the phone thing. And the mouse thing."

His brow skews like it's now his turn to gauge if I'm kidding or not. And, honestly, I get it. This verbal diatribe has been truly crazy, even by my standards. Is it the head injury? Or the fact that this man looks like a lumberjack fresh out of medical school?

"Okay. Well, bye!" I practically shout, then turn and fling open my door, slamming it shut behind me before I can say another word. It's as if my broken brain has somehow amplified my penchant for oversharing. Or maybe it's always been this bad, and I'm only just now realizing it.

Regardless, there is no coming back from this. It's me and the mouse, together forever from here on out.

Just as I start to work out how to reduce all my movement to off-peak hours, I hear a knock on the door.

When I open it again, Doctor Sweater is there waiting, with one arm braced against my doorframe.

"Hello again," I say, trying to sound upbeat.

"Would you mind going over all that one more time?" he asks gruffly.

"Oh. Sure." I clear my throat. "Okay, well, I saw you at the hospital and asked you about Goldie Hawn—"

"Yeah, I remember that part."

"Right. So just the bit about how my brain was bleeding, and how I don't remember the last year, and that there's a mouse in my apartment?"

He frowns. "Yeah. That."

"I'm seeing a doctor tomorrow about the memory thing," I reply quickly. "All I have to do is figure out my phone passcode so I can confirm the appointment. And call to schedule a car to pick me up. And use the Maps app to find a grocery store because there's barely any food in my apartment. I don't even have any tea, and I always have tea when I'm stressed, so that's probably not helping the situation. Or the fact that all I've eaten for the past few days is Jell-O and dry toast." Oh no, I can feel tears starting to burn my eyes again. I try to blink them away and smile. "But it's totally fine. Once I eat something, I can handle the rest."

Doctor Sweater's lips bend into a grim line. Thank God for his thick stubble. It softens what would probably otherwise be incredibly intimidating.

"So you need a grocery store," he replies.

"Yes. I need a grocery store," I say, relieved he's able to glean that much information from my babble. "Is there one nearby?"

"There's one on North Street."

I nod as if I know where that is. Or where I even am right now.

His eyes narrow on me, like he can see how close I am to tears. "Do you want me to walk you over there?"

My heart flutters awake at this reintroduction to hope. "You would do that?"

"It's on my way to work," he says. His voice is so matter-of-fact, as if this isn't one of the nicest things anyone's ever offered to do for me.

"Are you sure? I don't want you to feel like you have to escort me, or something. I can even hang back a few steps to give you space."

"Like . . . tail me?" he asks, one eyebrow arched on his forehead. It's only then that I realize how this might be the most unhinged thing I've said so far.

"Not *tail* you," I say, even though, yes, that's exactly what I meant. "But *follow* you. In a way that's not inconvenient."

"I wouldn't offer if it was inconvenient," he says, finally locking his door and sliding the keys into his bag. "Do you need to grab anything?"

It's only then that I realize I still have my coat on, with my wallet in one pocket and my keys in the other. I'm also still wearing my red Crocs with my blue hospital socks underneath.

"Nope, ready to go when you are," I say, working hard to manufacture as much fake confidence as possible. As if this entire outfit is intentional. "I'm Marnie Stephens, by the way."

At that, he frowns.

I want to ask him if this is the first time I've introduced myself to him. But after almost ten solid minutes of unadulterated insanity, I need to regain some of my pride, shake off the awkwardness.

Or, at the very least, reassure him that, despite the outfit and the verbal diarrhea, I am in fact very normal.

"Ben Morgan," he replies.

"It's nice to meet you, Ben Morgan," I say. Then I salute. With two fingers. What is *wrong* with me?

He stares back like he's wondering the same thing.

Forget off-peak hours, I think even as I try to smile. *I'm never leaving my apartment again.*

CHAPTER 5

As we make our way downstairs and out the building's front door, I get the distinct impression that Ben Morgan is not a fan of small talk. He keeps his focus ahead, the solid line of his shoulders tense under his canvas jacket. By the time we arrive at the corner, a crossroads where every direction seems to lead to a labyrinth of even more brick rowhouses, I'm starting to think he's forgotten I'm even here. Which is probably for the best. I need to keep track of the path we take before it becomes a jumble in my brain. Otherwise, there's no hope that I'll ever find my way back home again. I'll be left wandering the streets of Boston with nothing but a pair of red Crocs and a bad bob, and—

"How are you feeling?" Ben's voice breaks the silence like a truck rolling over a gravel path.

I blink up at him. He taps a finger against his temple.

Oh, right. My head.

"Well, they discharged me this morning, so the hospital thinks I'm okay," I reply. "I mean, there's still the issue with my memory, obviously. But I'm better than when you found me."

"That wouldn't be hard. You were in rough shape."

Part of me is desperate to dig into the details, pick them apart to see if there are any answers hiding underneath. But I'm also aware that asking Ben to catalogue exactly how he found me passed out downstairs, and then somehow managed to get me to a hospital all on his own, promises more embarrassment than clarity. Especially since I'm in the clothes I had on when I was admitted to the ER, which means I'm probably wearing the same outfit he found me in. I have to tread carefully.

"Do you know how long I had been there?" I ask.

"Not long. I only ran to the store to grab a few things before they closed. You were there when I got back," he replies, waiting for a cab to pass before crossing another narrow street.

I follow as I try to make this new information fit the empty spaces in my memory, but all it manages to do is remind me how much I still don't know.

"Well, I appreciate it," I say, trying not to sound too dejected. "Not just for getting me to the hospital, but for sticking around afterward."

"Just until they told me you were okay and someone had contacted your boyfriend."

Right. Matt. I'm almost embarrassed that I needed a reminder that he existed, let alone that I should probably be mourning our relationship right now instead of studying the width of my neighbor's shoulders.

"Yeah. Although I think he's my ex-boyfriend now? I'm not sure. I need to figure that out after the phone thing. And the doctor's appointment. And the mouse." The memory of the small ball of fur scurrying across the kitchen floor flashes in my mind and I shiver. "Is it normal to get mice in the building?"

"Not unless you leave food out."

My brain stumbles back to my apartment and the half-eaten toast on the kitchen counter that must have been sitting there all week and I try not to look too guilty. "So who should I talk to about it? The mouse, I mean."

"Gino, the super."

"The super! Of course. We have a super, don't we? Great, I'll call Gino." I'm so relieved, I actually let out a laugh.

"How?"

I blink. "Excuse me?"

"How will you call him? You can't get into your phone," he replies flatly.

Touché, Ben Morgan.

I nod as if I've thought of this, like we're partners on equal cognitive footing. "Well, if I can't figure out the passcode, I'll just bring it to an Apple Store. There has to be one nearby, right?"

Ben looks dubious. "In the North End?"

"Is that where we are right now?" I ask, looking around at the intersection we've entered. All four streets meet in the center at an odd angle, making the brick buildings around us feel off-kilter. Their bay windows, framed in copper that's succumbed to a deep verdigris green patina, seem to arch over us and the line of people outside an Italian bakery across the street.

"Yup," he replies.

"And it doesn't have a computer store or something?"

"The North End is like Boston's Little Italy. Good for food, not for technology. But there's a hardware store just down the block where you can pick up some mousetraps."

"Oh, I don't need traps," I say, waving off the suggestion as we turn left and pass a basketball court slotted between an apartment building and a church.

His eyebrows knit together. "I thought you saw a mouse."

"I did, but I don't want to *kill* it. I just want to make sure he's gone."

An elderly couple is walking toward us, so we pause beside the steps of the church to give them space to pass by with their walkers. Ben takes the opportunity to glance down at me, a look that seems to demand that I take him seriously. "You need traps."

"I'm a vegetarian, Ben. I cry during ASPCA commercials. Do you honestly think I'm going to willfully kill a small animal who accidentally stumbled into my apartment?"

He frowns. "Is that a trick question?"

The elderly couple finally passes, and they give us a warm smile. I give them one back, while Ben offers a tight nod before starting down the sidewalk again. I wait until they're out of earshot before I say, "What if I'm lying in bed one night and I hear one go off—SNAP. I'm supposed to not only live with the guilt, but also get up and get rid of it, too?"

"That's the general idea, yeah."

I scoff. "That's awful. I could never do that."

"All right. Then knock on my door and I will."

The offer is so matter-of-fact that it takes me a moment to realize he's serious.

"Really?" I ask.

He gives me another look as we stop at a crosswalk, brows drawn together so his eyes seem even darker than before. "Yes. Really."

His voice is startlingly deep and hits low in my stomach, sending a prickling heat across my skin. Oh God, is this another by-product of the head injury? An inconvenient attraction to my neighbor?

I blink away just as the WALK sign lights up and we start across the street. "Well, I guess that's the difference between you and me."

"The appreciation for pest control?" he says.

"And the thirst for innocent blood."

I think I catch a twitch at the corner of his mouth. It's almost like a smile, but not quite. Just enough to send a steady thrum down my veins.

We go around another corner and onto a street that is blessedly wider than the last. The brick buildings are low and tightly packed, and the businesses occupying the ground floors—a bank, a laundromat, a couple of restaurants with tables set up outside—are shielded every few feet by a tree with leaves turning different shades of yellow and orange. A group of tourists pass, taking photos of each other with what looks to be yet another church framed in the background, while on the opposite side of the road an elderly man sits on a stool outside a cigar shop, grumbling about something I can't quite make out.

Despite the picture-perfect moment, Ben's pace is undaunted, and I match my steps to his as I try to recall our path up until now. Right, then right, maybe? Then two blocks and a left, then straight, I think. But as we pass yet *another* bakery, the directions become a jumble in my brain.

At the corner, we wait for the light to change, and I do another audit of my surroundings.

"What's the matter?" Ben asks when he catches me frowning up at a street sign where a dozen other signs have been hung as well—except instead of streets, they're labeled with the names of different Italian cities. Even worse, they're all pointing in different directions. Roma to the left, Firenze to the right, Pisa straight ahead. As if my brain needs another spatial challenge.

"Sorry. Just realizing I should have been writing down the directions along the way," I say, looking across the intersection again. "I'm sure it's just because I don't know the neighborhood. It's like trying to do a jigsaw puzzle with all the pieces turned upside down. How can I figure out each part if I don't even have an idea of the overall picture, you know?"

Ben stares down at me for a moment, his lips making that grim line again. "Your brain was bleeding a few days ago, Marnie. Give yourself a break."

Huh. Fair.

The light changes and we continue on. I'm trying to think of what to say next, how to ask any of the dozens of questions that pop into my brain at any one moment, when he stops halfway down the street in front of a green awning with NORTH MARKET written across the edge. It looks almost out of place, stuck between a dry cleaner on one side and a small shop called Wireless Warehouse on the other. Above the door there's an illuminated OPEN sign, with each of its three windows featuring a different faded poster of produce. None of it looks particularly appetizing, but right now, I'm too relieved to care.

I turn back to Ben, a huge grin on my face. "Thank you. Seriously, I never would have found this on my own."

It's impossible to tell if he truly understands just how much I mean it. His expression gives nothing away.

"Do you need help getting home?" he asks.

"No, it's totally fine. I'll figure it out," I reply, waving away the offer and ignoring the stab of anxiety at the thought of somehow navigating my way back again.

A moment passes while we both just stand there, looking at one another. The morning sun has risen above the buildings opposite us, and its light shines down on Ben's face from a new angle. I didn't realize it before, but his eyes aren't really that dark at all. There are flecks of amber woven in with the brown, and the rings around his irises are tinged with green.

His brow furrows, and it's only then that I realize I've been staring up at him for an embarrassingly long amount of time.

"Right, well, I should probably head inside. Wish me luck," I say. Then I give him another salute—*why?*—and pull open the door to enter.

A bell trills somewhere above me. It's warm inside and thick with the smell of bread and coffee. There's a row of fresh produce along the left wall, crates of tomatoes and lettuce and oranges piled high under harsh fluorescent lighting. Further down the aisle there's a deli counter with rows of meats and a dozen different types of cheese. Tall shelves lined with pasta stand next to it. It's all so beautiful I could start crying again.

Instead, I pick up a basket and start filling it with my favorites—kale and pears and a few sweet potatoes—then venture down the next aisle, grabbing two bags of ziti and a few jars of tomato sauce. When I find the tea section, I'm so excited I grab six boxes as if the entire city might run out of chamomile at any moment.

By the time I make it to the register, my basket is laden with so much food, I need to use both hands to hoist it onto the counter in front of the cashier.

"Hello," I say, offering him an overly eager smile.

His name badge says *Darryl P.*, and he's eyeing me cautiously as he scans each item. Maybe it's my enthusiasm for fresh produce. Or my bangs, which I haven't touched since I left the hospital and probably look like they're trying to jettison from my head.

"That will be ninety dollars and thirty-seven cents," he finally says.

I instinctually reach for my phone, ready to unlock it and offer my digital wallet. But then I remember I don't have my phone. Even if I did, I couldn't do anything with it.

My heart begins to pound as I pull my wallet from my coat pocket. When I open it, there's only one debit card and I don't recognize the bank emblazoned on the front of it.

"I don't know if this works," I say, holding it up.

Darryl P. cocks an eyebrow at me, then at the card in my hand. "Is it stolen?"

My mouth falls open. "No, it's not stolen. It's *my* card. I just don't know if there's any money in this account."

"There's an ATM around the corner. You could check the balance."

For a split second I truly believe this is a genius idea. But then I remember that if I don't remember the passcode to my phone, there's a good chance I don't remember the four digits needed to get into my bank account, either.

"I don't know my pin," I say. "I mean, I *might* know the pin. I just don't know if I know. I hit my head and can't remember much from the last year, and normally it wouldn't be an issue since I never change my cards or passcodes, except I apparently changed the one on my phone, so . . ."

"So you have a debit card that you didn't steal but you can't access because you don't know the pin?" He laughs to himself, and I can picture Darryl P. telling this story to his grocery store employee friends tonight at the local bar. *You'll never believe the story this one tried to pull on me to use a stolen debit card.* Oh, the laughs that will be shared.

"Can you just swipe it to see if it'll go through?" I ask, trying to smile.

"Depends," he says with a shrug. "Is your signature gonna match the back of the card?"

"Just . . . run the card, please," I say through gritted teeth.

He considers for a second, then presses a few buttons on the register until the machine instructs me to tap my card on the reader in front of me.

I do, ignoring the panic clawing at my chest as we both stare down at the screen, waiting. Who knew a grocery store purchase could trigger this much anxiety?

Another moment passes, then, miraculously, the screen lights up with the word "approved."

Darryl P. doesn't look totally convinced, but I don't care. If this is as close to magic as I get today, I'll take it.

I emerge from North Market, a teeming shopping bag in hand, feeling triumphant. Sure, I don't know if I have a job or a boyfriend, or what I've been doing over the past year of my life, but I have a working bank card! And tea! The day couldn't possibly get any better.

Then I see Ben is standing right where I left him, and my heart stumbles. His feet are planted firmly on the sidewalk like he's taken root there, even though he clearly hasn't since he has a new shopping bag in his hand with *Wireless Warehouse* printed across the front.

"You're still here," I say, stopping in front of him.

His brow creases like he's the one who should be confused. "Should I not be?"

"No, I just didn't expect you to stay. You already walked me all the way here, and honestly, that's above and beyond what I expected . . ." My tongue trips over everything I want to tell him. How grateful I am for his help. How excited I am about my bank card and all the items in my shopping bag. But his expression suggests he's genuinely confused by my reaction, so I keep it short. "Anyway, thank you."

"It's fine," he says, like it's nothing. As if walking his neighbor half a mile to the grocery store is on par with his usual Monday morning. Then he holds out the plastic Wireless Warehouse bag to me. "This is for you."

I blink. "What is it?"

"They sell prepaid phones next door. Nothing fancy, just something temporary until you figure out your passcode."

I reach out and take what might be the best gift I've ever received in my entire life.

"You got me a burner phone?" I ask, my voice wobbly with emotion as I look inside the bag and see a box with a photo of a flip phone on the side.

He frowns, the full shape of his lips down-turning in such a way that I don't know whether to feel ashamed or turned on. "Not a burner phone, just a basic model with prepaid minutes so you can call and text until you don't need it anymore."

I smile up at him. "I'm pretty sure that's the definition of a burner phone."

This time I'm absolutely sure the corner of his mouth twitches up. "Just don't use it for any illegal activity."

"I won't. I promise."

"Very reassuring," he replies dryly, adjusting the leather bag over his shoulder. "Ready to head back?"

"Don't you have to go to work?"

"I have time."

I'm tempted to accept the offer, but I also know I've already given him more than he bargained for on this short walk, so I wave him off. "It's okay. I got it."

He's watching me like he knows that I do not, in fact, got it. "You remember the way?"

Nope, not even slightly, I want to say. But I reply, "I think so. It can't be too complicated, right?"

He frowns again as he flips the leather flap on his bag over so he can rummage inside. It's not that I'm trying to look, but I also can't help a quick glance at the contents. There's a laptop, a leather satchel neatly tied closed, and a paperback book whose title I don't catch before he pulls out a pair of tortoiseshell glasses along with a notebook and pencil. Then he puts on the glasses and starts writing.

A minute passes. Then another. He's too tall for me to see what he's doing, and I refuse to stand on my tiptoes—I have already been through too much—but I still lean in to see. I can't quite read what is on the paper, but I do get a whiff of sawdust and sandalwood from his jacket.

"What's that?" I ask.

He doesn't answer immediately, only finishes the line he's working on, then rips the page out and hands it to me.

"Directions."

I look down at the grid paper and see that, yes, that's exactly what they are. He's even added little arrows to show which way to turn at each step.

When he catches my expression over the rim of his glasses—eyes wide, mouth agape—his head cocks to the side slightly. "You said you should have written them down, right?"

"I did, yeah."

"There you go," he says, as if the topic has been resolved. Then he slides his pencil and notebook back in his bag, along with his glasses. "I put my number there in the corner. Text me when you have the phone set up and I'll send you Gino's information. He's old, so he moves pretty slow, but he's thorough."

"I will," I reply. "Thanks."

A moment passes and I'm not sure if I've missed a cue, if I'm supposed to say something else. Before I can decide, he takes a step backward.

"I'll see you around, Marnie," he says.

Then he turns and heads down the street and around the corner.

It takes another minute for me to recover enough to look back down at the directions. I read over each line carefully before I take a deep breath and follow them. Walk to the corner, then turn right. Pass the cigar shop with the man sitting outside, still grumbling to himself. Take a left at the street sign with numerous arrows jutting out, pointing to different Italian cities. Pass the basketball court, through the off-kilter intersection, then turn left.

Fifteen minutes later, I see our building there just a few doors down and can't help but smile.

Sure, Ben Morgan might think I'm insane, but he also got me home, safe and sound. And, with tea.

CHAPTER 6

To celebrate my new 617 area code, I do a thorough sweep of the apartment to make sure the mouse is gone, make myself a well-earned cup of tea, and put on a true crime documentary I'm not all that interested in watching, but is sure to drown out the sound of ABBA still playing downstairs. Then I curl up on my faded sofa and flip open my new phone, which I've convinced myself is very cool and retro and not at all embarrassing.

I know I should call Matt so we could figure out a time to meet up. I should also call the hospital to confirm my appointment tomorrow, and the bank to find out just how much money I have in my account. But that can all wait. Right now, the only person I want to talk to is Sara.

I type her number into the small keypad, the same one I've had memorized since we both started working at Probus Recruiting five years ago—or six now, apparently. Back when she and I were just two junior recruiters who shared the same small cubicle across from the bathrooms. By the end of that first month, we were best friends, and over the next few years, we saw each other through so much, I'm not sure how I went so long without her. Even after she was promoted out of our department a few months before I was due to move, she still helped line up a position for me at the Boston office, because that's just who she is. Sara solves everything.

I press call, just as another rusty gear clicks into place in my brain.

Wait. Do I still work at Probus? Did the Boston office know about my accident, or did they simply fire me after I didn't show up for a week? Had Sara tried to cover for me? Did Sara even know? What if—

The phone connects.

"Hello?" Sara answers. Her voice is so familiar when nothing else in my life is that a sudden rush of emotion swells in my chest and all I can do is burst into tears.

"Oh my God, Marnie! Is that you?" she says. "I've been trying to call you for days! I was so worried! Are you okay?"

"I'm fine," I say, my voice wobbly. "I mean, not *fine*, obviously. But I'm okay. Sort of. Just . . . happy to hear your voice."

"Really? Because it sounds like you're crying so hard you're doing that sob-hiccup thing," she says. I can hear the smile in her voice.

"You're worth the sob-hiccup," I reply, trying to smile, too.

"You have no idea how much I've been freaking out. Matt called us a few days ago and told us about the accident, but he was cagey with details, which is just so annoying. And whenever I tried calling you, it always went to voicemail, which had me even more worried. Well, first I was pissed off, *then* I was worried."

I laugh. At least now the mystery behind the seventeen missed calls is solved. "Sorry. I can't unlock my phone. I don't remember the passcode."

"What do you mean, you don't remember the passcode?"

I tell her the whole sordid story in one long diatribe, all the broken bits and scraps that I have no idea what to do with. From the hospital to the new apartment to my retro burner phone. In true Sara fashion, she doesn't interrupt, not until I deliver the final, devastating blow.

"And I cut my hair!"

An audible gasp fills the line. "No."

"*Yes*. It's so short, Sara."

"Why would you do that without consulting me first?"

If I was being honest, I would tell her that is the only thing about this situation that does make sense. During our five—six—years of friendship, Sara has become the closest thing to family that I have left. She had been there as my grandmother's health declined, opened up her home to me when I had to sell the bungalow. She had helped plan the funeral, forced me to keep coming to work when the grief was too much. She's the best listener I had ever met, the big sister I never had. But in true big sister form, she also tended to think she knew what was best, sharing her opinion and advice whether I asked for it or not, so for my own sanity, I had learned to keep some decisions to myself. And choosing to lop eight inches of hair off would definitely fall under that category.

But now isn't the time for honesty. It's the time for lots and lots of tears.

"I don't know, Sara!" I wail. "I don't remember an entire year. That includes haircuts!"

Sara lets out a sympathetic sigh, like she recognizes that this is a rare moment to bypass the typical advice and head straight for compassion. "If it makes you feel better, I would be crying, too, Marn," she says. "And not just about the hair."

It does make me feel better. Sara is always so put together, so on top of everything. If this would reduce even her to tears, maybe I'm not doing so badly.

Then I catch sight of my bangs shooting out at a right angle from my forehead and give up on trying to console myself.

"Have you talked to Matt yet?" Sara asks carefully.

"Just for a few minutes in the hospital," I mutter, wiping my eyes with the sleeve of my sweater. "And before you ask: Yes, he told me about the breakup."

"He told you over the *phone*?"

I smile despite the tears. That's one thing I've always loved about Sara: She expects only the best from everyone, even in the face of inconvenient medical emergencies.

"Well, he didn't really have a choice. He's out of town at this conference, so it was either that or I show up at an apartment that's not ours and figure it out on my own."

"Fine. I'll give him a pass," she huffs. "So how are you feeling about it? Are you okay?"

I know what she expects me to say. That I'm gutted, that these tears are for Matt just as much as for my lost memories. And part of me wants that, too, if only so I could have one emotional reaction that feels normal.

"I'm still working that out," I reply, being as honest as possible.

"Of course you are. You don't even remember breaking up with him."

Ostensibly, this is true. I can almost feel the absence in the corner of my brain where the breakup *should* go. But it doesn't feel empty because of a lack of memory. Not entirely. There's a lack of emotion, too. A space where the pain and heartache should be, but they're missing. All that's there is the echo of all the awkwardness and stress that had accumulated between me and Matt during that last year in LA.

It had been a subtle shift. Anyone on the outside wouldn't have even noticed. But I did. As soon as Sara and Garrett were married, it felt like the same expectation was waiting on the threshold for us, but neither of us wanted to answer the door. So we just pretended it wasn't there. The same way we pretended not to notice how work monopolized our time, how we barely talked anymore. And when we did, how we didn't really have that much to say.

Maybe that's why we broke up. We got sick of pretending.

"Did you and I talk about what happened?" I ask her.

"Are you kidding? I feel like it's all we talked about for months. How the move was really stressful for both of you, and he was working these long hours, while you were miserable at Probus. It was a rough time, but I thought you two would get through it. Then one day you called and said you broke up. You moved into your own apartment, and then a few weeks later you told me you quit Probus and took a job in sales and distribution—"

"I work in sales and distribution?" I blurt out, interrupting her.

The idea that I quit Probus isn't totally shocking. Since Sara got promoted, leaving me alone in our windowless cubicle, I had struggled to remember why I'd spent so long there to begin with. I never wanted to work in an office, proofreading résumés or creating PowerPoint slides that no one would ever look at. It had simply been the most straightforward way to pay my grandmother's ever-growing pile of medical bills. After she was gone, I promised myself I'd start chasing my dreams again. That's half the reason I agreed to come to Boston with Matt; I needed a fresh start.

So why would I quit one office job just to take another?

"Yeah, for a beverage company or something like that? Meanwhile, Matt started dating this woman who was totally not his type, and it was like living in bizarro world."

All thoughts about my apparent career change suddenly dissolve. "Matt has a girlfriend?"

"*Had* a girlfriend. They broke up," Sara replies reassuringly.

I pause, waiting to feel something—sadness or anger or even just annoyance. Instead, there's just that odd hollowness in my chest.

"He's still crazy about you, Marn," Sara continues. "In fact, you two just met up to talk about getting back together!"

The information sits at an odd angle in my brain, not quite slotting in where I know it should. "We did?"

"Yes! Right before the accident. I'm telling you, it wasn't a breakup. Just a reroute."

"A reroute?"

"You know, like GPS. If there's a crash or traffic or something, it reroutes you. Yeah, it's not the road you planned to take, but you still get to the same place."

"And where's that?"

"The house across the street from mine, married to Matt so our kids grow up together and everyone lives happily ever after, obviously."

I let out a dry laugh. That had always been Sara's plan. Since the first moment she mentioned her boyfriend's best friend, the expectation had been written in stone: Sara and Garrett, Marnie and Matt. Two sets of best friends who live the rest of their lives together. Our collective happy ending.

After a moment, Sara sighs. "God, this sucks. I wish I could jump on a plane right now and come to see you but I'm in the middle of this stupid pitch deck about building out our New York team. It's asinine but I need to do it if I'm going to get this promotion."

"I thought you just got promoted before I moved?"

"I did, but this is for a VP title. I need to lock that in before Garrett and I start trying for a baby."

I smile even as new tears prick my eyes. "A baby?"

"Don't you dare! We can't talk about it or we'll jinx it." Sara's voice is firm, the way it always is when she demands I knock on wood after saying something provocative, or when someone spills salt and forgets to throw it over their left shoulder. "If it happens, it happens. In the meantime, we need to focus on you and how you're going to get better, and then you and Matt will get back together, and everything will be great."

I roll my eyes, but only because I know she can't see me. "Okay."

"So, what's the plan?"

How do I admit I have no plan? That part of me is still hoping my grandmother was right and the universe will intervene, magically fixing my brain, maybe even show me what I'm supposed to be doing with my life, too. I know my grandmother would love to hear about my renewed faith, but unfortunately, Sara is too pragmatic. She needs dates and milestones, something concrete and quantifiable.

"Go to this appointment tomorrow and hopefully figure out how to get my memories back," I reply, trying to sound confident.

She hums to herself. "Hope isn't a strategy, Marn."

I sigh. That has been Sara's signature phrase since the moment I met her. "And then I should probably get a hold of my bank to see if I have any money. I haven't been able to access my email or get online to check."

Silence fills the line and I can almost hear Sara's brain working.

"All right," she finally says. "I know what you should do."

I smile. This is Sara's forte. According to her, everyone needed a plan, and if you didn't have one, she was more than happy to come up with one for you.

"Okay, let's hear it."

"You move back here," she says. "You can stay with us in the spare room and start looking for a job in Los Angeles. I bet Probus would even have you back!"

My stomach drops. It's not just the idea of working at Probus again that makes me cringe, but retreating to California, moving back in with Sara, returning to a life that I had already been looking to escape.

"I can't," I say. "At least, not right now. All my doctors are here and I need to work out a plan with them to get my memories back."

"Okay, fine. I'll accept that excuse. But only because I need you to remember why you cut all your hair off."

I groan. "It's so bad. There are *bangs*, Sara."

"FaceTime me so I can see."

"I can't get into my phone, remember? I'm using a prepaid one until I can get to an Apple Store. Which is somewhere in Boston, but I have no idea how to get there!" Suddenly, I can feel tears start to burn my eyes again. "And to make everything worse, I think the head injury sent all my emotions out of whack, so now I'm crying all the time and . . . and . . ." My voice falters as I hold back a sob.

"And your hair will grow back, and your brain will heal, and everything will be okay," Sara finishes for me, her tone so assured I can't help but believe her. "In the meantime, we have *so* much to catch up on."

We talk for another hour. Sara deftly avoids all mention of her and Garrett's attempts at starting a family, though it's clearly implied in each anecdote: the house they just put an offer on in Calabasas. The large SUV they're getting when they trade in Garrett's sports car. We could probably have talked all night, but halfway through a story about Garrett's demands for a man cave, I hear another voice behind her.

"Oh shit. I have to go. I have a meeting and totally forgot," she says.

There's a flurry of hurried goodbyes, then she hangs up.

I let my head fall back into the sofa cushions and try to recall everything she told me, parsing out the information that can help piece together the past year. First, I quit Probus. That should be good news. But if I finally got up the nerve to leave, why did I take another office job? Is there some local beverage company out there that's livid because one of their sales managers hasn't shown up for work all week? Second, Matt is still crazy about me. We might have even been talking about getting back together. Except, if that's true, why did we break up to begin with?

It's just a reroute.

I understood why Sara thought of it that way. Before Matt and I had even gone on our first date, she talked about us getting married as if it were an inevitability. Somewhere along the way, I think I had started to believe that, too.

So why didn't this hurt more? Shouldn't I be spending days in bed, nursing my heartbreak? Instead, there's just a dull ache, like an old bruise pressed long after it had started to heal.

I look back down at my phone. The obvious answer would be to call Matt and ask him every question currently swimming around my brain. But it's barely noon on a Monday, which means he's at work. Or he's still in Toronto, which means he'll have his phone on silent while attending some panel discussion about computer languages or something. He might even be on the panel himself. In any case, I have enough experience with calling Matt in the middle of a workday to know it only leads to his voicemail.

So instead, I text.

MARNIE

hey, it's Marnie!

having issues with my other phone so this is my new # in case you need to reach me

hope the conference is going well–let me know when you're back and we can grab that coffee! xo

While I wait for a reply, I call the hospital and confirm my appointment, then I pull my bank card from my wallet and dial the number on the back. The silver lining to Sara's revelation about my new job is the fact that I *have* a job. Which means I probably have at least a little bit of money to pay bills. All I need to do is talk to someone who can pull up my account and tell me how much. Maybe they could even see who issued my paychecks so I know who to call to explain my unexpected absence.

Unfortunately, after ten minutes, I'm ready to cry all over again. Regardless of what I say or the numbers I type when instructed, the automated voice on the other line refuses to connect me with a live person.

"I'm sorry, I didn't get that," the stilted voice says for what feels like the fiftieth time. "If you'd like to speak with an agent, say 'agent.'"

"AGENT," I say again, this time through gritted teeth.

"Got it. You want to hear the branch hours for our location in Somerville. We're open from nine—"

I hang up before I throw my phone out the window. Then I stand up, empty mug in hand, and head for the kitchen. I need more tea.

Ben's directions are still on the countertop where I left them when I got home. I barely notice until I stop at the sink to fill the kettle and my eyes snag on his phone number scrawled in the corner.

His handwriting sends an odd thrum down my spine. While I wait for the water to boil, I type his number into my contacts, and open a new text message.

MARNIE

thanks for your help today!

got home safe obv

I'm about to put the phone down, but then pause and start typing again.

MARNIE

this is Marnie Stephens, btw

from across the hall

I leave the phone face down on the counter when the kettle begins to whistle, and pour hot water into my waiting mug. Just as I'm about to reach for another bag of chamomile, a loud, tinny *ding* echoes through the apartment. I jump, only to almost immediately realize that, no, it's not some insane fire alarm. It's the sound of a text message coming in on my burner phone.

I pick it up and flip it open.

BEN MORGAN

No problem.

He's attached the contact information for Gino, the building's super. I smile and type out my response.

MARNIE

thank you for remembering!

BEN MORGAN

You're welcome. Knock if you need anything else.

Ben Morgan texts with the perfect punctuation of a serial killer. Thank God I didn't know that before our walk to the store earlier or I definitely would have convinced myself I was going to die.

MARNIE

i promise not to abuse the privilege 😉

I finish making my tea, then open the contact information for Gino and press call. It rings three times before it connects, but there's only silence on the other end.

"Hello?" I say after a moment.

I hear a reedy voice on the other end: "Hello?"

"Is this Gino?"

"Hello?"

"Hi, is this Gino?" I repeat a bit more loudly.

"Hello? This is Gino."

"Hi, Gino. I'm Marnie Stephens. I live in apartment 3A."

"Okay."

"Sorry to bother you, but I think I saw a mouse in my kitchen today."

"Okay."

I wait, hoping he'll connect the dots on his own. When he doesn't, I ask, "Is that something you can take care of?"

"Okay."

It takes another ten minutes before we finally agree on a time for him to stop by on Wednesday morning. At least, I think we've agreed. I'm trying to confirm one last time when my phone dings with another text message. I glance down at my screen long enough to see that it's from Matt, and my heart dips down into my stomach.

"That's great, Gino," I say, not exactly sure what he's talking about now, only that I need to get off the phone to reply to the text. "I'll see you Wednesday at nine."

"Okay," he says.

"Okay."

I wait, wondering if there's a more substantial goodbye coming, but then the line cuts out.

If that was Gino's version of goodbye or my new phone simply dropping the call, I have no idea. I also don't think it will accomplish much to call him back and find out. Instead, I open my messages.

MATT

Thanks for your number

I got back today, actually

Could grab coffee this week if you're around

MARNIE

sounds great!

i have a doctor's appt at the hospital tomorrow—maybe we could meet up before?

MATT

Sounds good

There's a coffee shop right there on the corner of Cambridge St & Blossom—meet you there?

MARNIE

perfect! should we say 10-ish?

Matt sends back a thumbs-up emoji.

I stare down at the screen, waiting for more. Matt always treated text conversations like he would in-person ones, which usually meant adding a goodbye at the end. But after another moment, I realize there's no goodbye coming. This is it.

And that's fine. A limited response makes sense in the context of whatever happened between the two of us. I just wish I knew exactly what that was.

It's not our purpose to understand the universe's plan, my grandmother's voice echoes in my head. *Just trust its magic and enjoy the ride.*

That sounded so wise when I was eleven. So whimsical. I only wish it still did at thirty.

I mean thirty-one.

Damn it.

CHAPTER 7

The muffled sound of ABBA's "Dancing Queen" wakes me up the next morning. I pull my duvet up around my chin and squeeze my eyes shut, willing myself back to sleep. Yes, I should probably be excited about meeting Matt for coffee in a few hours, and my doctor's appointment afterward, but this bed is so comfortable, and I had been having the best dream about long blond hair and megayachts. Then a car horn blares from somewhere outside, followed by a long string of profanities. My eyes snap open and I remember: *Oh yes, I am in hell.*

As if to prove my point, "Dancing Queen" ends, only to immediately begin again from somewhere downstairs.

I roll over to my stomach and open my eyes to look around at what is apparently my bedroom. Is that music coming from the apartment downstairs? How thin are these walls? Am I still dreaming?

When the song starts for a third time, I get up and shuffle over to the kitchen to make a cup of tea. I fill the kettle and put it on the stovetop, then lean a hip against the counter and stare at the items tacked up on the corkboard while I wait for it to boil. There's a napkin from a coffee shop called Strange Brew. A receipt from the Brattle Book Shop. Two movie theater ticket stubs for *Rear Window*.

I've always tended toward sentimentality. When I was six, I had a crush on Justin Webber, a boy in my first-grade class whose mother packed a Jolly Rancher in his lunch every day. Once, when no one was looking, I discreetly saved the wrapper from one and hid it under my pillow. In my mind, that was the safest spot imaginable—until my grandmother changed my sheets a few days later. I cried myself to sleep that night, but I also learned an important lesson: If I wanted to hold on to small, seemingly insignificant mementos, I had to keep them somewhere safe. Like a corkboard.

I stare at the items tacked up there now. What had I been up to this past year?

The kettle begins to wail. I absently reach into the cabinet for a mug, placing it on the counter and throwing a tea bag in before I really look at it.

When I do, I pause. It's white, with blue text on the side that is too faded to make out from numerous washings. But I know exactly what it says: PARADISE COVE BEACH CAFÉ. In an instant, a flood of memories come back to me: walking down from my grandmother's bungalow barefoot, ordering a strawberry milkshake to drink in the beach chairs and only being able to make it through half of it. For a brief moment I can actually feel the sand between my toes. Smell the ocean salt and taste the ice cream. All from a completely ordinary mug.

I fill it with steaming water and cradle it in my hands as a kernel of an idea plants itself in my brain. I turn back to the corkboard.

My memories are in my brain somewhere, I know they are. I just need to find the right thing to trigger them.

~

The idea is still rattling around in my brain an hour later when the car that picked me up for my doctor's appointment comes to a stop outside the hospital. The coffee shop where I'm meeting Matt is just across the street, but as I step out onto the sidewalk and see Mass General looming in front of me, all other thoughts bottom out of my head.

I only left yesterday, yet my body has a visceral reaction to being back, like it remembers exactly how I arrived there, even if my brain doesn't. I cross the street to the coffee shop, working so hard to ignore how my heart pounds, how my hands shake as I cling to my purse, I almost walk past Matt without noticing him.

He's standing by the doorway, his blond head bent down as he stares at his phone, so he misses my double take.

I'm not used to seeing him in a suit. Back in LA, the most his job required was khakis and a button-down, and even that was only when there was a client lunch. Most days he was in a T-shirt, huddled behind a computer, writing code to secure huge data centers all over the world.

Apparently, the folks in Boston are more demanding about dress code. His navy blue suit and maroon tie render him almost unrecognizable. I probably would have walked right by him if it wasn't for the way he was leaning against the lamppost, one leg crossed over the other. Matt has a very specific lean, one he claims he adopted to try to blend in after a growth spurt in fifth grade shot him towering above his classmates. From then on, he was tall and lanky, but now more grown-up, too.

"Hi," I say, stopping a few feet in front of him.

He looks up, his blue eyes wide with surprise, and for a moment I worry he's not there to meet me at all and this is just a random coincidence. Then his gaze meets mine and he smiles. His blond hair is shorter than the last time I saw him, when he left for Boston and I kissed him goodbye at the airport. But that wasn't the last time I saw him, was it? Suddenly, the reality of where I am and what's happened hits me all over again.

"Hey," he says.

I almost step forward to give him a hug, half expecting one of his signature kisses on the top of my head. But he doesn't open his arms like I'm used to. Instead, he just slides his phone into his pocket. It almost feels awkward, like running into an old friend from college you haven't seen in years, and now you're struggling to remember why you were friends at all.

He seems to be thinking the same thing because he shifts his weight and clears his throat.

"Sorry, I was just going through a few work emails," he says.

I nod. "Everything okay?"

He shrugs one shoulder as he lets out a long sigh. "Probably not."

I smile. Finally, a hint of the Matt I remember. "Sounds like you need some coffee."

He smiles, too, then motions toward the nearby door.

Inside, the coffee shop is sterile and gray. Even if you didn't know the hospital was nearby, you could tell by the clientele, a scattering of white coats and blue scrubs, all with an air of exhaustion. Matt and I go to the counter, where I order a tea and he orders a latte. Then we navigate the haphazard collection of tables and chairs to a long metal counter along the window. It's a moment that's almost normal, similar to thousands we've had before, but this time there's an unfamiliar politeness, manners that never existed between us but now feel required.

"Is this spot okay?"

"Sure, does it work for you?"

"Yes, this is good. Do you want to sit—"

"Oh, sorry . . ."

"No, no, you go ahead . . ."

By the time we settle into our seats, the air is heavy with that same stiffness from the sidewalk.

It's ironic, in a way. When we were getting ready to move, I had prepared myself for at least a little bit of awkwardness. Matt and I had spent our entire relationship as part of a larger whole: Garrett and Sara, Matt and Marnie. In Boston we would be on our own, defining exactly what Matt and Marnie, the singular unit, would be.

I guess we never figured it out.

"Thanks for meeting up," I say, as if the moment calls for it. And who knows? Maybe it does. "Especially right after being out of town. Work is probably crazy right now."

"It's okay. Work is always crazy. Besides, this is important," he says, then takes another sip of his latte.

Silence descends again. My innate desire to fill it is almost unbearable, but I also don't know where to start. I want to prod him, push and poke for any answer I can get until I arrive at wherever we ended up. A place he knows how to navigate while I'm left completely in the dark.

"I'm sorry, by the way," he continues after a moment. "For that phone call while you were in the hospital. You were already dealing with a lot, I should have just shut up and waited for the right time to tell you everything."

"To be fair, I'm not sure there's a right time to tell your girlfriend with retrograde amnesia that the two of you broke up after moving across the country together," I say.

He nods, his smile returning for a moment. "Very true."

I let another moment pass before I ask, "So what happened?"

He releases a long breath, as if he had been holding it until we arrived at this question. And even though I don't have the courage to ask outright, I know he reads between the lines: *Why did we break up?*

"I don't know if it was just one thing," he replies. "Just . . . a lot of things piled up."

Part of me wants to roll my eyes at another one of Matt's signature nonanswers. Words strung together that don't really tell you anything at all. But I have to admit there's truth in there, too. Even before Boston, Matt and I had been feeling the strain. Living together had been punctuated by expectation and stress. On top of Sara's not-so-subtle hints that we should just get engaged already, I was struggling with the day-to-day monotony at Probus, while Matt put in extra hours in the hopes of getting a promotion. When it finally came through, he warned me about how much more he would be working, how he wouldn't be present as much as he might want.

Full disclosure, he'd said at the time. It had eventually become an inside joke, a code for when we had a confession to make, however small.

Full disclosure, when I was at the coffee shop today, I spent eleven dollars on something called "cloud coffee."

Full disclosure, I was up until two a.m. playing Call of Duty.

Then, when the promotion required him to relocate to Boston and he asked me to come with him, I almost wished I could use our joke as a lifeline, a way to talk about my concerns, my fears.

Full disclosure, I don't know what I'm doing with my life and I worry that I'll just be swallowed up into yours.

I never did, though.

"Was it the move?" I ask.

Matt seems to consider as he strums his fingers against his cup. "The move was stressful, yeah. You arrived a few weeks after I did, and I'd already fallen into a rhythm at work. Long hours, weekends, it was bad. When I was here alone, it only affected me. But then you arrived and we never saw each other. It all just got really hard."

The comment feels awkward, like it's missing some key component, but I can't quite place it.

"When was the last time we saw each other?"

Matt sighs. "We actually met up for drinks the day of the accident."

A spark of recognition flares in my brain. Sara had mentioned something like that, hadn't she? How Matt and I met up right before my injury to talk about getting back together.

"But I thought you were in Toronto," I say.

"I left the day after. I didn't know what happened to you, or I wouldn't have . . ." He sighs again, this time with a shrug. "Anyway, I didn't know anything until the hospital called me."

I stare down into my tea, trying to organize a thousand different questions spinning in my head. "But if we broke up six months ago, why did we meet for drinks?"

He leans back, like he's thinking very carefully about what words to say next. "We hadn't talked much since the breakup. There was a lot that we didn't get a chance to say."

I have no idea what that means, but before I can ask, his phone rings, sending a tinny melody through the air. He pulls it from his jacket pocket and glances at the screen. Whatever name he sees there makes him nervous, a microexpression that no one but me would probably notice.

"Sorry, it's work." He flashes me an apologetic smile, then turns to take the call, leaving me with a view of his profile.

When Sara first told me she was going to set me up with Garrett's friend Matt, she had described him first and foremost as ridiculously handsome. *He has such a strong nose*, she had said. *A politician's nose*.

I never knew what she meant by that, but ultimately, it didn't matter. All that mattered was that Sara thought he would be perfect for me. And just a few weeks later, Matt became a regular fixture in my life, slotting in so seamlessly, I barely noticed the change. How had I extracted myself from that so spectacularly?

Matt hangs up and sighs. "Sorry, we have a new client who needs an epic amount of hand-holding. They're coming by the office this morning, so I need to head in."

Then he's on his feet, putting on his coat, and I suddenly feel panicked. I don't know what I had been hoping to glean from this meeting, but it was definitely more than a cup of tea and a few of his signature nonanswers.

"Do you think we can get together later this week?" I ask.

He pauses, and a strange emotion passes over his face. Not regret exactly, but something pained. Like he had hoped to escape this line of questioning.

"I don't know if that's a good idea," he says delicately.

"Oh." I blink, trying to recover, but I have no idea what the right response is. Should I try not to look hurt? Or act like I know why? I can't pick one, so instead I just sit there, trying to keep a neutral, easy expression on my face, while my bangs point out sideways from my head.

He pauses. "It's not that I don't want to, Marn. I just think it's better if you have some space to work through all of this. But that doesn't mean you shouldn't call if you need something. Regardless of what happened between us, I still care about you."

Then give me something, I want to say. *One concrete bit of information to help make this make sense.*

But I don't. I just watch as he gets his things together, then disappears out the door, leaving me with a half-finished tea and no idea what I'm supposed to do next.

If my grandmother were here, she'd know what to do. There would be a crystal I needed to wear or a mantra to repeat. *Be present and let the magic find you*, she'd say. There was a time when I would have believed her, too.

But my grandmother isn't here now. And there's no magic I can find to save me. I have to save myself.

CHAPTER 8

After I finish my tea, I walk across the street and take the elevator up to the fifth floor of Mass General. It climbs slowly, and as each floor number lights up above the doors as we ascend, I feel what I think is a panic attack growing in my chest, crowding my lungs as I try to gulp down air without drawing too much attention from the two nurses standing beside me.

When I left here yesterday, I had really hoped I wouldn't need to come back. The bit of my brain that still worked wanted so badly to believe I would wake up this morning with my memories magically restored, that I had somehow put a mental block on everything that would have to happen next if they weren't. More tests, more appointments, more reminders of just how broken I am.

A loud *ding* saves me from that particularly sobering thought just as the doors open on the fifth floor. I step out, take in a few more deep breaths, then turn down the hall to see the neurology clinic just ahead. The waiting room is wrapped in glass walls so I can see row after row of chairs and a long desk near the back. There's a nurse seated behind it, and he gives me a warm smile when I enter.

"Checking in?" he asks as I approach.

"Yes. Marnie Stephens?" I reply.

He types something into his computer. "I just need your license and insurance card."

Right. I reach into my tote bag and pull out my wallet, sliding my license from its sleeve. Then I look for my insurance card. I have insurance, right? I had it when I worked at Probus Recruiting. I had even celebrated the fact that, after years of temping, I finally had a job that offered benefits. But I don't work for Probus anymore, I work in sales and distribution at some mysterious beverage company. That's if I still have a job at all.

I'm about to start panicking when I find an insurance card tucked behind a Walgreens rewards card. It's not the same one I had in California. I'm not even sure if it's valid, but I still hand it over to the nurse. It feels like I'm holding my breath as he types the information into his computer—*click*, *click*, *click*. He pauses. Then, miraculously, he smiles and hands both cards back to me.

"You're all set," he says. "Have a seat and we'll call you when we're ready."

I thank him and turn back to the waiting room.

The chairs are all covered in the same fabric, beige with specks of dark brown, like whoever picked them out wanted you to forget them as soon as you left. It's kind of ironic, considering. I pick the one closest to the desk, situating myself with my bag in my lap. And I wait.

The minutes pass slowly. There's a woman sitting across from me in a Patriots sweatshirt, scrolling on her phone with the same glassy-eyed focus I feel like I've had since I woke up. Same for the man on the other side of the room, who's staring slack-jawed at the aquarium on the far wall. We're all waiting for our names to be called, the world's least exciting lottery.

I'm so desperate for something to do, I'm about to pick up the two-year-old copy of *Golf Digest* sitting on the small table next to me when a nearby door opens.

"Margaret Stephens?" another nurse calls out from the doorway. When I stand, she smiles. "Come on back."

I follow her down a long corridor lined with doors, each one shut and only the muted hum of conversation audible as we pass, until she finally ushers me into a room at the end.

She takes my blood pressure and my heart rate and tells me the doctor will be with me shortly. Then she's gone and I'm left staring at a poster on the opposite wall explaining the parts of the brain.

After twenty minutes, it's clear to me why *Overboard* didn't feature Goldie Hawn's outpatient cognitive therapy appointments after she was discharged from the hospital: This is all painfully boring.

A knock on the door echoes off the walls of the small room a moment later, and a doctor appears through the doorway. Her scrubs are a vibrant turquoise that flatter her complexion. Her tight curls are short, and she's wearing a pair of silver hoop earrings. She tilts her head to look at me over the rim of her red glasses and smiles.

"Hello, Margaret. I'm Dr. Janine Herman. I'm a neuropsychologist who works with the neurology team here at Mass General."

"It's nice to meet you, Dr. Herman," I say, shaking her hand. "You can just call me Marnie."

"And you can just call me Janine," she replies. "You might not realize, but I was in the ER the night you were admitted."

I feel the heavy roll of my pulse. I still have such an abstract perspective on my injury and everything that happened afterward. It's a blank page only half filled with bits and pieces of information supplied by the doctors and nurses who were there, but without any real frame of reference. Like people describing a movie they saw, not my actual life. It's so frustrating and scary that before I know it, I feel tears welling in my eyes.

"I'm sorry," I say, doing my best to smile even as my bottom lip trembles. "I usually don't cry like this, but I can't seem to stop lately."

"No need to apologize. No doubt your emotions are a bit of a roller coaster. But that's normal. That's why you're here. Dr. Buterman took care of the injury, so now I'm here to help you with the recovery." She sits down in the chair in front of me and crosses her legs. "So how have you been doing?"

I had promised myself that I would try to be brief, but once I start talking, I can't seem to stop. I tell her everything: how I didn't recognize anything in my apartment, how I met Ben and he showed me where to find the grocery store. I even bring up the mouse, though I'm not sure how that fits into the broader story of my brain.

Once I finally shut up, Janine leans back and sighs. "I know you might not believe this, but you're doing phenomenally well."

I let out a feeble laugh. "Really? Because this does not feel phenomenal."

"You've been through a lot," she agrees. "And I can see how that gap in your memory would be your main concern right now. But trust me when I say that it's impressive to be doing this well after an injury like yours, which leads me to believe that your *memories* haven't been affected by the injury, just your ability to retrieve them. If that's the case, then we have to give your brain time to heal. Develop a plan to help in your recovery."

"You mean a plan that will help me get my memories back."

She pushes her reading glasses up to the top of her head. "Recovery isn't linear, Marnie. You'll have good days and bad days. The most important thing is to be patient with yourself. As your neural networks stabilize, I'm confident things will start coming back to you."

It feels so ambiguous. So passive.

"So I'm supposed to just . . . wait?" I ask, hoping I don't sound too dejected.

Her lips purse as she seems to consider. "Not wait, per se. But making demands of your brain right now could do more harm than good. That said, you don't have to take a back seat in the process, either. Something as simple as spending time with friends and loved ones could promote memory recall, especially if they're nearby and know your daily routine."

The hope that had begun to float up in my chest quickly sinks to the floor. The only person I know in Boston is Matt, and he just made it very clear that spending any time together is off the table.

"Anything else?" I ask.

"Well, there's data to suggest that visiting places that are familiar to you helps with recovery as well, but since you're new to the city, that might be hard," she says carefully.

I'm about to remind her this wouldn't just be hard; it would be nearly impossible. Even if I wasn't struggling with directions right now, I still don't know the city, let alone how to navigate it. But then my mind flits back to my apartment. The movie tickets on the corkboard. The bookstore receipt. The coffee shop napkin.

"What about places I *think* I've been before?" I ask.

Janine cocks her head to the side. "I'm not sure I understand."

"It might be nothing, but since I've been little, I tend to keep mementos from moments I want to remember," I say, trying to find the right words to make this sound constructive and not completely crazy. "They usually seem pretty insignificant, like a candy wrapper, but they mean something to me. And I've found a few things like that in my apartment—movie tickets, napkins, receipts, all from places in Boston. I know I kept them for a reason. I just don't know why. But maybe if I went back to those places, it could trigger something in my brain. Unlock my memories. What do you think?"

Janine smiles. "I think you're onto something." Then she turns back to her tablet. "Okay, let's put together a plan and then schedule a follow-up appointment for next month to see how you're progressing. How does that sound?"

I nod. For the first time in what feels like ages, excitement stirs in my chest. I can get all my memories back—all I have to do is follow the clues I left around my apartment. If Goldie Hawn could do it in *Overboard*, I can do it in Boston.

Maybe I'll even pick up some purple shampoo while I'm at it.

CHAPTER 9

By seven o'clock that night, I have a hot cup of chamomile tea and a handwritten list of every unfamiliar object in my apartment that could potentially have sentimental value:

- A receipt for Jane Eyre from the Brattle Book Shop from the corkboard
- A piece of red-and-white string
- A napkin from a coffee shop called Strange Brew with 304 written across the top
- A finished roll of 35 mm film in an envelope ready to be sent to someplace called Photo-Rama

- A program for the autumn events at the Boston Public Library taped to the fridge
- Two movie ticket stubs for Rear Window at the Brattle Theatre
- A map of the Isabella Stewart Gardner Museum from my desk
- A metal dog from Monopoly that was sitting on the windowsill

I cradle the warm Paradise Cove Beach Café mug in both hands and stare down at the list, then into an old shoebox I found in my closet, where I have all the items piled together. Suddenly, I feel a twinge of pity for my grandmother after she threw away Justin Webber's Jolly Rancher wrapper all those years ago. How was she supposed to understand the significance of something anyone else would assume was junk? Because right now, that's what this looks like: a small box of junk.

It's not junk, though, I remind myself. These are memories. *My* memories. All I have to do is visit the places associated with them and those memories will come back. Simple as that.

For a half second, it honestly feels that easy. But as my gaze flits over the contents of the shoebox—the Monopoly dog, the random piece of string—I realize the colossal kink in this plan: I don't know where half these items came from. They obviously mean *something* to me, but without any other tangible details to go on, it's virtually impossible to decipher them.

And that's fine, I remind myself. I don't need to know where *all* this stuff came from. If Janine is right and all I have to do is visit a few places to trigger my memories, then I just need to focus on the items that have locations attached. And figure out how to get to them. And what I'm looking for once I do. And then, how to get back home.

Before I reach peak levels of panic, my phone starts to ring on the cushion next to me. When I look down, I see Sara's name lighting up the screen.

"Did you have coffee with Matt today?" she says before I can say hello.

I straighten, my eyebrows stitching together. "How do you know about that?"

"Garrett, obviously. He just called me and said Matt texted him, so now I need to know why *you* didn't call me immediately afterward."

I roll my eyes. "Because nothing happened. Honestly. We grabbed a coffee and talked for a few minutes. That's it."

"That's it?" She sounds utterly disappointed.

"He had to go to work, and I had a doctor's appointment."

"Okay, fine. When are you meeting up again?"

"I'm not sure we are," I say. "Matt didn't seem to think that was a good idea."

Sara scoffs. "Why not?"

"I don't know. It sounds like his job is really demanding right now. Or maybe he's seeing someone else and doesn't want to give me the wrong impression."

"Impossible," she says. Her voice is so resolute, I almost believe her. "But whatever, I'll have Garrett give him a call and ask what his problem is."

"Sara—"

"How did the doctor's appointment go?"

I sigh. "It was fine."

"We're talking about a traumatic brain injury, Marnie. You have to give me more than 'fine.'"

I smile, letting my head fall back into the sofa cushions. "Well, my brain is healed, so that's a good thing. And we came up with a game plan to recover my memories."

"A plan! Yes!" she exclaims. "What do you have to do?"

"I'm supposed to visit places that are familiar and wait for something to trigger my brain so my memories come back."

"Okay, but how can you do that when you don't even remember moving to Boston?"

"Because I keep finding all these mementos from Boston around my apartment. Movie ticket stubs. A piece of string. A receipt for a copy of *Jane Eyre*."

Sara is well aware of my sentimental menagerie of items—I kept the cork from the bottle of drugstore prosecco we opened when I moved in with her prominently displayed on our bookcase for years—so I know she'll immediately understand. "So you're going to those places to see what looks familiar? God, that's so brilliant."

"Only if it works," I reply.

"Of course it will work," she says. "Now tell me what we're working with."

I go through the list with her, detailing each item until we get to the end and she lets out a gasp. "Wait. You kept all these things because they're from moments you wanted to remember, right?"

"Right."

"What if they're moments you wanted to remember with someone else?"

My brow furrows. "What do you mean?"

Sara groans. "Isn't it obvious? These are from dates with Matt!"

"How can you possibly know that?"

"Because I just *know*. He always said he was going to read *Jane Eyre*, right? Who else would you buy a copy for?"

She has a point. I had been begging him to read it ever since we started dating. After we moved in together—and my copy was readily available on our shared bookshelf—he said he would try, but he never found the time. Did I buy him his own book after the breakup? One last parting gift that could be sitting in his apartment right now.

"Matt's the only person you know in Boston, Marn," Sara continues. "And if you two were toying with the idea of getting back together, then it makes sense that you'd go out a few times, too."

The thought rolls around in my head, not knowing which way to go.

"Maybe that's why he doesn't think it's a good idea to get together again," Sara continues. "He's waiting for you to remember so it's not, like, emotional manipulation or something. When you think of it that way, it's really kind of selfless."

I smile. "You should write romance novels."

"No way." She scoffs. "I'm much too cynical. Besides, I'm within spitting distance of this VP job, I *know* it."

There's a knock on the other end of the line, then the sound of a door opening.

"Oh shit, my four o'clock is here. I gotta go," Sara says. "Call me later!"

She hangs up and I leave my phone on the cushion beside me, taking a sip of my tea as I do another audit of my carefully curated box of memories.

Are these all from moments I shared with Matt? The idea doesn't ring true, but that doesn't mean much since nothing in my life rings true right now. All I can do is follow this list until something triggers my brain and my memories come back. Then I'll know for sure, one way or another.

Now I just need to decide where to start.

I reach inside the box and pull out the small Monopoly dog. When Sara and I lived together, she told me her Monopoly theory: If you feel like you're falling in love with someone, you should play a game of Monopoly together. If you came out the other side still liking the other person, then it was meant to be. The idea sat in the back of my brain ever since, waiting for the right moment to test it with Matt, but that never happened—or if it did, I don't remember it. It's also nearly impossible to know where this particular dog came from since there are probably thousands of Monopoly games in Boston.

I place the dog back inside and pick up the receipt from the bookshop. The address is printed at the top, so at least I know where to go. Then I notice something else: the date of purchase. I not only know where to go, but exactly when I was there last.

It feels like a nudge from the universe, one of those signs my grandmother always told me to watch out for. Sure, I have no idea why I bought a copy of *Jane Eyre* when I already own one, or why it would mean so much that I memorialized it on my corkboard, but those are all details to work out later. For now, I have an address and a date.

I lean down to examine the receipt for the Brattle Book Shop again, looking for any other details that could be helpful.

The good news is it's in Boston. The bad news: I don't know Boston at all. If this were Malibu, or even LA, I might have a chance, but the idea of an aimless wander around an unfamiliar city is enough to send my fragile optimism into freefall.

I flip open my phone and type the address into the small browser window. A map pops up that's almost impossible to decipher, so I try to follow the directions list. This *might* work, as long as I don't make a wrong turn. If that happens, I'll never find my way back.

I close my phone and glance at my front door. Maybe I could ask Ben for directions. He had offered, hadn't he? His text had explicitly said *Knock if you need anything else*, with perfect serial killer punctuation. And this would definitely constitute something else. He wouldn't even have to leave the building this time, just write down directions like he did before. Easy enough, right?

I've just about convinced myself to go knock on his door, when I hear footsteps out in the hallway. A moment later, there's the rough edge of Ben's voice, though I can't make out the words. Not that I'm trying to listen. Only, it's impossible not to. Apart from the distant echo of ABBA's "The Winner Takes It All" from downstairs, it's only me and my own thoughts, and those are getting me nowhere tonight.

Then I hear something else. It's another voice, but this one is lighter, soft and melodical. A woman.

I'm on my feet in an instant, tiptoeing across the room as if they could possibly hear me, then I press my eye to the peephole.

Ben has his keys out, ready to unlock the dead bolt, while a woman waits beside him. Their bodies are distorted by the fish-eye lens, but I can tell she has long brown hair pulled back in a low ponytail. She's talking, using her hands to animate her words, while Ben nods, his broad shoulders barely concealed under his faded work coat. The door muffles any chance I have to hear what the woman is saying and, a moment later, Ben gets the door open and they both disappear inside.

Huh. Ben Morgan has a girlfriend.

I stare out the peephole for another minute, on the off chance that maybe, *possibly*, she might leave. But the door stays shut. And that fact sends a small, strange ache through my chest.

CHAPTER 10

"You want me to kill it," Gino says, his giant salt-and-pepper eyebrows skewed in opposing directions.

"No, I don't want to kill it," I say, trying to maintain my smile, though it's becoming more difficult than it was fifteen minutes ago when the building super arrived at my apartment.

As promised, Gino rang my buzzer promptly at nine a.m. Wednesday, then hobbled down the hall from the stairwell with a canvas bag almost as big as him. Despite being well into his seventies, Gino's full head of hair is the same shade as his eyebrows, an even mix of black and white and gray, all perfectly combed back the same way it probably has been since he was eighteen.

He dropped his bag inside my apartment with a thud and waited patiently while I explained exactly what had happened a couple of days before. I tried to be concise, and he seemed to follow. There was a wave of the hand, a nod, and a confident "Okay."

But since then, we've barely made it past the front door. It's been propped open, letting in the draft and forcing me into what's swiftly becoming my favorite oversized wool sweater and a scarf, as I've described the mouse three times and we're only just getting to follow-up questions.

"You already killed it?" Gino asks.

"No," I sigh, tethering together the last of my patience. "I don't want anything dead. I just want you to go through the apartment and see where he's coming in."

"And set traps?"

"I don't know." I gnaw on my bottom lip. "Do you have traps that are humane? Ones that catch them, but won't kill them?"

"Yes."

I smile, relieved. "Oh, that would be great. Are they the ones that have a trapdoor so when the mouse crawls in, they—"

"They're glue traps."

My expression flattens. "Glue traps."

Gino nods. "Yes."

"Those don't kill them?"

"Nope. They just stick," he replies, illustrating how with one of his hands playing the part of the glue trap and the other the struggling mouse. "Sometimes they start chewing through their little legs to break free but—"

"No, no. No," I cut him off, squeezing my eyes shut to somehow erase that image from my mind. "Absolutely not. No glue traps."

"Okay. No glue traps." He holds up both his hands in surrender. I can tell he's starting to get annoyed. "So what do you want me to do?"

I steal a quick glance around the apartment. However unfamiliar everything still is, the idea of a mouse crawling over any of it tightens a knot in my stomach. But not as much as hurting said mouse. Maybe it was my grandmother's insistence that every living thing was important, or maybe it was because I saw Cinderella too many times as a child. Either way, traps are a no go.

I turn back to him. "Is there a mouse rescue we can call or something?"

Gino frowns and starts back toward his canvas bag.

"What?" I ask, following him.

He's mumbling now in what I'm pretty sure is Italian, shaking his head as he gathers up his things and heads through the door.

"Wait!" I follow him out into the hall. "What about the mouse?"

"Dio aiutami!" he calls out, looking up at the ceiling as if the fluorescent light there might help.

He disappears down the hall toward the stairwell just as I hear another set of footsteps, an odd shuffle. Then the door across from mine swings open and Ben is there on the threshold, disheveled in a way that's entirely too vulnerable for a random Wednesday morning. His hair sticks up as if he just lifted it from his pillow, and his beard stubble is scruffy and uneven. Even more distracting, his sweatpants are dangerously low on his hips, creating a gap between the waistband and his T-shirt so a flash of skin peeks through.

"Hi. Hello," I say, my eyes snapping to the hallway, the doorframe, the piece of fuzz in his hair. "Hi."

He stares at me from under his brow, then turns as Gino disappears down the stairwell. "Was that Gino?"

"Yeah. We didn't wake you up, did we?" I wince, my eyes darting over his shoulder, waiting for the mysterious girlfriend I saw through the peephole last night.

"Did he put down some traps?" Ben asks, completely ignoring my question.

My stomach does an odd stumble at the sound of his voice. It's somehow even rougher than before, like sleep left it with a serrated edge.

"We decided to go in a different direction," I reply carefully.

Ben's mouth flattens.

I offer him an apologetic smile, hoping it offsets any irritation at not following his advice, then quickly add, "Hey, while I have you, do you know where the Brattle Book Shop is?"

His brows knit together. "The Brattle Book Shop?"

Good God, his voice is borderline pornographic right now.

I clear my throat. "You don't need to go with me or anything like that. I just need to know how to get there and the map on my burner phone is really hard to see, so maybe you could write the route down like you did before?"

I think he might be about to ask me why it's urgent to go to a bookstore on a random weekday morning, and I have no idea how to answer without sounding slightly insane.

But instead, after a few beats of silence, he just sighs. "Give me five minutes."

Five minutes later, there's a rap on the door. I smooth down my hair, which had gone wild when I tried to change quickly by pulling off my sweater and scarf at the same time and finally gave up. The left side of my bangs are still sitting at a weird angle against my forehead, so I hide them under a knit hat just before I open the door.

Ben's standing in the hall, his broad frame filling my field of vision. The sweatpants are gone, replaced by a pair of dark olive-green chinos and work boots, and he has his canvas jacket pulled over a thick gray sweater.

"Ready?" he asks. His voice has smoothed out a bit but is still deep enough to lodge somewhere low in my belly.

"Yup." I step into the hall, my attempt at nonchalance coming out a bit too high-pitched, then lock the door behind me.

We emerge onto the sidewalk and take a left, passing two drivers who are hanging out their windows, yelling obscenities to each other while pointing their cars into the same spot on the street.

"No work today?" I ask when we reach the corner.

He itches at the stubble along his jaw as he waits for a car to pass. "Not today, no. I just wrapped up a project, so I have the day off."

"What was the project?"

"A building over in the Back Bay."

I wait for him to elaborate, but he seems happy enough to leave his involvement ambiguous.

"Did you *build* said building?" I press.

"No. Said building is two hundred years old. They're renovating it and needed someone to come in to supervise the framing and staircases."

My eyes narrow as my brain ties together each strand of information.

"Do you work in construction?"

"Not exactly," he replies as if he doesn't want to answer at all. "I'm a carpenter."

I blink. "A carpenter?"

He nods once. "Mostly on historical restoration projects. I also teach a preservation carpentry workshop twice a week. Sometimes on the weekend."

I don't know why I feel completely blindsided by this information, but I am. It's like living next to Clark Kent and finding out he's Superman. Or, in this case, some other very hot lumberjack-type superhero.

He catches my shocked expression and frowns. "What?"

"You're like . . . Paul Bunyan. Or Dean Proffitt," I say. It comes out almost wistful.

"Who's Dean Proffitt?"

"Kurt Russell's character in *Overboard*."

Ben's brow furrows.

"You know the movie *Overboard*," I say, rolling my eyes. "It was on TV in my hospital room when you were there."

"Watching TV wasn't my main concern at that moment," he replies offhandedly.

"Right," I say, working hard to play it cool even while praying that the chill in the morning air curbs my flushed cheeks. "Well, it's a classic. Kurt Russell plays a carpenter who is barely scraping by in this small town, and he wears this T-shirt without sleeves, so his arms are showing . . ." I realize that my rambling is only making this conversation more awkward, so I clear my throat and move on. "Then, Goldie Hawn arrives and hires him to redo the closet on the yacht."

"As one does," Ben deadpans.

"And he ends up making the most amazing closet with this little lever thing for her shoes and everything, except he makes it out of oak, which Goldie isn't happy about. Then she delivers that iconic line: 'The entire civilized world knows that *all* closets are made of *cedar*.'"

He frowns as he cocks his head to the side. "I'm pretty sure that's not true."

"No, obviously that's not true. That's the joke," I say.

His expression tells me he doubts that very much.

I wave my hand in front of us in an effort to move on. "Anyway, she ends up falling off the boat and getting retrograde amnesia, except instead of just forgetting a year like me, she forgets *everything*, so she has to move in with Kurt Russell as a domestic servant."

Ben's eyebrows bob up. "This was on while you were in the hospital?"

"To be fair, it's hard to avoid. *Overboard* is always on basic cable," I say with a sigh. "Long story short, Goldie and Kurt end up falling in love, and from that moment on, Kurt Russell has been America's favorite carpenter."

Ben stares down at me, like he's trying to figure me out. It's a look that's becoming familiar: eyes slightly narrowed, mouth quirked at an odd angle. Like he's mildly suspicious, but also too intrigued to question it. "I'm not sure he's America's *favorite* carpenter."

I scoff. "What other famous carpenters are there?"

His head tilts slightly like he's not sure if I'm kidding. "Jesus is the usual go-to."

Oh. Right.

I nod, considering. "Well, equally as impressive."

The corner of his mouth quirks up again, close to that almost-smile I caught the other day, and my pulse trips.

We walk in silence for another block, enough time for me to notice how autumn has begun to settle in, and how Boston wears it well. The scattered trees in our neighborhood are capped with an array of yellow and orange leaves, while pumpkins have suddenly appeared on almost every doorstep.

"Do you want to walk or take the T?" Ben asks after another minute.

My eyebrows knit together. "The what?"

"The T is the subway."

"Oh." Have I taken the subway at some point over the last year? Maybe, but without the memory, it feels too overwhelming to even consider now. "I don't mind the walk."

Ben doesn't look convinced. "You sure? It's about a mile."

I know what he's really asking: *Are you okay to walk a mile?* Marnie Stephens, Malibu High School Cross Country Champion, now treated like she's an invalid.

"I'm fine," I say.

He nods and lets the topic drop.

The air is cooler than it was a couple of days ago, the slight bite feeling good against my cheeks as we turn down a road I'm pretty sure I haven't been down before. This one seems to lead out of the cramped streets of our neighborhood and into a long park that cuts right through the city, with tall buildings looming just beyond.

We follow the sidewalk straight ahead as the park stretches out on either side of the road. The smells of the city suddenly mix with freshly turned dirt and grass.

"What do you need from the bookstore?" Ben asks when we reach the next corner.

Of course he wants to know why I'm dragging him out of his apartment on a Wednesday morning. I had just been so laser-focused on my assignment, I hadn't considered that other people might ask me about it. I had simply hoped that it would work out. That the universe would cut me this one break, and the memories would simply come back.

I hadn't anticipated needing help. I hadn't anticipated Ben.

"It's just this idea I had," I say. "A way to trigger my memories so they come back."

I'm almost impressed at how I'm able to leave it at that, but then I notice he's still looking at me, waiting for me to continue.

It's a subtle gesture but still jarring. Maybe it's because I've spent so long trying to tone myself down, convinced that my chronic chattiness is an annoyance. I'm so used to looking for cues that the other person is zoning out that I'm confused to find him genuinely listening.

I look away, as if something ahead is more interesting than the dark mix of browns and yellows in Ben's eyes.

"Apparently there's a chance that revisiting familiar places can trigger memories for people with retrograde amnesia. The only issue is that I don't even remember moving to Boston, let alone what in the city could be familiar. But I know I must have memories from at least a few places, because I have all these random mementos scattered around my apartment, things that aren't from my life before the move, so they must be from memories I made after. Memories I made here."

"Like what?"

"A piece of string. A coffee shop napkin. A Monopoly dog."

That line between his eyebrows is back as he stares down at me.

"You know, the little metal dog that comes with Monopoly?" I say. "You move it around—"

"I know what a Monopoly dog is."

I throw my arms out at my sides. "Well, there was one on my windowsill. Except I have no idea where it came from, and trying to figure that one out is impossible, so I'm focusing on the mementos that are tied to specific places."

Ben seems to think about it, distracted for a moment. Then he asks, "And did you get this idea from your doctor or Goldie Hawn?"

"I really wish I could say Goldie, but this one came from my doctor," I reply wistfully.

His lip twitches again. "And how does the bookstore work into it?"

"There's a receipt on my corkboard from there. For a copy of *Jane Eyre*, which doesn't make sense."

"Why not?"

"It's my favorite book of all time. I borrowed it from the library when I was twelve and read it twice in one weekend and was so sad to have to give it back. Then the next week, I was down on the beach and there in the middle of the sand was this beautiful hardcover copy of it. Like . . . magic." I slide my teeth over my bottom lip. "That same book is on the bookshelf in my apartment right now. So why did I buy another copy? And where is it? I looked through my bookshelves and I can't find it anywhere. There's no way I returned it, so where else could it be?"

I'm lost in thought, playing out all the possibilities, so I almost don't notice Ben's expression, his concern bordering on shock, until we stop at the corner.

"What?" I ask.

"You read *Jane Eyre* at twelve?"

"Is that a problem?"

"The main love interest keeps his wife locked in the attic, Marnie."

I frown. "Okay, let's not—"

"And isn't he also Jane's boss?"

"Charlotte Brontë wrote it in 1847, Ben." I wave my hand in the air between us, like that helps my argument. "It was a different time."

His head tilts slightly. "A time when people kept their spouses in crawl spaces?"

The fact that his lips are barely curled up on one side is the only clue that he might be kidding. I'm annoyed that I can't keep from smiling, too.

"Yes, Rochester shouldn't have locked Bertha in the attic," I say. "But that doesn't negate the rest of the novel."

One eyebrow is cocked high on his forehead as he stares at me, like he's pretty sure it does.

"It's called *Jane Eyre*, because it's about Jane Eyre. She's one of the most complex heroines ever written," I argue. "Yes, she's judgmental and an introvert and difficult to get to know. But at the heart of it, she just wants to be loved. Not by everyone, just one person who sees her for who she truly is."

Ben watches me, but the amused look in his eyes has faded. Now it's like he's trying to find something specific in my expression, studying me for some hint of what I'm really trying to say.

The silence grows and I can feel my cheeks warming. "Let's just find the bookstore, okay?"

As we continue on, the buildings get taller, sending long shadows over the street so I can't feel the sun anymore. I follow Ben around another corner, silently bemoaning the fact that I didn't bring another layer, when I realize we've arrived.

The buildings surrounding us seem to miraculously part, leaving an empty lot between two of them. Except it's not empty. There's row after row of bookshelves lined up across the pavement, each one almost overflowing with different titles. It almost feels like a mistake, literature exposed to the elements and city traffic. But no one walking by seems to find it odd. There are even a few patrons roaming the outdoor shelves as if this is normal.

"Is this it?" I ask, gawking from where we've stopped on the sidewalk.

"Almost," Ben says, and continues forward.

That's when I notice the storefront just a few steps away, adjacent to the lot. There's a long sign above the front window shaped like a giant pencil with BRATTLE BOOK SHOP written across it.

Ben holds open the door for me, then follows me inside.

I'm met by the smell first—dust, paper, and something faintly sweet. Then I see the books waiting on every surface, the motley collection of posters hanging on the walls. In California, all the bookstores near me were modern and airy, with wide windows that spilled sunlight over clean, meticulous spaces. This feels like an amalgamation of a dozen different elements that on their own wouldn't equate to a bookstore, but here they somehow work. The marble staircase with its antique iron-and-wood banister leading up from the linoleum tile on the first floor. Piles and piles of books sitting on the long desk ahead of me, while rows of bookcases lie just beyond. I'm tempted to start combing through them when a voice calls out.

"Can I help you with something?"

I turn to see an older woman standing behind the front counter, near the register. Her curly gray hair is barely contained by a banana clip on the top of her head.

"Hello." I smile, wide and bright, as I walk up and pull out my wallet to produce the receipt. It's bent at odd angles, and I try to smooth it out against the wood countertop. "I made this purchase back in March."

She looks at the receipt, then up to me. "We don't accept returns after thirty days."

"Oh, I would never return a book. Do people really do that?" Then I laugh, hoping she'll join me. Instead, she just looks confused and my confidence falters. "No, I don't need to return anything. I was just wondering if you remember the purchase?"

She raises her eyebrows at me from behind the rim of her red reading glasses. "From six months ago."

When she says it like that, I realize how insane it sounds. How insane *I* sound. "Sorry, I know it's an odd request. But I already own a copy of *Jane Eyre*, so I'm trying to figure out why I bought another one."

"You don't remember?"

Wow. I never imagined such an innocuous question could land like a punch in the gut.

"Right. Good point," I say, working to maintain my smile as I scramble for an apology that will let us leave as soon as possible.

"I'm sorry, we'll get out of your hair. You're probably busy, and it was a long shot, so—"

"What about this particular edition?" Ben asks, leaning forward and resting his hand on the wooden counter. His fingers splay across the top edge of the receipt, like he's unconsciously measuring its angles. "Do you have another copy in stock that we could take a look at?"

"Oh, no, it's okay," I say, bringing my hand up to his arm to pull him back. "It's not that important."

He turns his head slightly, just enough to look down to where my fingers gently grasp the sleeve of his canvas jacket. Then he slowly slides his gaze up to mine.

"Yes," he says. "It is."

His dark eyes are trained on me and, for a moment, I can't move. I can only stare back, trying not to focus too much on the way his jaw ticks under his stubble, or how his hair falls over his forehead.

Then, just like that, he turns away, bringing his attention back to the woman behind the counter.

She looks from him to me, then back at him, before giving us both a smirk and typing away on her computer.

"There's a copy in the literature section," she says a moment later. "This floor, all the way back."

Ben thanks her and then motions for me to go ahead.

It's a maze among the stacks, and I'm not sure I'm heading in the direction of the literature section, or if we've ventured to geopolitics. All I know is that Ben is behind me, so close that I can actually feel his presence as we turn into the next aisle, then another. It's like trying to navigate our neighborhood all over again—long, dark passageways, half of them ending in dead ends. I think we've finally found the right spot a few minutes later, but my hope dims as I scour the shelf where the book should be. The titles of the other Brontë sisters are here: *Villette* and *The Tenant of Wildfell Hall*, *Wuthering Heights* and *Agnes Grey*. But no *Jane Eyre*. I turn around to suggest we ask the woman at the front desk for help again, but stutter to silence when I realize my face is just inches from Ben's chest.

He smells like sawdust, I think. *Like sawdust and sandalwood and soap.*

I immediately push the thought away and turn back to the bookshelf. "I don't think it's here."

"Are you sure?" his voice rumbles behind me.

I do another quick scan of the titles lined up in front of me, then sigh. "I'm sorry."

"What are you apologizing for?"

"This," I say, my arms flopping from my sides, a pathetic attempt to motion toward the entirety of the bookshop. "I dragged you all the way here for nothing."

"I don't mind."

"But I do," I say, turning enough to look at him over my shoulder. "I already knew this would be a long shot, but this is ridiculous. And now—"

My words stutter to a halt as his hand comes up from his side toward me, like he's about to cradle my cheek in his palm. My heart trips and I hold my breath, waiting . . . until he reaches past my shoulder to pull a book from the shelf behind me.

I clear my throat, feeling a bloom of heat rising up my neck, and look down at the paperback in his hand.

Jane Eyre is written across the front in simple white font, along with Charlotte Brontë's name, while the rest of the cover features a Victorian oil painting of a young woman standing in the corner of a library. The colors are muted, the design simple, but something about it feels significant. I just can't pinpoint what.

"Does it look familiar?" Ben asks.

"I don't know. Maybe," I murmur to myself. "Then again, it's a mass market paperback. I've probably seen it a dozen times before."

Ben doesn't rush me. He just holds it out for me to study, letting me do a slow audit of every inch.

But after a few more minutes, I admit defeat. I don't remember this book or why I bought it. I don't remember anything at all.

I'm back at square one.

CHAPTER 11

I'm fighting back tears the entire walk home. Despite Janine's assurances earlier in the week that my emotional roller coaster is normal, I don't *feel* normal. I feel raw and exposed, like the slightest jostle will send me over a tear-soaked ledge.

Thankfully, Ben doesn't seem to notice. He walks beside me, unbothered, as if I haven't wasted his morning trying to track down a book that's sold at literally every bookstore within a fifty-mile radius.

What did I think was going to happen? I would walk into some random bookstore and magically remember everything that happened over the past year?

Yes, a small voice in my head admits. Even though I knew I wasn't guaranteed to remember anything, I still held on to the hope that maybe some part of my grandmother's advice was true. That the universe was looking out for me, that magic would finally appear right at the moment I needed it most.

But instead, I'm back where I started, feeling so gullible I'm almost angry.

It's overcast by the time we reach the North End again. I haven't said much the last few blocks, and when we stop at the corner at the end of our street, Ben finally looks down at me.

"You okay?"

I know I should say I'm fine. After all, he didn't sign up to deal with my mess. But I can't quite muster the energy to lie.

"My grandmother always said the world was full of magic. All you had to do was look for it," I reply. "I know that sounds ridiculous, but I really needed it to be true today. I needed something to be familiar. It didn't have to be huge, just . . . something." I shake my head. "But I didn't remember anything. And yes, I knew that was a possibility before we left, but I still got my hopes up, so now I'm not only disappointed but *mad* that I'm disappointed. Today was . . . it was just . . ."

"Today was a bad day," Ben finishes.

I exhale. "Yeah."

A moment passes.

He shifts his weight so he's facing me fully. "What are you doing right now?"

I shrug. "I'm probably going home to stare at the wall and feel sorry for myself."

His head cocks to the side. "Can that wait twenty minutes?"

"I don't know, it's a really good wall."

The corner of his mouth tugs up even as he nods to the sidewalk ahead. "Come on."

I follow him as he turns right, and within a few steps we're maneuvering down a narrow street between a hair salon and an Italian restaurant. The brick walls on either side feel like they're almost bowing above us, but then we're spat out on another street similar to the one we just left.

"Where are we going?" I ask.

"Modern Pastry."

"Is that the bakery we walked past on the way to the grocery store?"

"No, that's Mike's. Modern is one block down."

I throw my arms out at my sides. "How many bakeries can one neighborhood have?"

He throws me a hard glare, but there's something playful in his eyes. It sends a hot prickle over my skin. "This is the North End, Marnie. We take our baked goods very seriously."

I want to laugh, but he's moving again, long strides that take us another two blocks until we turn onto Hanover Street and find Modern Pastry, glowing like an oasis. The windows are bright and the sign above beckons with buzzing neon.

It's crowded, so Ben directs me to wait outside. I watch him through the window as he approaches the long glass display case, featuring an array of cookies and cakes, and places his order with a woman behind the counter. A moment later, she passes him a small white pastry box with a wink.

When he emerges, I want to ask what he got, but he doesn't stop, just nods for us to continue down the street. We barely pause as we turn down what feels like an alleyway that I'm fairly certain I've never seen before, and head onto a street I'm positive I haven't. Within five minutes, I'm completely lost. But I also don't care. Every concern I had that first time I followed Ben through this neighborhood is gone. All I can focus on is his broad frame, how it seems to span the narrow spaces we navigate until, suddenly, we emerge onto a small cemetery. There's row after row of old slate headstones, each set at a different angle, and as we walk past, I can tell that most of the names carved into them have worn away.

"Where are we?" I ask.

"Copp's Hill," Ben replies, as if that explains everything.

I want to stop, examine the graves more, ask what this is doing here a few steps from restaurants and shops. But before I can, Ben continues forward and crosses another small street.

I think it's a continuation of the cemetery, but it's not. It's a small stone terrace. There are a few iron benches set across it, each facing out at the sweeping view ahead. I hadn't realized the neighborhood was slightly elevated, and that from here you can see out onto the harbor, the boats and ships slowly floating past, the overcast sky reflecting back on them from the water. Just below us is another small park, but this one has a few long bocce ball courts. There's a small group of older men playing, laughing and yelling at one another.

Ben heads over to the nearest bench, but I don't move. All I can do is stare out at the view, mouth agape.

"Wow."

"I know," he says, sitting down on the bench's edge.

After another minute, I walk over and sit down beside him, leaving space for the white pastry box he places between us.

"All right. You ready?" he asks. His voice is low and suggestive, and my pulse trips over itself.

"For what?" I ask.

"Your entire life to change."

I laugh. "I think so?"

There's that now-familiar tug at one corner of his mouth. Then he unties the string keeping the pastry box closed and reaches inside. A moment later, he pulls out what looks like a massive cornucopia made of flaky pastry, lightly dusted with powdered sugar and filled to bursting with whipped cream. He hands it to me, then pulls out his own, holding it up to tap against mine.

"Cheers," he says, and takes a massive bite. He only manages to fit one corner in his mouth, and the rest of it leaves powdered sugar in his stubble.

I attempt to do the same, trying to get a bit of the cream sticking out the end.

"What do you think?" he asks as he chews.

My mouth is full, and for a moment, all I can do is close my eyes as the pastry and cream combine into an almost decadent combination of flavors. I groan.

That seems to be enough to satisfy him, and he takes another bite.

"What is this thing called?" I ask once I swallow.

He chews for a moment, then says, "A lobster tail."

I already have my mouth around it, ready for another bite, when I still.

Ben catches my expression and shakes his head. "There's no lobster in it. It's just shaped like a lobster tail."

"Oh, thank God." I let out a relieved sigh.

"Do you have a problem with lobsters?"

"No. I love lobsters. They're the reason I'm a vegetarian," I say, then take another bite.

His head cocks to the side, like he's about to question my logic, but I cut him off.

"No one should eat lobster. It's unethical."

"You realize you live in Boston, right?"

"They mate for *life*, Ben." I lean forward, maintaining a steady gaze so he understands the gravity of the situation. "Imagine you're a lobster, okay? You've searched your entire lobster life for your soulmate. Then, at long last, there she is. You both just know. Because everything that has happened in the history of the universe has brought you to this one moment. You've found your destiny. And then, you're both wrenched from the ocean and stuck in a fish tank somewhere, forced to watch as one by one, your lobster friends disappear until one day, it's your soulmate taken away from you and plopped into a pot of boiling water just because it's somebody's date night or . . . something."

My words trail off once I realize I'm rambling. This is usually the time where I would get a strange look from Matt, or Sara would laugh and move the conversation along.

But Ben doesn't do either. He's quiet, his expression pensive, like he's actually listened to every word.

"All right," he says after a moment. "No more lobster."

"I didn't mean for you to stop. I'm just telling you why I don't eat it," I say.

"Then you shouldn't have made such a good argument," he replies, taking another bite of his pastry. There's a piece of whipped cream at the corner of his mouth that he doesn't know is there, and I suddenly want to reach over and run my thumb over his lips to wipe it away.

He turns and catches me staring.

"You okay?" he asks after he swallows.

"You've got something right there," I say, using my pinkie to point to the corner of my own mouth.

His tongue darts out to clean up the stray bit of cream, and I try to ignore how the motion makes my pulse feel like warm syrup in my veins.

"Better?" he asks.

I nod.

Silence descends as we both take another bite and stare out across the water. The gray sky mutes the already muddy colors of the buildings on the opposite shore. The boats moored nearby bob with the current, their masts lolling from side to side like metronomes.

"Thank you," I say after another minute. "I needed this."

"My mom used to get me one of these whenever I was having a bad day."

I try not to look surprised by this nugget of personal information. "Yeah?"

"Yeah. She says every good wallow deserves a good pastry. If she knew I had a rough day at school, she'd stop by the Italian bakery near her work and pick one up for me."

The image of Ben Morgan as a child is such a novelty, I can't help but smile. "What happened at school to necessitate a lobster tail?"

His gaze travels out across the water as he chews, like he's letting himself mull over a memory.

"We moved back to my mom's hometown when I was in eighth grade. We didn't have a lot of money, and I wasn't a very outgoing kid, so I was an easy target for bullies. I kept to myself a lot, always had my nose in a book, and tried to stay under the radar. It worked most of the time."

"And the other times?" I ask.

"I had five different pairs of reading glasses thrown out the window of our school bus before I figured out that it was probably smarter to walk home." He sighs and puts his lobster tail down on a napkin, then brushes his hands together to get rid of the crumbs. "When kids learn how to be cruel, they become experts fast."

I try to imagine a young Ben awkwardly adjusting those same tortoiseshell glasses I've seen him wear a few times, trying to ignore barely whispered taunts from his classmates. It sends a sharp ache through my heart. "I got called Sand Witch in middle school."

Ben pauses. "Like the food?"

"No, like an actual witch who lives on a beach," I say. "It was more of a dig at my grandmother than at me. My parents died when I was six, so I went to live with her in Malibu. She was a product of the hippie movement and never grew out of it. Long hair, always in a different caftan, talking about auras and magic. She even tried to form a solstice circle with some of the PTA moms when I was in fifth grade. The two of us were so close, I just saw it as normal. I didn't understand why other kids found it so funny, but I learned. Because all those traits started getting assigned to me, too. The ditzy California blonde, the weird flighty hippie girl. It didn't really stop until I graduated high school."

He's quiet for a moment, his dark eyes locked with mine. "Sounds like you could have used a lobster tail."

I smile. "It would have definitely helped."

He nods to what's left of the pastry in my hand. "Is it helping now?"

He somehow manages to make the question sound offhand, but with a slight edge that hints that the answer is vitally important. Like I'm important.

I turn away so he can't see how *that* thought warms my cheeks.

"Yeah," I answer, working to sound casual.

"Yeah?"

I shrug. "A smidge."

The corner of his mouth quirks up. "I'll take a smidge."

Then he picks up his lobster tail and takes another bite, and so do I.

~

I don't pay attention to the walk back to our building. I'm too engrossed in our conversation, which has somehow moved on to my vegetarianism. Ben is staunch in his defense of beef, and I'm in the middle of making a passionate case for tofu, complete with hand gestures that make my tote bag swing in every direction as we turn the corner to Sheafe Street. I barely register that we've arrived at our building until I see a woman standing out front, arms crossed as she watches us approach. She looks familiar, and for a moment I think it's a memory coming back, but within a few steps I realize that she's the woman I saw with Ben through the peephole. And she does not seem happy to see us.

"Hey, Lauren," Ben murmurs, like he already knows he's in trouble.

"You're a half hour late and all you've got is 'hey'?" she replies.

His hand comes up to scratch his jaw. I think I even catch a wince. "Yeah. Sorry about that."

Lauren just rolls her eyes. "Whatever. Hurry up, I don't want to get stuck in traffic."

She starts down the street, and I can only assume she doesn't look back because she knows Ben will follow.

He curses under his breath as he brings his attention back to me. "Sorry, we—"

"No, I'm sorry. This is totally my fault. I dragged you to the bookstore and never even considered that you might have plans with . . . someone," I say.

Ben nods, and for a moment it looks like he's going to say more, try to offer an excuse or apology, so I cut him off before he can try.

"I should go," I say. He doesn't owe me anything. In fact, I almost feel like I should run after Lauren and say sorry to her for ruining her day. Instead, I take a backward step toward our building and force myself to smile. "That wall's not going to stare at itself, right?"

I give another one of my weird salutes. This time he gives me one back. It makes my heart do an odd tumble, and I'm so embarrassed, all I can do is turn around and speed walk to the front door.

CHAPTER 12

A muffled version of ABBA's "Money, Money, Money" wakes me up the next morning. This is better than "SOS" playing on repeat yesterday when I got home, so I take it as a sign that today will be better. Or, at the very least, I won't have another awkward encounter with my neighbor's girlfriend.

I stare up at the ceiling, listening to the muffled crescendo as ABBA sings about living in a rich man's world, then the song ends with a flourish. There's a moment of silence when all I can hear is a distant siren echoing down the narrow street outside my window. I close my eyes, letting myself enjoy it. This is the closest I've had to peace in days. Maybe it will last a few minutes, maybe even until I make myself some tea. But just as soon as the thought materializes, the opening chords of "Money, Money, Money" reverberate through the floorboards again.

When the song hits its second verse, I shuffle out of bed and head toward the bathroom. If I shut the door and turn on the shower, I can almost pretend I can't hear it.

At least the blaring chorus of "SOS" last night had masked any possibility of hearing Ben and his girlfriend return to his apartment. It hadn't stopped me from occasionally peeking through my peephole to check, though.

But what had I been hoping to see, exactly? Did I want to catch a glimpse of them together? Absolutely not. But still . . .

I stare at my reflection in the mirror above the bathroom sink as the shower heats up. My hair is still a disaster, only made worse by whatever position I was sleeping in last night. Half of my bangs are literally standing straight upward. But I don't attempt to fix it; I just step under the hot spray and close my eyes.

I don't know why I'm surprised Ben has a girlfriend. Of course he does. I would be more surprised if he were single, disappointed in every woman in Boston for their lack of effort and good taste. But that doesn't change the fact that he has someone—a lobster to be paired with—while I decidedly do not. I'm on my own, facing another day with nothing but a broken brain and a shoebox full of memories disguised as junk.

When I'm done in the shower, I wrap myself up in my bathrobe and wander out into the living room to where the box still sits on the sofa, with the carefully itemized list of its contents on top of it. I've crossed off one: the Brattle Book Shop receipt. Next on the list is the napkin for a café called Strange Brew with the number *304* written on the top corner.

I flip open my phone and type the name into the small browser. A moment later, the results pop up, but I can barely read the small text, let alone the map on the pixelated screen. I give up, falling into the sofa cushions with a groan.

I can't go anywhere without a functioning Maps app. And for that, I need to find an Apple Store and get my phone fixed. But to do *that*, I need a functioning Maps app. It's the world's most inane paradox.

Maybe I could just hail a cab and tell the driver to take me to an Apple Store? That wouldn't be too crazy, right? Of course, a cab would require payment and I'm still not sure how much I have in my bank account . . .

I straighten as inspiration hits, clearing the confusion in my head. That's it: the bank. I swear I saw a branch when I went back and forth to the hospital a few days ago. All I had to do was find one, go in, and explain my predicament. By the end of the day, I could have access to my account, a statement that tells me where any potential paychecks came from, maybe even some cash in hand for a cab to take me anywhere I want to go.

That's it. All I have to do is find my bank. I can do this on my own, right? At the very least, I can try.

I put on my coat and knit hat, and leave my apartment a half hour later with my burner phone in hand.

This is fine, I think as I start down the stairs. Y*ou don't need help. You used to navigate the 101 every day during rush hour! You can find one bank branch in Boston.*

The pep talk must be working, because when I get to the second floor and hear the sound of "Mamma Mia" echoing off the cement walls, I pause.

And if I can conquer the 101 and venture out into a city I don't remember to find a bank, then I should be able to knock on my neighbor's door and ask them to turn down their music. Right?

I step into the second-floor hallway. Even if I didn't know apartment 2A was directly below mine, the music blaring from behind its brown door is a dead giveaway. The song is in the middle of its second verse when I knock. A moment passes, and I begin to think that no one is even home, when the door swings open. A man stands on the threshold in a bathrobe and sweatpants, and it takes me longer than it should to recognize him—he's the same man from the lobby who I tried to introduce myself to when I arrived home from the hospital. He's taller than I remember, and there's a towel wrapped around his head now. His eyes, ringed with the remnants of yesterday's mascara, take me in without a word.

"Hi," I begin, struggling to keep my voice cheerful as I practically yell over the music. "Do you remember me? We met downstairs last week. I'm Marnie."

He leans his shoulder against the doorframe and tilts his head, like he might be trying to remember, but also isn't trying that hard, either. Behind him, the refrain of "Mamma Mia" echoes down the hall.

"Sorry to bother you," I continue. "It's just . . . I live in the apartment above yours."

He waits, and I wonder if he honestly needs this spelled out for him.

"And I've noticed you listen to a lot of ABBA?" I have no idea why I phrase this like a question.

"I'm not listening to ABBA," he replies flatly.

I blink. "Are you serious?"

He stares back, his expression blank as the song reaches its crescendo.

"Okay," I say, working hard to keep my approach diplomatic. "Well, whatever it is that I'm hearing right now, it's a little loud, don't you think?"

"Do you have something against music?"

"No, I love music," I reply assuredly. "When I was growing up, my grandmother had a huge record collection and used to go through different phases where she would play the same album over and over. Not ABBA, but lots of other stuff from the seventies and eighties. Kate Bush and Joni Mitchell and Fleetwood Mac . . ."

My breath catches on the memory—at my grandmother's funeral, when her only two requests were that no one wear black, and that we play "Gypsy" while her ashes were scattered along the beach. The memory is so potent and unexpected that my eyes begin to tear.

My neighbor only stares at me, his confusion growing.

"She really loved Stevie Nicks," I say. My smile suddenly hurts to maintain. "You know the song 'Gypsy'? That was her favorite. It was on the album *Mirage*, although I think a lot of people assume it came out earlier—"

He closes the door in my face before I can finish. My expression wilts as I hear the lock slide into place only a moment before the opening notes to "Mamma Mia" fill the hall again, just a touch louder than before.

Right now, I almost miss the 101.

I try to gather the crumbs of my confidence as I continue down to the lobby, but give up as soon as I open the front door and step out onto the street. There's a row of cars in front of the building, all beeping at a moving truck at the end of the block with its hazards on. A few drivers are hanging out of their windows yelling—at the movers, at each other, at random pedestrians walking by—and for a split second, I consider turning around and going back inside.

You can do this, I repeat. Then I turn to start down the street, and slam right into a man walking with two bags of groceries.

"What the hell are you doing?" he yells as he continues forward.

I smile and apologize, but really, I want to panic. Every fiber of my body is telling me I should and that makes me so angry, so unbelievably disappointed in myself that I want to scream. Instead, I keep my head down and march forward.

By the time I make it to the end of the block, it's clear the neighborhood isn't as easy to maneuver without Ben. The streets are clogged with traffic, and the sidewalks are so crowded I have to wait at the corner to let a tour group pass by. It's only after they do that I realize I didn't keep track of which direction I was going. I continue forward, undaunted, and turn left. Then right. Then another left, I think. Or was it another right? Trying to navigate back to where I've just been suddenly feels like an impossible puzzle in my broken brain.

If I went left, then it's a right, but at the intersection?

"Move, motherfucker!" a driver bellows at a van double-parked ahead.

I keep walking forward, barely avoiding a group of college students waiting outside another bakery.

When I look up again, I'm on a street that I've definitely never been down before. I don't remember passing the wine shop on the corner, or the restaurant across the street called Capobianco's with a ham leg hanging in the window. The café next to it doesn't look familiar, either. I squint against the sun, trying to read the wooden sign above the door. When I finally do, my pulse soars.

Strange Brew. The café from the napkin in my memory box, the one with the number *304* written on one side.

It feels impossible. Miraculous, even. The first scrap of magic in what feels like ages. I've never been so thrilled to mess up so thoroughly.

I barely remember to look both ways as I cross the street and push open the door. The smell of coffee beans greets me, the spurting and hissing of an espresso machine. Sunlight pours through the front windows, landing on the raw brick walls and long wooden counter.

There are only a few people in the coffee shop—two men bent over their computers at two different tables, and a couple standing nearby waiting for their drinks. Meanwhile, behind the counter, a green-haired barista pours a carafe into two mugs. Above him there's a chalkboard covered with neat handwriting, and I stare up at it, pretending to find it interesting while I work to curb my pulse.

The sheer joy of finding this place has quickly been usurped by one question: Now what? I could order and sit down, wait to see if something looks familiar, or maybe I should—

"OH MY GOD, MARNIE!"

I whip around, darting my eyes to the other customers to see who yelled my name. Then I make eye contact with the green-haired barista only a second before he's enveloping me up in a big hug. "We were so worried about you! Are you okay? Can I hug you? God, you look awful."

I'm so confused, all I can do is blink and say, "Hi."

"How are you? How's your head? Did you break anything?" He continues his line of questioning as he pulls away, keeping his hands on my shoulders. "Becca felt awful, but I told her it wasn't her fault. Not completely. It's not like she purposely mopped the floor just before you walked across it, but you know that. I told her you *know* that."

I stare at him for a minute, then look down. The floor of the coffee shop is polished cement.

"Wait. Did I fall *here*?" I ask.

"Oh my God, you don't remember." He gives me an exaggerated frown. "Yes, right over there by the seasonal display. One minute you were walking with a latte, then *bam*. Your head met the floor. Honestly, I can't believe you got up like it was nothing. I thought you'd have a concussion or something. But afterward you seemed fine! It wasn't until I came in for my shift on Tuesday that Becca said some guy called to say you were in the hospital."

I blink. "Which guy?"

"I don't know. You'd have to ask Becca. She's taking a few mental health days because she thought she killed you, but she should be back soon."

My mouth falls open, but I don't know where to start asking questions. My brain is too tripped up on all the details that don't seem to fit together.

After a moment, his eyes widen. "Are you having a stroke?"

I let out a long breath. "No."

"Did you have a stroke?"

"No. When I hit my head, it injured my brain and—"

He nods sympathetically. "Like a concussion."

"Not really. There was bleeding—"

"My brother got a concussion once playing Little League," he continues. "Took a ball straight to the temple. When he woke up he thought he was Jason Varitek, then he puked all over home base."

I blink. "Is he okay?"

"Yeah, he's a corporate attorney now."

"That's . . . good." I have absolutely no idea where to go from here.

"How about you? Are you okay now?" he asks, leaning down a bit as if this will help him focus.

I pause for a moment before saying, "Well, everything in my brain has healed, but I'm still having an issue with my memory. I don't actually remember the fall, or anything that's happened over the last year, really."

"Wow. Okay, well my name is Bobbi," he says slowly. "B-O-B-B-I."

"Right." I force a smile. "And I'm here a lot?"

"Oh yeah. A couple of times a week at least."

I glance over at the two people on their laptops, still working away. "Do you have any idea what I do?"

He narrows his eyes, like this is a trick question. "You make . . . coffee?"

It takes a moment for my brain to process the information. "I work here?"

"Not, like, *here*," he says, motioning to where we're standing in the middle of the room. Then he waves toward the counter. "But, like, over *there*."

But I've never worked in a coffee shop before, I want to say. *I don't even like coffee*. My gaze flies around the room, looking for something, anything, familiar. For one detail to stick out and make all of this make sense.

"Are you okay?" Bobbi asks, watching my reaction.

No? Yes? Maybe? There is no correct answer to that question.

"I work here," I repeat. "Making coffee."

"And matcha," he quickly adds. "We serve matcha, too."

My mouth feels like it is permanently ajar now, but I can't help it. What had Sara said? My new job was in sales and distribution for a beverage company? At the time, it had sounded impossible, but then, I hadn't considered this angle.

"Are you worried about your shifts?" Bobbi asks. "Because Helen got them all covered through Monday. She's so scared that you'll sue for unsafe work conditions, she not only kept you on the schedule, but called to make sure all our health insurance policies were up-to-date."

Huh. Well, at least that solves the mystery behind the health insurance card in my wallet.

"That's great," I reply flatly.

The bell above the door rings out just as a family of four wanders in with a stroller.

"Let me go take care of this order, then I'll grab your schedule for next week. Sound good?"

I nod, not trusting myself to form actual words.

Bobbi retreats to the other side of the counter as a muted Noah Kahan song plays from the speakers above.

Okay, I think, looking around as I release a shaky breath. *So I never found the bank. But on the bright side, I have a job! And I found a location from my list! That has to count for something, right?*

I want it to. But I can't move past the fact that after spending five years building a career in recruiting, I am now a barista. And I don't even like coffee.

Is this the magic my grandmother always talked about? Because this doesn't feel like magic. This feels confusing and lonely, like I somehow ventured off the universe's path and am now so lost I can't find my way back again.

But there has to be a reason *why*. At least one that would explain the napkin. I let my eyes do another long audit of the room, waiting for something to snag my attention. The brick walls, the mismatched chairs, the chalkboard menus. It all looks worn and comfortable, but it also feels like the first time I've been here to notice that.

I sigh and pull off my knit hat. In the periphery I can see my bangs shooting out in different directions, but before I can tamp them down, my gaze catches on a low bookcase in the far corner. The shelves are full of board games, angled and bent to fill every available space. The ones that don't fit are piled on top, requiring you to really commit to your choice if you were going to find a way to get it out without knocking over the others. Scrabble, Trivial Pursuit, Monopoly, something called Farkle . . .

Wait.

My attention zeroes in on the Monopoly box. It's barely a box anymore, its edges and corners devoid of their original shape, replaced by new creases and curves that reveal the brown cardboard beneath the faded packaging.

I rush over to the corner, dodging the tables between me and the bookcase until I'm there, on my knees and pulling the box from the shelf. An entire narrative is spinning alive in my head as I lift the lid—Matt and I laughing over a couple of scones, rolling the dice in the hopes of avoiding the hotels on Boardwalk—and I know, I just *know*, that this is it, the corner piece of the puzzle in my head. Matt and I played Monopoly here together. And if that moment was important enough to immortalize in my collection of memories, then it has to help sort out the rest of them, too.

I push my bangs away from my face so I can focus on the mess of colorful money in front of me, community chest cards, and metal playing pieces. There's a top hat and a battleship. A race car and a thimble . . . and there, sitting in the corner, a small metal dog.

I stare at it, irrationally angry at its presence, when Bobbi appears beside me.

"Here you go," he says, holding out a piece of paper with a calendar printed on it. "Your shifts through the end of the month!" He looks down at where I'm kneeling on the floor, surrounded by a mess of pink and blue money. Then his gaze slides to my forehead, lips pursed. "Is that what you're doing with your hair now?"

CHAPTER 13

"You work at a coffee shop?" Sara asks, her voice loud. For some reason, she always yells her side of the phone conversation when she's using her hands-free headset, as if the Bluetooth affects volume. "Like, making coffee?"

"Yes," I reply, though my voice is muffled. After getting home from Strange Brew and calling to relay the entire story to her, I had fallen face-first onto my pink-and-white gingham duvet.

"But you don't like coffee."

"I know," I say, turning over to stare up at my ceiling.

"And you told me you worked in sales."

"Maybe I'm with corporate?" I offer.

Sara snorts. "Why did you lie to me? Were you embarrassed or something?"

I wince. Technically, it wasn't a lie. And knowing how Sara would have critiqued my choice to quit Probus only to take a job as a barista, I can understand why past me might have bent the truth a little. But pointing that out right now wouldn't accomplish much, other than make her defensive, so I offer the only other explanation I've come up with.

"Maybe I'm having a midlife crisis."

She scoffs. "You're thirty-one, not fifty. And don't worry, Probus will have you back in a heartbeat. You could even call the office here and line up a job before you move back."

I glower at the ceiling. Even though Sara and I worked together for five years, I don't think she ever really appreciated that I never wanted the same things from it that she did. While I was happy just to have a job with benefits, something to pay the bills while I took care of my grandmother, Sara had long-term goals that set her up for a lifelong career. I always admired that, but I also never wanted it, no matter how much she told me I should.

"I'm not sure Probus is the answer here," I reply.

"Oh, come on. You didn't *hate* it."

She's right, I didn't hate it. But I hadn't loved it, either. It was just a means to an end, a temporary stopgap to stay afloat until the bills abated, until my grandmother was stable. Until I saved enough and could finally start living the life I had always dreamed about.

The only problem was that the bills never went away. My savings account was always stagnant. And my grandmother, who had promised me magic and signs and a mystical, cosmic plan, died, leaving me with no plan at all.

That's why I had been so eager to come to Boston with Matt. It might not have been perfect, but at least it was something, an opportunity for change that I desperately needed. Maybe even the sign from the universe that I had been waiting for. But if that were true, why did it end up imploding my entire life?

"No, I didn't hate it," I reply, pushing myself to sit at the edge of my bed. "I'm just not moving back to LA right now."

"Why not? What's so great about Boston?"

I try to ignore how the comment stokes my frustration. She means well, I know she does, but right now I don't need her advice. I need her support.

"Sara—"

"Tell me you'll at least *think* about it."

"Fine." I sigh. "I'll think about it. Now can we talk about something else?"

"Sure," she says. I can hear the smile in her voice. "Have you had any more morning meetups with a certain hot guy that I should know about?"

I know she means Matt, but Ben's face flashes in my brain before I can stop it. The slope of his shoulders when he leans against a doorframe. The sound of his voice, low and rough, especially when he first wakes up . . .

I quickly push him away, back to the corner of my brain. I have enough problems without daydreaming about my neighbor, who also happens to have a girlfriend.

"Let's talk about you," I say, standing up and leaving a Marnie-size imprint across my duvet.

"Do not bring up the promotion. Or babies," she warns. "I'm not jinxing anything."

"I don't know what you're talking about," I say, smiling. "I'm talking in the most general terms about how you as a human being are doing."

"I am good. As a human," she replies carefully. "Hopefully I will be better in a couple of weeks. That's all I'm saying."

"Then that's all I need to know. As a fellow human being."

She laughs and so do I, and for a minute the three thousand miles between us don't feel so big.

"So what's next in that box of yours?" she asks.

I walk out to the living room, where the shoebox full of mementos sits on the sofa. The list is still taped to the top, except I've crossed out the Brattle Book Shop and Strange Brew.

"Next is the Isabella Stewart Gardner Museum," I say.

"Oh, that sounds fancy."

"It might be. I have no idea."

"Here, let me look it up." I can hear her typing away on her keyboard and then she hums to herself. "Oh yeah. Very fancy. Kind of romantic, too. Matt has good taste."

I ignore the comment. "How far away is it?"

"Let me see . . . from you it looks like it's about three miles, but there's traffic, so a cab would take a while."

I also have no idea if I can pay for it, since I haven't found a bank yet, I think.

"What are the other options?"

"You could take the subway?" she says. "It's on the green line. Whatever that means. There's like four different ones."

"Four?" I ask, panic tripping my pulse.

"Wait. Maybe five. There's one that splits off or something? I don't know what this map is telling me."

I groan and let myself collapse onto the sofa.

"What are you going to do?" Sara asks.

A moment passes, then I turn my head up enough to look at my front door. "I could ask my neighbor."

"Your neighbor?"

"He helped me find the grocery store the day I got home from the hospital, and the bookstore the other day."

"Perfect. Ask him."

"Actually, that might be a bad idea."

"Why?"

Because I've seen him in sweatpants that were quite frankly obscene, and the image keeps popping up in my mind at very inopportune moments.

"Because after the bookstore we ran into his girlfriend outside our building, and she didn't look very happy to see the two of us together."

"He's got a girlfriend?" Sara almost sounds relieved. "That's great! Now you don't have to worry that you're leading him on."

I roll my eyes. "Right. But I don't want her to get the wrong idea, either."

"Oh please. What is there to be jealous about? He's helping you revisit places you went on dates with your ex-boyfriend."

Is that what I'm doing? I've been so focused on getting my memories back, I'd almost forgotten about Sara's suggestion that they all lead back to Matt. To be honest, I'd barely thought about him at all. But if I'd learned anything over the past few days, it's that I can't trust my brain to tell me what's real right now. All I can do is follow the plan.

"Maybe," I say.

"I'm just saying, if he offered to help, you should take him up on it," Sara replies.

"Even if he's distractingly hot?" I ask with a wince.

She laughs. "*Especially* if he's hot."

CHAPTER 14

I spend the next morning trying to convince myself that I don't really need Ben's help to find the museum. There's a subway map in the drawer of my nightstand, and after I make myself a cup of tea, I pore over it, a desperate attempt to make sense of the disparate lines of the MBTA. Part of me knows I could avoid the entire exercise and just walk across the hall to ask Ben, but two issues stop me. One, the memory of how he previously opened the door still pops up in my head despite my best efforts to forget it, and two, I'm not totally convinced his girlfriend isn't over there.

I'm still no closer to understanding the green line later that afternoon, or why there are five of them, or why some of them appear to be buses. But I also come up with an idea that solves at least one of my issues. I may not want to rely on Ben's help, but if I need to, at least I can avoid the view.

I pick up my phone and call his number. After two rings, it connects.

"Hello." His voice sounds deep and rough, but thankfully not tinged with sleep.

"Hi. It's Marnie."

"I know. Your name pops up when you call."

Right. Of course it does. I texted him before, didn't I?

I clear my throat, working to sound like the thought of him taking the time to program me into his contacts isn't sending my brain into a tailspin. "I'm not catching you at a bad time, am I?"

"I'm just finishing up at work."

I have no idea if this means it is a bad time or not, but I plow on anyway. "Okay, well, I was wondering if you had a second to give me some directions."

"Where do you need to go?"

"The Isabella Stewart Gardner Museum?" I hate that I sound needy, but I also don't know how not to. Trying to navigate my own brain when I only have partial memories and half-truths is terrifying.

A moment passes before he says, "The Isabella Stewart Gardner Museum."

"Yeah. On Huntington Avenue?" I ask.

"I know where it is."

"Oh, good. Well, I thought I would take the subway—"

"The T."

"Right, the T. I just want to be clear on which train to take, though. It's the green line, right? But I'm confused about which one goes where and—"

"You're going by yourself?"

"I can manage, honestly. I just need—"

He cuts me off. "When are you leaving?"

I look down at my pajamas that I have yet to change out of.

"In a few minutes?" I say, wincing.

"All right. I'll text you directions."

"To the subway?"

"To the North Bennet Street School. I'll meet you in the lobby in fifteen minutes and we can go."

My eyes go wide. "Oh, I don't need you to walk me to the subway or anything. I just need—"

He doesn't wait for me to finish. "Fifteen minutes, Marnie."

Then he hangs up.

~

I'm halfway through Ben's directions before I realize that I'm starting to recognize the neighborhood. After I turn right off our block, I know where to find Prince Street because I know Bova's Bakery is there on the corner. And I know I've turned the right way because I remember the playground there behind the tall chain-link fence, how it teems with kids during the week at lunchtime. And on Hanover Street, I know when to turn left onto Richmond because that's where there are all the signs pointing in the directions of different Italian cities. By the time I turn onto North Street and see the North Bennet Street School across from me, I feel like jumping up into the air to celebrate. But my wide smile is already getting a few looks from passing strangers, so I restrain myself and go inside.

The brick building looks old from the outside, but once I walk through the front doors, the sunlit atrium is thoroughly modern. There are a few people milling about, and the sound of their laughter and conversation echoes off the cement floors, making the otherwise industrial space feel alive and welcoming. The smell of wood and oil floating in the air only adds to the atmosphere.

"Can I help you?"

I turn around to see a woman approaching. Her hair is cropped short and she's wearing an oversized pair of coveralls.

"Is it that obvious?" I ask, offering her a smile.

She laughs. "You look a little lost."

"I'm meeting someone here. Ben Morgan?"

She nods toward the elevator. "I think he's just finishing up his workshop. Up on three, second door on the right."

I follow her instructions, letting myself revel in the opportunity to take an elevator, and get out on the third floor.

The second door on the right is open, room 304, but I still hesitate before walking in. Then I hear Ben's voice, low and rumbling, coming from inside.

The smell of sawdust and pine welcomes me when I finally step forward. It's a huge space, running almost the full width of the building, with harsh fluorescent lights overhead. Tools line the long walls, exploiting every inch of purchase around the tall windows. There are a dozen tables spaced out across the room, each one crowded with angled pieces of wood, heavy chisels, random gloves, and paper. It feels warm. Almost inviting.

I take a few steps in but pause when I see Ben. He's standing at a table near the back of the long room, bent over a set of plans with the sleeves of his gray sweater pushed up to the middle of his forearms and a pair of glasses perched on his nose. Beside him is a man a few years younger than him, listening intently. I can't hear what Ben is saying, exactly, but the young man is nodding along as Ben carefully traces his finger down the lines in front of him to make his point.

The young man finally smiles as Ben straightens. They seem to be wrapping up, so I start forward again, my feet kicking some of the wood shavings across the floor. It's loud enough to draw their attention. Ben meets my gaze from over the rim of his glasses, his dark eyes so intense that I almost trip.

"Hi," I say lamely, waving one hand.

The line between his eyebrows deepens with concern. "Has it been fifteen minutes?"

"Fourteen. But to be fair, I left early," I say, holding up my hands. "Just in case I got lost."

His expression turns doubtful. "Did you follow the directions?"

"Yes."

"Then what were you worried about?"

I smile as I throw my arms out dramatically. "Do you know how many bakeries I passed that I wanted to stop in?"

The corner of his mouth twitches. "Give me a minute and we can go."

I wander further into the room, stopping at the desk in the far corner. I recognize Ben's coat over the chair and his leather messenger bag on the seat. On top of the desk is a mess of papers, a few small tools. A notebook, a cell phone, and a thick paperback with a faded cover. I crane my neck to read the cover.

The Count of Monte Cristo.

Before I can study it further, I hear the shuffle of papers behind me. I turn as Ben folds up the plans in front of him. The young man takes them, his eyes darting to me, then back to Ben before gathering up his things and heading for the door.

I don't want to blatantly stare as Ben walks toward me, but it's hard not to. It's like seeing a wild animal in their natural habitat. He's large but at ease as he saunters over to the other side of his desk, like he's in no particular rush. He reaches for his messenger bag and starts to gather items from his desk. The notebook, the cell phone, the paperback.

"*The Count of Monte Cristo*," I say. "Is it good?"

"It's one of the best books ever written."

I throw him a dubious look. "Ever?"

He nods.

"What makes it so great?"

"Well, for starters, no one is hiding a wife in their attic."

"Ha ha," I reply flatly, even though I really want to smile. "I'm serious. I feel like this is the one book that all men love but I have no idea why."

He pauses. I can almost see how his brain condenses everything he wants to say into one concise sentence. "It's about hope and forgiveness. And revenge."

"For a thousand pages?"

"There's a lot of revenge."

I laugh as he turns to lead us out of the workshop.

"Do you want to borrow it?" he asks when we reach the hallway.

"Aren't you in the middle of reading it?"

"I'm rereading it. Should be done soon."

"Sure. But fair warning, my brain is still a little broken, so I can't promise I'll finish it. Or remember to give it back."

The corner of his mouth tugs up as he holds the door for me. "That's all right. I know where you live."

We take the same path as we did to the bookstore, turning left down Hanover Street, through the North End Park, but then we veer off in a different direction. I'm trying to keep track, memorize the landmarks as we go, but downtown is crowded—not just with people, but buildings. They feel like they've been squished together so haphazardly, I could wake up tomorrow to find them completely rearranged, and it wouldn't be all that surprising.

"What's at the museum?" Ben asks as we cross another street. I can see the sign for the subway stop at the end of the next block.

"I don't really know," I say, squinting against the midday sun. "But there was a museum map pinned up on my corkboard, so I'm assuming I went there at some point."

He nods once and I brace myself for follow-up questions, but none come.

"It might be nothing," I continue. "I mean, look how the bookstore turned out, and this time I don't even have a specific thing I'm looking for. I have to just wander around hoping I see something familiar—and if I don't, what then?"

"You'll have spent the afternoon at one of the best museums in the country," he says flatly.

I roll my eyes even as I smile.

We reach the subway entrance a minute later and I'm about to turn to thank him, ask him to go over the trains with me quickly, but he walks right past me into the station.

"Wait, what are you doing?" I ask, following close behind.

He looks at me like he's the one who should be confused. "What does it look like I'm doing?"

"I thought you were just walking me to the train station."

"The T stop."

"What?"

"The train station is called the T stop."

I shake my head. Nothing about this city makes sense.

"Fine. I thought you were walking me to the T stop."

"I am."

"Okay, but why are you paying to get on the train?"

"Because you need to get on the train to go to the museum."

At this point, I can only assume he's being deliberately obtuse, but he's through the turnstile before I can stop him, and I have no choice but to follow him toward an escalator heading down.

Once we arrive on the train platform, we're enveloped by the crowd already waiting there. A moment later, a loud screech echoes through the tunnel as the train appears, a long chain of metal cars with gleaming red lights to herald its arrival. It stops before us and slides open its door.

The car is already half full, but Ben moves us forward, wedging us in the far corner. I can barely move, so I stare straight ahead at where my hand grasps the nearby metal bar. Ben's hand is just an inch or so above my own, close enough that they almost touch. His hands are huge compared to mine, each finger marked with small nicks and calluses. Like he spends a large portion of his time sanding and shaping, making things beautiful at the cost of his own skin.

I try to recall Matt's hands, but the only detail I remember is that he has long fingers, courtesy of years of piano lessons. They're nimble, almost elegant, and used to dance across my skin, back when discovering each other's bodies was a novelty. Nothing like Ben's broad palms and scars that seem to cut across other scars. I wonder if he has scars on the rest of his body, too. Lines and nicks in the skin across his chest or—

A deafening screech fills the car as the train does another jerky turn, jostling me from my thoughts. Yes, okay, my cheeks are warm, but it's also a very crowded car. There's no reason for Ben to think it's from anything other than the people pressing in on us from all sides. Yes. It's definitely that.

When we emerge from the train, it's three o'clock. The museum closes at five, but Ben doesn't seem like he's in a hurry as we cross the road.

Then I realize why. The museum is just ahead, a modern glass-and-metal structure abutting an older brick building. We enter the atrium-like lobby, welcomed by an almost otherworldly quiet, like someone has sealed us up from the rest of the city. For the first time in days, I feel my shoulders relax.

Ben approaches the ticket counter, already pulling his wallet from his back pocket, but I grab mine from my bag first.

"Here, let me get it," I say, reaching past the expanse of his chest to hand the woman my card.

"Marnie—"

"No, really. I insist," I say, smiling at the woman while silently praying to the universe—and to the nearest branch of my bank—that it goes through. "It's the least I can do. You came all the way over here and it's expensive for a random Friday. Maybe not if it were like a date or something. Not saying this is a date, because... obviously." I give him a combo shrug-nod, as if this is the universal sign for *I know you have a girlfriend and I promise I'm not a threat, so maybe you could pass that on to her*.

"Right," he says, his brow creasing.

The card blessedly goes through, and the woman hands us our tickets before we head toward a towering courtyard. Plants and trees crawl up what looks like a Venetian palace, while arched windows into different galleries across four floors peer out across its greenery.

"Is this place real?" I whisper, almost to myself.

"I know. It's pretty incredible," Ben replies, looking around like he's equally impressed.

"Was this someone's home, or was it always a museum?"

"A little bit of both," he says. "Isabella Stewart Gardner built it as a museum, but she also put her own apartment on the fourth floor. It's essentially a museum of her private art collection, and she lived upstairs. That's why none of the galleries have any central theme. It's all based on what she liked."

I smile. "That sounds like my grandmother."

He turns to me. "Yeah?"

I nod. "Her house was this beautiful mess of things she had accumulated over the years. She traveled a lot when she was younger, then she settled in Malibu and bought this bungalow overlooking the Pacific. It sounds impressive, I know, but she bought it in the eighties for next to nothing. The entire place was about a thousand square feet, but she managed to fit all sorts of things in there."

"Did you bring any of it with you?" he asks.

A stab of guilt hits my chest. "Not really. Most of it is in a storage unit in California. I kind of wish I had, though. Maybe the apartment would feel more like me."

He cocks his head to the side, like he's waiting for me to continue.

"I just mean . . ." My words dissolve as we wander into a nearby gallery. What *do* I mean? The thoughts are still forming in my brain, this mess of feelings that's so hard to articulate. "It doesn't *feel* like home yet."

"Why not?"

"Well, for one, there's the ABBA. My downstairs neighbor listens to it nonstop."

"You mean Brian?"

I pause. "Is that his name?"

Ben nods.

"Well, Brian listens to ABBA nonstop."

"Does he?"

My mouth falls open. "Are you telling me you can't hear it?"

"Only when I'm in the stairwell."

I roll my eyes. "Count yourself lucky, because it's a constant soundtrack in my apartment. It's like he's rehearsing for Broadway or something."

"He is."

I almost trip across the gallery's brick floor. "Are you serious?"

"Yeah. He's a dancer and just got a chorus part in a national tour for *Mamma Mia!*"

That explains a lot, I think.

"Well, apart from the ABBA, there's also all this stuff I don't recognize," I say. "Growing up, everything my grandmother had in her house had a story, a *reason* for being there. I've always been the same way. I'm sentimental over the most useless things. And now . . ."

"You don't remember why you have any of it."

I throw out my arms as I shrug. "So it's weird. I'm surrounded by objects that obviously mean something to me, but I have no idea why. It's like I have a collection of someone else's memories."

He's quiet for a moment, his gaze locked on an abstract portrait of a young woman as he says, "My mom does that."

"Collects other people's memories?"

"Sort of. She collects other people's photo albums." Ben says it like we're discussing the weather.

"With pictures and everything?"

He nods. "We used to go to a lot of thrift stores and garage sales growing up, and when my mom came across an old photo album full of pictures, she always bought it. My sister and I would beg her to stop, but she said that those books were full of moments that somebody wanted to remember. And if no one else was around to, then she would."

"I love that," I say with a smile. "What's your mom's name?"

He looks down at me, and I notice a new softness around his eyes. "Joyce Martin."

"Joyce Martin," I whisper, like we're sharing a secret. "Keeper of lost memories."

He lets out a short, dry laugh. It crinkles the corners of his eyes and sends goose bumps over my skin.

"I wish people still kept photo albums," I say, walking to the next painting, a sweeping landscape with an obelisk in the center.

"Didn't your grandmother?"

"She did, but after my parents died, she stopped. I think it was probably too painful."

Another moment passes before he asks, "Do you remember them?"

I shake my head. "Not really. I didn't think that was weird until somebody at school pointed it out. Like I had done something wrong by not remembering them. Like it was my fault. I was so embarrassed, I went home and I tore through my grandmother's bungalow, looking for something that proved they existed. Then my grandmother pulled this box out from her closet, like she had been hiding it away. Photos from when my mom was a little girl, of my parents on their wedding day. These tangible images that I could carry in my back pocket so they could get creased and worn down from every time I showed them off. It felt like proof that they existed. That those moments happened, whether I remembered them or not. That probably sounds silly, but to a sixth grader, it was very important," I say.

Ben's head cocks to the side. "It doesn't sound silly at all."

I nod as his words burrow into my chest, healing something I didn't even know was still aching. "Anyway, that Christmas, my grandmother gave me a 35 mm camera. It's one of the few things I brought with me when I moved, so maybe that means something."

I look up and meet his gaze again. His dark eyes have taken on a new facet in this light, like honey held up to the sun.

"Maybe it does," he says.

I smile.

We wander the first floor, and I lose myself in the art—Sargents and Manets and Botticellis hanging together in a gloriously random collection. But there's also the intricately carved crown molding. The damask wall coverings. The cracked brick floor. And all of it is accentuated by the smell of the gardenias and freshly turned dirt in the courtyard.

After a while, we find ourselves in a long gallery with light blue wallpaper visible between the landscapes and portraits tightly crowded along each wall. But one in particular catches my eye.

The painting is tall and has a boy at the center with dark hair and eyes. He's dressed smartly, though his waistcoat is a bit askew. His hair looks like it was brushed, but barely, and he's staring out at us just as a child today might in a photo their parents forced them to take. Begrudging compliance.

I lean forward to read the plaque:

STANDARD BEARER OF
THE HARVEST FESTIVAL, 1884
ANTONIO MANCINI (ITALIAN, 1852–1930)
OIL ON CANVAS

"Why does that look like you at twelve years old?" I ask as Ben appears at my side.

Ben hums, a deep, noncommittal sound. “My mom used to say the same thing.”

I blink up at him. “Seriously?”

He nods. “Always said it was her favorite. She used to bring my sister and me here a lot growing up.” He stares at the painting for a minute before catching my surprised expression. “How do you think I knew so much about the museum?”

“I don’t know, I guess I assumed it was a Boston thing. Like how you all know so much about Paul Revere.”

The corner of his mouth tugs up as he turns back to the painting. “My mom’s a middle school art teacher but has her master’s in art history. She always tried to inject some history into everything we did, even if it was just self-portraits out of Popsicle sticks.”

“Does she live nearby?”

“Yeah, she retired a few years ago and moved to Rockport. Just north of the city.”

His voice distracts me so much it’s worrying. It’s rough, like sandpaper on an itch deep in my belly. There are different levels to it, too, slight variations to its depth that trigger different reactions from my pulse.

I let out a deep breath, dislodging the thought as I turn back to face the painting again. “So this is your mom’s favorite. Where’s yours?”

~

We wind through a maze of hallways and galleries, past a few silent patrons milling about before closing time.

Finally, we end up in a room draped in heavy green damask. There is art hanging on every wall, situated to fit as many frames as possible. Ben stops in front of a huge frame hanging in the center of the wall. It's empty, so you can see clear through to the green velvet tapestry behind.

"This is your favorite?" I ask.

"At first it was a joke. My mom told us to pick our favorite painting, and when we got back home, she'd help us re-create it. I was twelve and a dick, so I picked an empty frame. She didn't challenge me, though. When we got home, she let me steal some spare wood in my dad's old workshop to make a frame. I even stained it and etched in the name there." He nods to the plaque displayed at the bottom of the frame that reads REMBRANDT. "Then she asked me why that was there. When I didn't have an answer, she made me research it. So I did. The painting that's supposed to be here is *Christ in the Storm on the Sea of Galilee*. It's this incredible scene of a storm about to tear apart a small fishing boat. Everyone on board is panicking, but Jesus is on deck, completely calm."

"Because he knew he could fix it," I say. "He's a really good carpenter."

Ben's mouth quirks up with another hint of a smile.

"So where's the painting?" I ask.

"Nobody knows."

My eyebrows stitch together. "Excuse me?"

"It was stolen in 1990."

"And they never got it back?"

He shakes his head. "Two men dressed like cops forced their way in. Tied up the security guards, threw them in the basement, then went around and grabbed what they could before the real police showed up. Cut paintings right out of their frames. No one has seen the men or the paintings since."

I look around, noticing now that this isn't the only empty frame in the room. "Have they kept the empty frames up this entire time?"

Ben nods.

"But what if they never come back?"

"Then they don't." He turns to me, his expression pensive. "But it doesn't cost anything to hope, right?"

CHAPTER 15

The sky is dark when we emerge from the T stop at North Station. The cool air bites at my cheeks as we walk toward our building, and it feels so good I barely notice that muscle memory kicks in when we reach our neighborhood. I know to turn left at the same time Ben does.

The smell of car exhaust fades under the aroma of garlic and cheese as we pass a pizzeria with its door open. The din from its small dining room spills out to the road, mingling with the sound of a church bell somewhere nearby. Just ahead, a bakery on the corner has all of its lights on, bright white and shining like a beacon.

The streetlamps come on a moment later, sending a muted glow across the cracked pavement, and I steal a glance up at Ben's profile. Even with the stubble, which at this point probably constitutes a beard, I can see the sharp angle of his jaw, how it's at odds with the softness of his mouth.

He has a girlfriend, a small voice in the back of my head reminds me.

I quickly turn away. I haven't thought about Lauren since we left the museum, but the moment I remember, I can't think of anything else. Guilt gnaws at my belly, not just because I've spent the entire afternoon with another woman's boyfriend, but because at some point, I'd forgotten why I'd gone to the museum in the first place. I'd been too busy enjoying myself. I wasn't being flippant just with Ben's relationship but with my recovery.

By the time we reach Prince Street, I have turned the problem over in my head so many times that I blurt out, "I don't think I'm going to need help finding my way around for much longer."

His eyebrows bob up. "No?"

"Nope. I recognized most of the streets when I was walking to meet you earlier. I even found that coffee shop from my box of memories yesterday."

His gaze stays on me, waiting for me to continue.

"It's this place called Strange Brew," I explain. "There was a napkin in my memory box from there. It had a number written in the corner that I thought might mean something, so I stopped by."

"And?"

"Apparently I work there. Which is confusing because I've never been a barista before. Not that I have anything against being a barista, it's just that in California I worked in recruiting. I was supposed to keep doing that after I moved here."

"Recruiting," he repeats, like he might have misheard me.

"It wasn't my dream job or anything," I reply. I hate how defensive I suddenly sound. "But my company lined up a position for me in their office here, so I accepted it."

"Why?" he asks, his voice cutting straight through to the heart of it: Why keep working in recruiting if it wasn't what I wanted to do?

"Because it was a staff job with benefits and a 401(k)," I reply, forcing a smile so the admission sounds less pathetic. "You know, the important things."

"Were you happy, though?"

The question lands like a lead weight in the center of my chest. I want to say yes, or at least offer a more nuanced version of the truth, but it would still be a lie. And I don't want to lie to him.

"No," I admit. "I wasn't."

He nods, not in agreement, but as if he understands. "My mom always says you can't fake happiness."

No, I want to say, stealing another glance up at him. *You can't.*

We walk for a few minutes before he asks, "Why did you go to the coffee shop on your own?"

"I didn't want to bother you in case you were busy. Or, you know, if someone found out I asked you to go to a coffee shop with me and they thought it was a date or something."

He glances down at me, and there's a new crease in his brow.

"Because I don't want to come between anything, especially when you're volunteering your time to help me," I say quickly. "Or have her thinking that I'm trying to insert myself—"

Ben stops, the solid line of him now planted in the center of the sidewalk, as he cocks his head to the side, like he's trying to see my train of thought from a different angle. "What are you talking about, Marnie?"

"It's nothing, just . . ." I sigh, then squeeze my eyes together as if that will make this less awkward. "I don't want your girlfriend thinking I'm trying to steal you or something, especially since I already feel like I'm using you a little bit. Ruining your relationship would just be the icing on this awful cake, you know?"

"No, I don't know," he says.

"When we got home from the bookstore the other day, your girlfriend didn't look too happy to see us together. To be honest, she looked like she was ready to gouge your eyes out. Or mine. Maybe both."

It takes a moment, but the confusion in his expression clears. "You mean Lauren?"

"Yes," I say. "Lauren."

"Lauren's not my girlfriend, Marnie."

I pause. "She's not?"

"She's my sister."

My eyes widen as my mind reviews our thirty-second interaction under this new lens. "I thought . . . the way she was acting, and then the way you were acting . . ."

"She was waiting on me to get some furniture out of my workshop. She and her husband bought this old house near my mom earlier in the year and they're trying to open an antique shop up there. I get her deals on stuff that comes up through my projects."

"Oh," I say, working to realign these new facts in my head. "So not your girlfriend."

"Not my girlfriend."

"Is there *a* girlfriend?"

He narrows his eyes a bit, like he's trying to decide the best way to answer. "I don't really do relationships."

I nod as if I understand, completely ignoring the sharp jab of disappointment between my ribs.

"I get it," I say, trying to sound casual. "Considering I don't even remember leaving my last relationship, I'm not looking for one right now, either."

I hate that he doesn't question it.

We walk the rest of the way back to our building in silence. When we arrive at the front door, Ben steps ahead, using the streetlamp to find the right key on his ring. I try not to study the soft silhouette of his lips when he's concentrating, the line between his brows. I fail miserably.

"Hey, Ben?" I say.

He looks up, pinning me in place with his gaze. I didn't realize how close I was standing. Too close. But I don't step back to give us space. I'm too invested in how he's looking at me, a perfect mix of curiosity and apprehension. The varying shades of brown and yellow in his eyes.

"I just wanted to say thank you," I say.

"For what?" he asks.

For listening and showing up and helping me figure out how I got here, I think. *For never making me feel like I'm a burden or a chore*. There were a million reasons flying through my head, and I know if I start listing them, I'll never stop. So instead I just smile and say, "For today. For everything."

"You don't have to thank me, Marnie," he murmurs, his voice so deep now I can almost feel it in the air.

"Yes, I do. All I wanted was directions, and I ended up hijacking your entire afternoon. And evening. You could have had plans."

"I didn't."

"I know, it's just . . ." I try to gather my thoughts, work to break the tension that has landed in the middle of the sidewalk. "You've been so nice and helpful, and I truly appreciate it. But I also feel like I've used you a little bit."

His head tilts to the side, considering me for a moment. "It's all right, Marnie. You can use me anytime."

Then he blessedly turns to the door again, completely missing how I stare back at him, wide-eyed and slack-jawed, like I could self-combust right there on the sidewalk.

CHAPTER 16

"Okay, let's go over the basics." Bobbi walks me over to the enormous espresso machine behind the counter at Strange Brew. "What do you remember?"

I stare at the array of knobs and tubes and panels. I'm only ten minutes into my first shift and already mentally preparing my resignation letter. "I'm not sure."

He nods sagely, like he's encountered this before. "Right. Then let's start with a cappuccino. That's one part espresso, one part steamed milk, one part foam. With me?"

"Sure," I say. Meanwhile, my palms are so sweaty, I have to wipe them against my Strange Brew–issued brown apron. It's just past ten a.m. on a Thursday and even though Bobbi assures me there's always a lull around this time, I still can't stop looking at the door, positive that a group of thirty stressed-out college students is about to appear and force me into action.

"Now, all you have to do is slip the portafilter into the grinder and press one if it's a single shot—that's our standard—then fit it here under the grouphead, but make sure it's tight or it'll make a mess. Then press this button and steam the milk while it brews. Just remember to check what kind of milk the customer wants. Or if they want a double shot."

"Or a double long," Claire, the other barista working today, says as she emerges from the storage room, a sleeve of coffee cups in hand. She's barely five feet tall, but her platform boots bring her heavily lined eyes level with my chin. "Gina from the post office likes hers with a double long."

"Right." Bobbi nods again. "Gina likes hers with a double long."

"What's a double long?" I ask, eyes wide.

"It's just a doppio, except with more water," Bobbi explains.

My brow furrows. "What's a doppio?"

"A double shot," Claire says over my shoulder.

"Great. Got it," I say, even though it feels like I might burst into tears.

Bobbi turns to look at me and his smile dissolves the minute he sees my expression.

"Are you sure?"

"Yup," I say. My bottom lip is wobbling now. "Sorry, I can totally do this. It's just hard to keep track of information since my fall. Like directions or instructions, or anything that has to be followed in order, you know? And my emotions are a little all over the place, too, so . . . so . . ."

Claire cringes and turns to head back to the storage room, while Bobbi carefully removes the portafilter from my hand.

"Let's just have you work on clearing tables today," he says, offering a placating smile.

I don't even mind. A bit of the tension in my shoulders dissolves and I nod. Clearing tables. Yes. I can do that.

I try to get a hold of myself as I wander the dining room, collecting plates and wiping away crumbs, but the tears stay right there, just under the surface, ready to burst out of me at any minute. I hate it. Before the accident, this job would have probably seemed like a breeze, someplace to show up to keep my insurance while I figured out whatever I was doing with my life. But now, every detail feels like it requires more brainpower than I'm capable of, resources I don't have access to anymore, leaving me feeling lost and overwhelmed.

If my grandmother were here, I know she would say this is a gift. *The universe is forcing you to be more present. Embrace it.* But I can't embrace anything when I'm holding a tray full of dirty cappuccino mugs in one hand and a sodden cleaning cloth in the other.

By the time the coffee shop closes at five p.m., my feet ache, my fingers are pruned from handling a wet rag for hours, and my scalp is unbelievably itchy from the knit hat I've been wearing to keep my bangs at bay. I don't take it off, though, I just shove my arms into my coat, then follow Bobbi and Claire out the main doors to the sidewalk.

Bobbi locks the front door, then stops to turn to me. "Oh, almost forgot, are we still doing that photography thing?"

I look at Claire, wondering if he's talking to her, but her attention is on me, too.

"What photography thing?" I ask.

"You know, that class at the Cambridge Arts Center that starts in December. You left the pamphlet in the break room," he says, waving back toward the dark café. "I'm going to register tonight. You're still in, right?"

He drops the information so casually, it takes me a minute for my mind to gather it up. I signed up for a photography class? It sounds impossible, but then I remember the 35 mm camera in my apartment, the roll of film still waiting to be developed, and it suddenly seems to fit.

"I think so, yeah," I reply before I can think better of it.

"Yay! It'll be like a field trip. Okay, see you Saturday morning! We'll tackle flat whites." He blows me an air-kiss before walking with Claire down Prince Street toward the T stop.

I watch them go, momentarily stunned, then turn in the other direction, burying my chin in my coat as the wind whips around the corner.

I'm taking a photography class, I think. I have no memory of signing up for it, or leaving a pamphlet in the break room so others would join me, but the knowledge that I did—that I'm not just a barista, I'm out there doing *something*—feels right. It feels vital. A glimmer of hope that my life here wasn't completely unrecognizable. That maybe I knew what I was doing. Or at least, I was trying.

The sky is already getting dark and the streetlamps are on, adding an otherworldly glow to the North End's narrow streets, but all I can think about as I turn down Sheafe Street is telling Ben.

Then again, maybe that's exactly the type of thing I shouldn't do right now. When he told me about Lauren a few days ago, I had felt so relieved, I hadn't taken a moment to consider what that could mean in the broader context of us. Before, when I thought he had a girlfriend, our relationship was neutral territory. Now those divisions are blurred, and every action has the potential of being so much more. I *want* it to be more. But that doesn't mean Ben feels the same. He might not have a girlfriend, but he also made it clear that he doesn't do relationships. And unfortunately, I've never been the type of person who can hook up with someone without completely falling for them, too. If something happened between us, I'd definitely get my heart broken. After everything I've been through over the past couple of weeks, I don't know if I could survive that.

The thought is so distracting, I almost miss the sound of my phone ringing at the bottom of my tote bag.

When I finally reach inside to grab it, I see Sara's name illuminated on the screen.

"Hey!" I answer a bit too loudly. But I can't help it, I feel guilty, like somehow she knows I was just thinking about somebody other than Matt.

"Hey." Her voice is high-pitched and cheerful. "What are you up to?"

"Just leaving work," I say, hugging my coat to my body as I turn down my block.

She gasps. "Did you get a job?"

"I already have one, remember? I'm a barista at a coffee shop near my apartment."

"Right, sorry," she says. "I didn't know you went back to work there. I thought you meant you got a *job* job. Like back at Probus or something."

A familiar annoyance sparks in my chest. It's the same one I always feel when Sara says something that not-so-subtly tells you exactly what she thinks about your choices.

"Well, after a full day on my feet wiping down tables, I can tell you that it is definitely a job," I say.

She groans. "I'm sorry. That sucks. But I have some good news for you."

"What's that?"

"What are you doing two weeks from today?"

I blink, working hard to remember the date. Halfway through my calculations I realize it doesn't matter anyway; I have no plans. In my new life, I am perpetually planless.

"Nothing," I admit. "Why, what's happening two weeks from today?"

"Drumroll, please," she says, and I can hear that she's tapping her hands on her knees. "Garrett and I are coming to Boston!"

A smile spreads across my face as I stop in the middle of the sidewalk just a few steps from my building. "Really?"

"Just for like, twenty-four hours. Garrett has a work thing, but I thought I would tag along. I have a meeting first thing on Monday morning, so we're literally flying in Saturday morning and leaving Sunday, but I thought that was still worth it, right? I need to see you, even if it's just a quick dinner."

The annoyance I had been feeling ebbs, and a smile spreads across my face.

This is good news, I think. And I really needed some good news.

"I can do a quick dinner. Maybe even a *long* one," I reply.

She squeals. "Don't tease. Okay, I'll text you our flight details and start looking into restaurants. We can do one of those Saturday night dinners like we used to!"

My smile falters. Saturday night dinners were a weekly tradition in LA, but they always included the four of us: Sara and me, and also Garrett and Matt.

"Sara—"

"I know it's not *exactly* like we used to, but come on, you and Matt are still our friends, right? And we miss you."

I unlock the building's front door and step inside. Normally, I wouldn't have a problem pointing out just how incredibly awkward this situation will be. But I can also acknowledge that this is an extenuating circumstance: The four of us haven't seen each other in a year—at least I don't think we have—and despite how the dynamics of the group have changed, we're all still family to Sara. Besides, I miss my best friend. If I have to have dinner with my ex-boyfriend to see her, so be it.

"Okay," I say.

"Really?" she gasps. "Oh my God, I'm so happy. Okay, you go relax. I'll text you all the details once I book reservations somewhere."

"Okay."

"And reach out to Matt! Maybe he can pick you up on his way."

I roll my eyes as I start up the stairs to the third floor. "We'll see."

"Okay, I gotta go, talk soon."

And then she hangs up.

I wish I was more excited, but I can't ignore the inevitable. This is going to be another one of Sara's master plans, some scheme to get me and Matt back together despite the fact I'm almost positive neither of us wants that. Which only makes the whole thing worse, since the only person who will end up getting hurt is Sara.

My brain is working so hard to come up with a solution as I climb the stairs to the third floor that I don't see the book that's waiting on the welcome mat outside my door until I almost step on it. When I bend down, I see it's Ben's copy of *The Count of Monte Cristo*.

And on the cover is a light blue Post-it:

Let me know what you think. —B

Suddenly, I forget to worry about Matt and Sara, or the ache in my feet and my pruned fingers. Because right now, only one thing really matters: Ben remembered.

CHAPTER 17

MARNIE

you dog-ear the pages

BEN

I what?

MARNIE

instead of using a bookmark like a normal person, you fold over the corners of the pages and now this book is riddled with creases

BEN

Ok.

MARNIE

you're going to ruin all your books

BEN

By keeping track of where I am?

MARNIE

by permanently damaging the pages when you do

BEN

You're burying the lede here.

MARNIE

which is?

BEN

If you know the pages are dog-eared in my book, that means you started reading it.

MARNIE

i did

BEN

And?

MARNIE

i really like it

except for all the ruined pages

BEN

I'm glad you're able to see past it.

MARNIE

some people call me a hero

BEN

I'm sure they do.

Where are you right now?

MARNIE

home

BEN

So you texted me from five feet away.

MARNIE

i'm on the sofa so technically i'm more like 12 feet away

BEN

Right.

MARNIE

now stop bothering me i'm reading

BEN

Okay.

MARNIE

hey Ben

thanks for letting me borrow your book

BEN

Hey, Marnie.

Thanks for reading it.

CHAPTER 18

"'Tonight you're going to see one of the Riviera's most *fascinating* sights,'" I quote, brandishing my best Grace Kelly impression while motioning elegantly down the road as we walk toward the newsstand ahead.

Ben shakes his head and throws a piece of popcorn into his mouth from the tub he took with him from the movie theater. "No."

I do my best to look insulted while also taking a long slurp from the remnants of my jumbo soda. "What are you talking about? That was a perfect mid-Atlantic accent."

"No, that sounded like a speech impediment."

"That's so insensitive. What if Grace Kelly really had a speech impediment? Maybe she adopted that accent to cover up the fact that she drops her *R*'s."

"Dropping your *R*'s is not a speech impediment."

"Says who?"

"Half of South Boston."

I laugh.

The past couple of weeks have developed a sort of rhythm all on their own. I didn't mean to memorize Ben's work schedule, how he has classes until three on Tuesdays and Fridays, and the occasional workshop on Saturday. How it fits with my own schedule at Strange Brew. At some point, though, I started expecting a text around 3:15—even earlier on the weekends—offering a walk to whatever destination is next on my list.

Last Monday, I met Ben in Beacon Hill where he had started overseeing the restoration of a townhouse on Acorn Street. We were supposed to go to the Boston Public Library, but he gave me a tour first, and before I knew it, we had spent hours exploring the space, seeing the hidden layers they were uncovering in the walls. On the way home I told him about the photography class in Cambridge, how I had called and discovered that I had already reserved a spot. I cataloged all the reasons I was terrified, but all the reasons I was excited, too. By the time we arrived back in the North End, I realized I hadn't shut up for ages, but Ben hadn't seemed to mind.

"You're an interesting person, Marnie," he said when I tried to apologize. "I like listening to what interesting people have to say."

It was a benign comment, said in such an offhanded way that I almost missed how those words burrowed into my chest, warming my bloodstream.

The Friday before that, we finally found a branch of my bank and I cornered the manager, detailing exactly what had happened to me, while Ben made sure that I provided my photo identification and social security card (which was thankfully in my desk).

It took over an hour, but I left with a balance statement ($2,238!) and a temporary debit card to use until my new one arrived in the mail. We celebrated by walking over to Haymarket, the endless lines of vendors set up along the street, and wandered the stalls, getting lost amid piles of radishes and apples and kale. It was so crowded, people pressing in from all sides, but not as overwhelming as I'd thought it would be when we first arrived.

"Just focus on the stall ahead. One at a time," Ben had said.

Which is exactly what we did. First apples. Then cucumbers. Then a selection of cheese. Then eggs. And the whole time, I watched Ben's back ahead of me, his shoulders squared, leading the way.

I left with my tote bag packed with a dozen apples, two pounds of cheese, and something called a kohlrabi. I couldn't have been happier.

Then today at noon, we took the T over to Cambridge to visit the Brattle Theatre, which, according to Ben, had nothing to do with the Brattle Book Shop except that they're both named after streets, which were, once upon a time, named after the same family. And since I'm learning to accept that nothing in this city makes sense, I just nod.

The ticket stubs from my corkboard were for *Rear Window*, but that wasn't playing. Luckily, there was a matinee for another Grace Kelly classic, *To Catch a Thief*. At twelve sharp we settled into our seats inside the theater. It feels like something set out of time, with its rows of low, narrow seats facing the movie screen, which is set deep on a stage at the front of the room. I looked around, trying to take in every detail, waiting for something to be familiar. Unfortunately, when the lights finally dimmed and Cary Grant appeared on-screen, the only thing I could focus on was how Ben's knee rested against mine.

He looks down at me now as we walk along the sidewalk back toward the T.

"Want to walk around here for a bit, see if anything looks familiar, or head home?"

I pretend like I have to think about it, like I haven't been secretly hoping we could prolong this trip since we left the movie theater.

"We can walk around," I answer, trying to sound casual. "If you're up for it."

He shrugs as if he's not opposed to the idea, then throws some more popcorn in his mouth.

"So, what do you have going on the rest of the week?" I ask as we turn the corner.

"I'm going to a Sox game with a friend. How about you?"

"Well, I have my next cognitive therapy appointment on Friday, so hopefully my doctor can tell me when all this is going to start paying off. Then my friend Sara is flying in from California with her husband on Saturday and we're going to grab dinner," I say. "She set Matt and me up so I think she's a little overly invested in finding out what went wrong."

It's meant to come out as a joke but Ben only nods.

"I'm glad she's coming out here," he says.

"I know. I've missed her. And that's saying something because I don't even remember the last time I . . ." My words falter when we turn the corner on a neat row of redbrick colonial buildings behind an iron fence on the other side of the street. "Wait. Is that Harvard?"

"It is," Ben replies, barely looking over.

"The Harvard of Elle Woods fame?"

His brow furrows. "I don't know what that is."

I roll my eyes. "You need to see so many movies."

He seems to accept this, then motions over with the popcorn. "Do you want to go in?"

I gawk up at him. "Can we?"

"Sure. We can't get into any of the buildings, but Harvard Yard is open to the public."

We cross the street and enter through the iron gate. A compact array of brick colonial buildings envelops us, their neat rows of windows looking down at us in a way that feels weirdly intimidating. But then, within a few steps, a sprawling green space opens up. The grass is bisected by a series of paths laid out at perfect geometric angles, and shaded by the tall trees scattered across the lawn. Their lanky branches shoot out in all directions, awash with red and gold foliage that softens the hard lines of the architecture around us. The perfect balance. I love it.

We walk slowly, no destination in mind, just following the straight paths that overlap each other. Students pass, backpacks thrown over their shoulders, conversations unfolding in low tones.

On the far side of the yard, a large sign sits in front of a building touting its recent renovation. I can't quite tell what they did since it looks exactly like all the others, but when I turn to Ben to ask, he's frowning at the sign.

"What?" I ask.

"I put in a bid to work on that."

"And they didn't take it?"

He shrugs, even though it obviously still bothers him. "It happens."

I look back to the redbrick building in front of us, and think of how much it could have been improved through his work. "I'm jealous."

"Of what?" he asks.

"You." I turn to look back up at him. He has the collar of his work coat popped up to protect his neck from the chill, but it still leaves his cheeks pink. "You love carpentry. You found your *thing*."

"My thing," he repeats, but in a more skeptical tone.

"The thing you're supposed to be doing," I say. "I'm jealous of that. I have no idea what my thing is. I didn't even really know I was supposed to be looking for it. When I was young, my grandmother talked about her life so much, I thought it was normal to spend a few years traveling halfway around the world to volunteer at an ashram, then leave to bake bread in Italy. So I grew up thinking I could do anything. That it wasn't so much about one particular job, it was about the *experiences*."

"A dynamic life," Ben says offhandedly.

My brow furrows. "What does that mean?"

"It's something Oscar Wilde said. I don't remember the exact quote, but the gist of it is, if you are born knowing exactly what you want to do, you'll inevitably become it. It's like a punishment. But if you wake up every day never knowing what that thing is, then you'll never be limited in what you can do. You'll live a dynamic life. That's your reward."

I smile. "Do you feel like being a carpenter is a punishment?"

He throws some more popcorn in his mouth. "I certainly never planned on it."

"What were you going to be?" I ask.

"A doctor."

I blink, not sure if I misheard him. "Are you serious?"

He nods.

How can he be so casual about this? It feels huge, like when I found out Dakota Johnson is a nepo baby. "What happened?"

A moment passes as he gives the question some thought. I've learned over the past few weeks that he does that a lot. Ben Morgan is careful with words. Every sentence feels deliberate, like he's weighed it, turned it over in his head, examined it from all sides, before it's uttered.

"My mom always made a joke about how she needed a doctor in the family. Then, in high school, I ended up doing well in biology and chemistry. My teachers told me how I would make a great doctor. So I went premed in undergrad. And when I got into medical school, my mom was so happy. I thought I was, too."

Ben's words from last week echo back in my head: *You can't fake happiness.*

He pauses in the middle of the path, like he's letting himself enjoy the memory. Then his expression clouds over. "The first two years were good, but it was all classwork. The third year is when you start the clinical rotations. Those are notoriously demanding, but I knew that. I was ready." He shifts his weight, and a muscle in his jaw ticks. "My first rotation was in emergency medicine. In the first twenty-four hours, I saw five people die. One was a six-year-old who had gotten hit by a car right in front of his house." His throat bobs. "All that training, years of work, and there was nothing any of us could do. Then we had to move on, build up a callus so it didn't affect us. I just couldn't. And I didn't want to learn to. So I talked to my attending at the end of the week and quit."

A gust of wind sends yellow and red leaves falling around us, but I barely notice. My attention is locked on Ben, the tension in his jaw, the hard line of his brow. How he's working hard to keep his emotions at bay.

"I'm so sorry," I whisper.

"My mom always thought I would go back. She used to tell people I was just taking a break, that it was temporary."

"But you love what you do now," I say. "That has to make her happy."

He lets out a heavy sigh. "I'm not so sure."

"Why?"

His head cocks to the side, like he's deliberating how much he should say. "My dad was a carpenter. He's the one who bought me my first set of tools. Who taught me how to use a marking gauge and a hand plane. He also had a lot of issues. And his way of dealing with those issues was drinking and arguing with my mom. Disappearing for days without a word. Then, one day, I noticed he had packed a suitcase, and I knew he wasn't planning on coming back." He pauses, letting his gaze travel across the lawn. "I chased him outside, begged him to stay, but he just kept walking straight to his car. He never came back."

I think back to the painting of the little boy in the museum, of that same boy begging his father to stay, to choose him, and my heart breaks in two.

"How old were you?" I ask.

"About ten. Lauren was just a toddler."

"Ben . . ." I whisper.

"Everyone always said I looked just like him. A carbon copy. They meant it as a compliment. They didn't know the details, why that messed with my head so much. I tried so hard to run away from it, to make sure I was nothing like him. But after medical school, I found my way back into his workshop in our garage. And it just . . . fit. I had spent so long running away from him, and in the end it didn't matter because I still ended up in the same place."

"You're not him, though. You know that, right?"

He lets out a dry laugh.

"I'm serious, Ben. You decide who you get to be. Nobody else."

He looks over to meet my gaze. His brow sets a dark shadow over his eyes, but there's a new softness there I haven't seen before.

"We're all out here winging it every day with no idea what the hell we're doing," he murmurs. "Sometimes we forget that goes for the people who raised us, too."

I nod, letting a moment pass before I say, "I think that's why my grandmother worked so hard to make me believe in magic and destiny. It made life easier to explain."

Ben turns to face me fully. "What do you mean?"

I shrug one shoulder. "I was six when I went to live with her. I didn't understand why my parents never came home, or what a drunk driver was. But the way my grandmother swooped me up in her arms and the things she said, the way she explained things, made sense at the time. Things were awful, but they wouldn't be awful forever, because magic was real. The universe had a plan just for me. And I was so swept up in it all, I didn't think to question whether she actually believed it or whether it was just something she said to make us both feel better."

"What do you think?" he asks, his voice soft.

A memory flashes in my mind. My grandmother waking me up at midnight on my twelfth birthday, wrapping a blanket around my shoulders before guiding me down the long path from her bungalow to the beach. *Jupiter has returned to the exact same spot in the sky as when you were born*, she'd told me. *That deserves a celebration*. Then she lit a bonfire and told me to set my intentions for the year. So I did, yelling them up to the stars like the universe was there, listening. The moment I was done, a shooting star flew across the sky, and all I could think was, *Yes, there really is magic here*. When I turned to tell my grandmother the same thing, I found her watching me, her long gray hair floating in the breeze, her pale skin almost glowing in the moonlight. But she didn't look magical. She looked old and frail. And sad. Even though she was smiling, there was so much sadness on her face that I didn't end up telling her about the shooting star at all.

"Honestly? I don't know. I wish I had had time to ask her, but she was diagnosed with dementia when I was in college. Within a couple of years, she barely recognized me anymore."

I try to offer him an apologetic smile, like I don't mean to burden him with the unabridged history of Marnie Stephens, but it fades when I see the look of concern on his face.

"Marnie," he says. There's a new gravity in his tone.

"It's okay," I say, trying to keep my voice level. "She died a couple of years ago, but I had been losing her for a long time before that. It's just hard sometimes because, yes, I miss her, but I feel so frustrated by her, too."

"Why?"

I sigh. It sends thin white tendrils of breath between us. "I guess it feels like I was sold a false bill of goods. If everything my grandmother told me about magic and destiny is true, then why did my parents die? Why did she always promise to leave me her bungalow, only for me to end up having to sell it to pay her medical bills? Why did a stupid fall wipe away a year's worth of my memories? Why do horrible things happen to good people every day? How is any of that magic?"

A moment passes as he studies my expression, as if he can see how my anger is just a thin mask for my grief. Then he smiles—the small, sad smile of someone who's been there, too.

"Maybe the magic is that we keep going," he murmurs, his voice so deep I can almost feel it in the air.

The tightness in my chest loosens, like his words have dislodged something I didn't even realize was stuck there. Then I offer him a small smile, too. "Maybe."

We stare at each other for a moment, caught in each other's orbit. I don't even know how much time passes, until a student across the lawn yells to another. Ben clears his throat and starts walking again.

When we reach the street a few minutes later, he asks, "So who is Elle Woods?"

"Only one of the most iconic blondes in film history. Besides Goldie. And Grace Kelly. Actually, Grace is probably at the top. She really nailed the perfect blond tone. And her cut was *perfection*."

He steals a glance down at me, tilting his head to the side. "Your hair right now looks pretty close."

I scoff. "Yeah, right."

"I'm serious."

"No way," I say. "Grace Kelly would never get a bob this short."

"Or drop her *R*'s."

"Tonight you're going to see one of Hahvahd Yahd's most *fascinating* sights," I say with the same elegant hand motion as before, but now with an affected Boston accent.

His mouth ticks up with that perfect almost-smile. "See, now that's not too bad."

I laugh, leaning into his side as we turn around and head back to the T station.

CHAPTER 19

I hit a major milestone after my shift at Strange Brew the next day: On my way home, I stop by the post office to send off the roll of film from the memory box to be developed, and I don't have to look up directions once. I'm so happy, I don't even mind that a gust of wind along Salem Street sends my bangs shooting out sideways, or that "Gimme! Gimme! Gimme!" is blaring in the stairwell as I pass the second floor on my way to my apartment. As soon as I walk through my door, I strip off my jeans and wool sweater and promptly get in my pajamas. Then I head to the kitchen.

It's only five p.m., so I start making myself a plate of cheese and grapes as a pre-dinner snack when my phone pings with a text. I dig it out of my tote bag and flip it open.

SARA

All set for dinner this weekend! Reservations confirmed for 7.

Can't wait to see my favorite people!

I don't realize Garrett and Matt are also on the thread until my phone pings again with another message. Then another.

GARRETT

Sounds good! Matt, you have the address, right?

MATT

Yup all set

SARA

Marnie, do you still need a ride??

Annoyance flares in my chest. I know what she's trying to do. No doubt Matt does, too. It's the world's least subtle setup.

But then the annoyance is swallowed up by guilt. None of this is different from how she orchestrated our relationship before, when I was all too eager to have my own someone so I didn't lose her to Garrett. If anything, it shows just how much she wants us to be happy.

Happy. The word echoes in my head. When was the last time Matt and I were happy? It shouldn't be hard to remember, and maybe if my brain weren't so broken, or if I could recall anything from the past year, it wouldn't be. But right now it's an effort. I'm wading through a bog of moments that were just fine or okay, trying to find something so elusive that I wonder if it existed at all.

There were plenty of times we had fun, like when we joined Sara and Garrett on vacation in Colorado, or when the four of us did that spontaneous road trip to Vegas. It feels like I should have been happy then. At the time, I thought I was.

You can't fake happiness. Ben's voice rolls through my head.

Another image pops into my head as I slice a piece of cheddar. Ben walking by my side through Haymarket, listening intently as I describe the perfect pear. Ben sitting beside me through *To Catch a Thief*, so close I can smell the sawdust from his coat, the sandalwood cologne on his skin. There are dozens of moments waiting for my attention, a long list of evidence that points to just one thing: I've been happy in Boston, because I've been happy with Ben.

And somewhere along the way, I started falling for him, too.

But what do I do about it? Tell him how I feel? Or will I just be setting myself up to get my heart broken? Is it better to stay where we are, this undefined place that feels like friendship but also so much more, or—

I pause halfway through that thought as something moves in the periphery.

Something small and fast and furry.

I turn just in time to see a mouse dart across the floor toward my bedroom.

What do I do, what do I do, what do I do?

I drop the cheese onto the counter and hold up the butter knife in defense. Then I tiptoe over to the front door, ready to open it, because that feels like the most rational thing to do right now. Maybe if he sees the available exit, he'll rethink his current course and make a clean getaway.

"I'm going to open the front door, okay?" I call out. "I won't hurt you; I just need you to leave. Please?"

I pause, listening. Waiting.

Suddenly I hear Ben's door opening across the hall. My heart does an odd tumble at the jingle of his keys, his gravelly chuckle, but then another voice pipes in.

". . . said she would meet us after, but still!" a male voice that is definitely not Ben's argues.

I want to keep eavesdropping, but suddenly there's scurrying behind me, like very small claws on very small paws running across my hardwood floor.

I scream and throw open my door.

Ben is in the middle of locking his dead bolt, his eyes wide as I almost fall into him. He looks so concerned I almost don't notice the man beside him until he blurts out, "Holy shit!"

"Sorry!" I gasp, still holding the butter knife in my hand. "I'm so sorry."

The man lets out a long breath while Ben's attention stays squarely on me. Despite the adrenaline coursing through my bloodstream, my pulse trips at the way his brows make a hard line over his eyes.

"What's wrong?" he asks.

I use the knife to motion back to my deceptively empty apartment. "He's back. He's in there right now."

The man beside Ben looks between us, concerned. He's wearing a Red Sox cap, but I can still see his curly black hair poking out the sides. "Wait, what's going on?"

Ben ignores him. "Where?"

"He ran into my bedroom." I have no idea why I'm whispering. "I mean, I *think* he's in the bedroom. He just moves so fast. Why does he run so *fast*?"

The man beside Ben narrows his eyes on me. "Is this a roommate?"

"It's a mouse," Ben says to him flatly. Then he turns back to me. "Do you want me to grab a few traps?"

I shake my head. "I don't want to kill him! I just want him to move out!"

"And we're sure this is a mouse," the man says.

"Shut up, Pete." Ben shakes his head.

"Hi." The man nods to me. "I'm Pete."

"Marnie, this is my brother-in-law, Pete," Ben says, already looking exasperated. "Pete, this is Marnie."

Before I can reply with my requisite "It's nice to meet you," Pete's eyes light up, like he's connected two disparate dots in his head.

"Wait, Marnie the *neighbor*?" he asks, a smile pulling his lips up as he turns back to Ben.

Ben frowns, throwing his brother-in-law a look that immediately shuts him up but doesn't dislodge his smug grin.

Under normal circumstances, I would only be too eager to overanalyze why Ben would have mentioned me to anyone, let alone a member of his family, but these are not normal circumstances. Something that could be carrying the plague is in my apartment right now, and I have no idea where.

"What if he can climb?" I ask.

"Hold up," Pete says, holding his hands up. "Can mice do that?"

Ben sighs. "I don't know. Probably."

Pete turns to me, looking almost as horrified as I am. "What if he's in your *bed*?"

I feel the color drain from my face.

Ben looks between us and sighs. "Jesus. Hold on."

He brushes past me into the apartment. Pete and I crane our heads to see past the open door, even utilizing the crack between the hinges to see what he's doing, but only catch the sound of the kitchen cabinets opening and closing, a gruff curse. A few minutes later, he reappears, wiping his hands against his jeans.

"I think it's gone," he says. "Did Gino figure out where they were getting in? I don't see any holes around your radiator, but maybe behind the stove—"

"They can get in from behind the *stove*?" Pete laments to himself.

"How is Gino supposed to move the stove to look?" I ask. "He's so old!"

Ben doesn't seem to be listening to either of us as he works something out in his head. It's causing the line between his eyebrows to deepen, a muscle in his jaw to tick. I can see it even under the thick stubble.

"All right, I'll go grab some traps—"

"No traps!" I interject.

He continues undeterred. "And we can lay them around every place where you've seen it so—"

"I already told you I don't want traps," I say, trying not to sound indignant.

"And I already told you to call me and I would take care of it."

"By killing a small, innocent animal?" I ask, motioning back toward the apartment with my knife again.

Pete looks momentarily confused, while Ben just looks exasperated.

"What's the plan, then?" he asks.

I don't have a plan. I've barely come to terms with the fact that the mouse is back and possibly burrowing under my duvet.

"I'll just . . . keep my door open for a couple of hours. I'm sure he'll run out at some point, right? It's not like he wants to live in my apartment. He's probably lost. So I'll just wait for him to leave."

In my head, this sounds completely rational. But judging by Ben's and Pete's expressions, I am insane.

"You're going to sit at home, alone, with the front door open all night," Ben says. Hearing him repeat my plan makes me realize they're probably right.

"Do you have another option?" I ask.

"Come out with us," he says, like it's the most obvious solution in the world.

"Oh, that's right!" Pete agrees, his expression lighting up as he turns back to me. "The Red Sox are playing the Kansas City Royals tonight. Lauren has to work late, so we have an extra ticket."

"Oh, no. I couldn't do that," I say, scoffing.

"Why not?" Ben asks.

I blink, trying to come up with an answer. The way he says it makes it sound so simple, as if the choice is obvious. But this is untrodden territory. We've never left this building together without the guise of my list as an excuse.

"What's it going to be, Marnie?" Pete asks after a moment. "Baseball or rodents?"

I sigh. "Well, when you phrase it like that, is it even a choice?"

"Depends," he says and smiles. "Are you a Yankees fan?"

CHAPTER 20

"Eat shit, Martinez!" a voice bellows from somewhere nearby as the sound of an organ playing "Charge" blares out of the speakers above Fenway Park.

More boos arise from the crowd in the bleacher seats around us. The sky has darkened and the lights above are on, illuminating the field below so the green grass almost glows.

"Hey, Martinez, does your wife know you're fucking us?!" someone else yells from behind us.

I lean toward where Ben is sitting to my right. "Who's Martinez?"

"The guy who just got walked," he says, nodding to first base as he throws a peanut in his mouth. "He came up through the Sox's farm system and built his career here, then requested a trade last year."

"Yeah, because the front office sucks!" Pete shouts, leaning forward as if the men on the field can hear him. "Typical nickel-and-dime bullshit they pull every year."

Next to me, Ben nods in agreement. I laugh around a mouthful of popcorn.

Even after I agreed to take Lauren's ticket, I still wasn't sure if I should come. But then Ben grabbed one of his Red Sox caps from his apartment and slipped it on my head, blessedly taming my bangs, and there was no possible way I could say no.

During the T ride down to Fenway, Pete attempted to fill me in on the complete 125-year history of the team, but as the train grew more crowded with fans all headed to the same place, more and more people began interrupting him, adding nuance to his anecdotes or challenging his statistics. When we finally arrived at the Fenway stop and the crowd emptied onto Comm Ave., we'd barely made it through the 1978 pennant race.

By then it didn't matter. Any chance I would retain the information was gone the minute we were enveloped into the mass of people on Lansdowne Street, the smell of grilled sausages and onions filling the air, along with the yells and jeers as fans passed one another beneath the shadow of the stadium.

I followed Ben and Pete inside through the turnstile, dodging our way through the crowd and up a flight of stairs. I was so wrapped up in the chaos I didn't realize we were actually entering the park itself until there it was, sprawling out in front of me, the field glowing under the bright stadium lights. Above it, the sunset painted the sky in vibrant pinks and yellows, extending out past the stadium walls. I couldn't imagine any of the other fans around us coming here and not being overwhelmed by awe.

Then the game started.

"Get off your knees, ump! You're blowing the game!" the elderly woman sitting in front of us yells.

Strike three is called, and Pete lets out a sigh of relief as he leans back in his seat.

"Finally! Jesus!" Pete yells, then he turns to me, his demeanor immediately shifting from belligerent to attentive. "Okay, rewind. You moved from California because your ex-boyfriend got a job here?"

I nod as I throw another piece of popcorn in my mouth. Over the course of the past five innings, Pete has made a concentrated effort to learn everything he can about me, like he's filling in the gaps of whatever information Ben had shared before. He didn't appear to know about the injury, though, or my memory loss, and I wasn't in a rush to tell him. It wasn't that I was trying to keep it a secret; I was simply enjoying the fact that, for one night at least, it wasn't the center of the conversation.

"Then you broke up with said boyfriend, and now you're living across the hall from this guy," Pete continues, nodding to Ben.

"Yup," I say.

"Well, that sucks," Pete says.

Ben throws him a look.

"Not you," Pete says, waving him off. "I'm just saying, if I moved here from California and didn't have a reason to stay, I'd go back in a heartbeat."

"You'd never get Lauren past Rhode Island," Ben says flatly.

"True," Pete murmurs, taking a sip of his beer.

I smile. "How did you two meet?"

"High school. We were in the same algebra class freshman year."

"Lauren turned him in for cheating on a midterm," Ben adds grimly, as if he's reprimanding a child.

"Yeah, she's a narc," Pete quips with a sigh, as if he's never loved her more. Then he turns back to me. "So what do you do, Marnie from Malibu?"

I take a big sip of my soda as I try to think how to answer that question. What do I do? It feels like, for the first time in years, I've been trying to work that out. But I have no idea how to explain that to Pete without launching into a diatribe that reveals everything else. *Well, I spent five years building a career in HR, but quit to become a barista and take photography classes in my spare time, which I'm really excited about even though I have no memory of why I did any of it.*

I swallow and still have no clue what to say, but thankfully Ben speaks first.

"They're starting Ronson again," Ben says, nodding out to the field.

Pete's head whips around to watch the pitcher jog toward the mound.

"Give it up, man!" he shouts. "It's over!"

Pete forgets to follow up as the inning begins, then we lose him to a rousing rendition of "Sweet Caroline" pumped through the speakers during the seventh-inning stretch. The entire stadium seems to be on its feet, swaying to the music and belting out the lyrics in every key except the one intended by Neil Diamond. When it's over, Pete leaves to find the bathroom, sliding past the other people in our row and heading toward concessions.

"I like Pete," I say after a moment.

"Don't tell him that," Ben murmurs, his gaze sliding across the field. "It'll go straight to his head."

I laugh.

"He can get intense with the questions, though," Ben continues, turning to face me. "Feel free to tell him to back off."

"It's okay. I don't mind."

I expect that to be enough for us to move on, but Ben's attention stays glued to me, his gaze focused on my eyes, my lips, my cheeks, like he's checking to see if I'm really okay. Doctor Sweater assessing his patient.

The thought turns my blood to hot syrup in my veins, and I look back to the field, pretending to be very invested in who is where, and not at all distracted by the fact that the seats at Fenway are so close that Ben's arm is tucked next to mine on the armrest. How I can smell sandalwood and soap even amid the mess of food around us. How I can feel the warmth radiating off him so much I can't even tell if the temperature has dropped with the sun.

"When was the first time you came here?" I ask.

"In high school. My best friend and I almost got arrested over in the grandstand."

I turn to him, incredulous. "Excuse me?"

The corner of his mouth ticks up. "I bought tickets off a scalper for Game 4 of the playoffs. It cost all the money I saved that summer, but I thought it was worth it. We get here, we actually make it inside, but when we get to our seats, there were already people in them." He shakes his head. "If we were smart, we would have kept our mouths shut, grabbed some food, and watched the game from the concession stand. But we weren't smart. We found a security guy and told him there were people in our seats. He took one look at our tickets and brought us downstairs."

"What's downstairs?"

"A prison."

My eyes go wide, and he's no longer able to temper his smile. It broadens across his face, and suddenly I can see him at that age: a teenager fumbling his way toward adulthood. "I'm kidding. It's just their security office."

"What happened then?"

"I think the fact that we essentially turned ourselves in was enough evidence to prove we weren't trying to scam anybody. We were just idiots," he says. "It helped that my friend Moe's face was painted like a red-and-white checkerboard, too. So they let us go and we watched the rest of the game from the Cask 'n Flagon over on Lansdowne Street."

I laugh, a bit of the tension releasing from my shoulders. The sound of an organ playing echoes through the speakers above us.

"Hey, Bobby! You sure you're right-handed?" someone nearby yells.

More people join in, and I laugh as they all start arguing with each other. After another moment, I turn back and catch Ben watching me. The corner of his mouth is still turned up, but there's that softness in his eyes that I haven't seen since that day in Harvard Square.

I'm happy right now, I think. Even if I never get the courage to tell that to Ben, even if we're never anything more than what we are right now, I will always remember that in this moment, with him, I was really and truly happy.

"You okay?" he asks.

I nod. "Thank you for inviting me tonight, Ben."

He leans in like he's about to tell me a secret. "Thanks for coming, Marnie."

CHAPTER 21

The Red Sox win, seven to three. Afterward, "Dirty Water" by the Standells—a song that sounds cynical but Ben assures me is a very beloved ode to the nearby Charles River—echoes across Fenway Park while Ben, Pete, and I spill out of the stadium onto Lansdowne Street. The reverie from inside continues with the crowd clogging the road, who sings and cheers and yells en masse all the way to the Kenmore T stop. I try not to focus on Ben's hand that's gently settled on the small of my back, keeping tabs on me in the chaos while subtly directing me where to go. He's just being considerate, I tell myself. Meanwhile the rest of my brain zeroes in on every one of his fingertips, the exact place I can feel them on my skin through my sweater.

We have to wait on the platform as three trains come and go, so full of fellow fans that there's no room for anyone else. By the time we do manage to squeeze in, someone is playing the Dropkick Murphys from a Bluetooth speaker, trying to get everyone to sing along, while at the other end of the car someone yells, "SHUT THE FUCK UP!"

I grip the metal bar above our heads and try to hide my smile in the sleeve of my sweatshirt. Ben is smiling, too, that crooked grin that seems to only affect one corner of his mouth. Beside him, Pete is trying to organize the packed car into rounds for the chorus.

We get off when the train pulls into Haymarket, and by the time we emerge out of the station and onto the street, Pete has decided that we're not going home quite yet.

"Lauren's waiting for us at Durty Nelly's," he says, reading a text from his phone. The street is dark but he charges ahead, his screen illuminating his face as he guides us down a narrow road lined with buildings that look like they've been there since the Revolution.

Just as my brain starts to get turned around, Pete whistles, waving us to the corner where a bar is waiting with its doors open.

As soon as I step inside, I'm met with a rush of sound. The bar is crowded, people in jerseys and jackets and the intermittent T-shirt all wedged shoulder to shoulder, talking and laughing so you can't hear any of the televisions mounted above. The ceiling is low and copper-tiled, refracting the blue and red and yellow light from the collection of neon beer signs on the walls as we enter.

Pete walks ahead, both hands aloft like he's a celebrity greeting his adoring fans.

"Seven to three, baby!" he yells.

Everyone seems to know exactly what he's talking about and begins to cheer. The only person who looks unimpressed is Lauren. She's sitting at the end of the bar near the door, a disappointed look on her face as she watches her husband soak up the applause.

"Is he already drunk?" she asks Ben as he and I approach.

"Pretty close," Ben replies grimly.

"Great," she murmurs. "Exactly how I wanted to spend my Thursday night after a long day at work."

Then Pete's eyes lock on her, and his face splits with a wide grin.

"My love, my light—"

"Don't you dare," Lauren says as if she knows what's coming.

"My bliss!" he exclaims, falling forward to envelop her in his arms.

She pushes him off her, cringing. "You smell like beer and regret."

He laughs, like this is standard operating procedure for the two of them, and Ben turns to the bar, looking for someone to take our drinks order.

"You're Marnie," Lauren says, as if noticing me for the first time. "The neighbor, right?"

"That's me," I say, doing an odd wave, silently praying she doesn't remember that I was with Ben a few weeks ago when he left her waiting for a half hour out on the sidewalk.

"You were with Ben a few weeks ago when he left me waiting for a half hour out on the sidewalk."

I cringe. "Yeah. Sorry about that."

"Oh please," she says, rolling her eyes as she nods to where Ben leans against the bar beside me. "My brother has never been on time a day in his life."

"Yeah, but he always picks up the bar tab," Ben replies.

"Not as magnanimous as you think when I'm stuck drinking seltzer because I have to drive him home." She motions to Pete, who's standing a few feet away singing along to "More Than a Feeling" now playing from the speakers overhead.

Ben chuckles. It's a lovely sound, rough and deep, and makes me wonder about the other sounds he makes when he lets his guard down.

And now I'm blushing.

A bartender arrives a moment later and takes our order—a lager for Ben, a seltzer for Lauren, and a Diet Coke for me—then disappears as Pete pulls Ben into a conversation he's having with a nearby group about the Red Sox's bullpen. Ben's expression turns grim, like this is the last thing he wants to do right now, but I can't help smiling. I love this. It's a side of Ben I haven't seen yet, a view into his life that I haven't been privy to, and it's so comfortable, so perfect that . . . oh God, I think I might be falling for him even more.

"Have you been to Fenway before?" Lauren asks, startling me out of my thoughts.

"No. I haven't even been to a baseball game before," I reply, working to appear relaxed.

"What'd you think?"

"It was incredible." I smile. "Thanks for letting me steal your ticket."

"Thank my boss. He's the one who decided to load me up with three hours of work at five p.m."

"Ouch. I'm sorry," I say. I remember those days at Probus. Sara and I would be packing up to leave, minutes from powering down our computers, when one of us would get an urgent email with some inane assignment that had to be completed immediately. We'd always stick around and help the other one finish it. At the time, it was almost fun, because we were there complaining together. But once she was promoted out of our department, the novelty wore off.

"It's fine," Lauren says, waving me off. "I'm planning to quit in a few months, so they're only getting me at fifty percent anyway."

"That's right. Ben said you were opening an antique shop."

"It's not really an antique shop. That's just the easiest way to describe it. Actually, it's more of an architectural salvage place. Pete works in construction and Ben is all over the city doing these renovation projects. Between the two of them, they see so many people gutting their homes of these beautiful original pieces just to put in something modern and impersonal. So I thought, why not take that stuff and sell it to people who will appreciate it?"

Lauren talks about her shop the way Ben talks about carpentry: with such deep love and admiration that I can't help but smile.

"That's incredible."

She scoffs. "Hardly. I spend most of my free time looking through old banisters and faucet handles."

"It still sounds like more fun than I've ever had at work," I say.

"That just means you need a better job." She laughs.

I laugh, too. Because maybe it is just that simple.

As the night progresses, the crowd grows, absorbing us into its fray. I don't even mind when our small group gets separated and I find myself seated next to an older man in a Ted Williams jersey who's explaining baseball's infield fly rule to me. I try to listen, but I can barely hear him over Pete, who is a few seats down arguing with a group of strangers about the Red Sox's chances in the playoffs, while Lauren sits next to him, rolling her eyes like she knows he's setting himself up for disappointment. The whole scene is punctuated by the smell of stale beer and sweat and fryer oil permeating the air.

It should make me feel claustrophobic and anxious, but it doesn't. I feel comfortable. Relaxed, even. There's a rough familiarity here, as though everyone intrinsically knows how to lean in close, how to cheer in unison, how to ride the same pulse that keeps the energy alive.

The man beside me is now describing the bench-clearing brawl he witnessed against the Devil Rays in 2000, waving his arms as beer sloshes from his glass, when I catch sight of Ben. He's on the other side of the room now, nursing a bottle of Sam Adams, when his eyes lock on mine.

You good? he mouths.

Without the sound, I can fully appreciate how his full lips form around the words, how the hard line of his brow softens ever so slightly with concern as he does.

I'm falling for you, I think.

I'm fine, I mouth back.

He doesn't look away, and neither do I. It feels like I'm locked into some impossible force. It's useless to try to fight it, and it suddenly occurs to me that I should stop trying. Just give in to it and—

"What do you think?"

I blink back to the man in front of me. I've totally missed whatever he's been talking about for the past couple of minutes, but smile anyway.

"Sorry?" I ask.

"I said it's getting crowded," he repeats. "What do you say we get outta here?"

He bobs his eyebrows at me, just so there's no doubt as to his meaning.

"Oh. Um," I stutter, so busy trying to think of what to say that won't hurt this man's feelings that I forget to curb my nervous tic. I automatically run my fingers through my hair, sending my bangs into high alert. "Well, I haven't finished my drink yet."

The man glances at my watered-down Diet Coke, then back to me. "I got plenty of soda back at my place."

I laugh a little too loud as my eyes dart around the room, hoping to find something, anything, that can extract me from this situation without embarrassment. Then, miraculously, the crowd parts as Ben approaches with his empty pint glass.

Relief sweeps through me as I smile at him like he's the Coast Guard and I'm stranded on a lifeboat.

His eyebrows stitch together, confused, but he doesn't question it as I loop my arm in his.

The older man eyes the two of us suspiciously.

"Oh, look! It's my boyfriend. Ben. Ben is my boyfriend," I reply a little too quickly.

I look up at Ben, maintaining my painfully broad smile while trying to somehow communicate telepathically: *Please play along because I don't think I can hurt an old man's feelings tonight. My heart can't take it.*

Something shifts in Ben's expression, but before I can decipher it, his arms come around my shoulders in a languid motion, pulling me close.

"Everything okay over here?" he asks, his voice dropping to an obscene octave. And just like that, all the blood in my body pools between my legs.

"Yup. Yes," I say, tripping over my own tongue. But I can't help it. My eyes are locked with his and every thought has emptied from my brain except for how warm he feels against me, how his eyes look like little explosions of heat and fire.

"Huh," the older man says, eyes narrowed like he still doesn't believe us.

I try smiling again, and do the only other thing I can think of: introductions. "Ben, this is . . ."

"Murray," the man says gruffly.

"Murray! This is Murray. And Murray, this is Ben. My boyfriend. My boyfriend Ben."

"Hold up!" Pete appears from behind Murray like some sort of smug guardian angel. "Did I hear *boyfriend*?"

Ben sighs, a sound of utter disappointment. "Let it go, Pete."

This only seems to egg Pete on more. "Are you kidding? This is great! Here I thought you were just neighbors. How silly of me! Everybody, let's cheers the happy couple! To Marnie and Ben!"

Ben shifts his weight to turn to his brother-in-law, a small motion that brings him a few inches closer to me. Close enough that I can feel the warmth of his body even through his sweatshirt.

The rest of the bar seems to be in on it now, all yelling their own encouragement.

"To Marnie and Ben!"

"To love!"

"Go Sox!"

Then someone bellows from the far corner, "Kiss her!"

My face is suddenly hot.

"Yeah, kiss her!" Pete cheers. "On the MOUTH."

"Jesus Christ," Ben murmurs.

A chant starts further down the bar. "Kiss her! Kiss her! Kiss her!"

"Should I kiss her?" Murray asks, looking around like he's genuinely wondering.

Ben turns his gaze to me, an apologetic expression that hints at what he wants to say.

Ignore them.

Don't worry about it.

We don't have to kiss.

Except, we *do.* I've been trying to stomp out the desire for weeks, but now that it's out there, I don't think I can survive the rest of the night *without* kissing him. Every inch of my body demands it.

Then, as if he just might be thinking the same thing, Ben's gaze drops to my lips.

I don't know who kisses who, only that his mouth is on mine, soft and perfect. My lips part, savoring the slide of his tongue, and I barely hear how the bar erupts with applause. The shouts and whistles and calls to get a room. All I can focus on is the feel of his body against mine, the smell of sawdust and soap that wraps around me, the sweet bite of lager on his tongue. I haven't had alcohol in weeks, and it feels like I could get drunk on this. Like I could devour him right here.

But just as quickly as it started, it's over. He draws back, and Pete is suddenly between us, holding up his beer and doing some kind of dance I can only assume is in celebration.

Ben tilts his head enough to look around Pete, meeting my eyes. It's that look he gave me at the hospital, apprehension mixed with concern. Except now, I know what his lips taste like, how his hands feel against my skin, and my body suddenly feels like it's glowing.

Cheap Trick's "I Want You to Want Me" comes on the jukebox then, and Pete pulls Ben and me into the center of the room where everyone else has started to dance, each person to their own version of the beat. I know I should feel self-conscious about the kiss, about my bangs, which are sticking to the sweat on my forehead, or how I trip over my feet. But all I care about is singing along to the lyrics I didn't even know I knew by heart. The feel of Ben's hand as he takes mine and spins me in a circle in time with the music. This moment that feels like the universe created it just for me.

The four of us pour out of the bar at one a.m., with Pete yelling drunken goodbyes to the other patrons over his shoulder.

"We're parked on Battery Street," Lauren calls out to Pete once we're outside.

There's no way to know if Pete hears her, or if he does, whether he's committed the information to memory. He's a few paces ahead of us, singing "Dirty Water" at the top of his lungs. Ben strides up beside him, helping him to stay on the sidewalk.

"Men are so embarrassing," Lauren murmurs to herself.

I let out a soft laugh.

We walk another few steps with only Pete's off-key version of the Standells filling the air before she says, "So, are you and Ben together or something?"

My cheeks are suddenly on fire. I don't know why I didn't anticipate the question, or stop to consider that Ben's sister was standing right there, just a few feet away when we kissed. I had been so consumed with the thought of his lips on mine, nothing else had even entered my mind. Not until right now.

"Oh, no. It's not . . . we're not . . . we're just friends. And neighbors, obviously. But definitely not *together* together. My personal life is a bit of a mess at the moment. And, you know, he doesn't do relationships, so . . ." I clear my throat, willing my words back down my throat.

She doesn't look convinced, and I can't blame her. Saying we're just friends doesn't magically erase our very public make-out session.

"Has Ben told you about our dad?"

I blink at her candor. "A little bit."

"So you know he left," she says. When I nod, she sighs. "Ben idolized him, then he was just . . . gone. And Ben was the one who had to pick up the pieces. He saw how heartbroken our mom was, how she struggled to make ends meet. He saw how much you can hurt a person, even when you think you love them. And as he got older, he worked so hard not to disappoint anyone that I think he started to believe it was easier on his heart to be alone."

I look ahead to where Ben walks beside Pete, the strong line of his shoulders helping to support his brother-in-law as they make their way down the street.

When I turn back to Lauren, I realize she's been watching me. And I gave away much more than I intended.

"My brother doesn't let a lot of people in," she says, her expression serious. "So don't make him regret it. Okay?"

The words feel heavy, like they're more than just advice. Like she wants me to make a promise.

"Okay," I reply solemnly.

She nods, the same way her brother does, as if it's a form of punctuation. A moment later, Pete's voice echoes down the street ahead of us.

"Seven to three, baby!"

Once we get to our building, Ben and I say goodbye to Lauren and Pete as they continue on past the corner and out of sight. Then a loaded silence descends as Ben unlocks the door and holds it open for me.

I can feel the weight of his presence behind me, warm and solid, as I ascend the stairs. It makes it hard to think straight, so I almost forget which apartment is mine by the time we get to the third floor. I blink between doors, finally recognizing my welcome mat and digging my keys out of my bag. But I don't unlock the dead bolt. I turn to face Ben.

His door is open, the apartment dark just beyond the threshold, but he hasn't entered. He's turned to face me, too.

"Thank you again. For inviting me tonight," I say.

"I'm glad you enjoyed it," he replies.

I don't move. Neither does he.

I know this should be the natural conclusion to the evening. I said thank you, and now I should unlock my door and disappear inside before I launch into one of my signature monologues that I know I'll regret. But that would mean sitting alone in my apartment, replaying our kiss over and over in my head until morning. And I don't want to do that, either. I want to keep his eyes locked on mine. I want to soak up the feeling of his concentrated attention, how it sends a prickly heat across every inch of my skin.

"I'm sorry," I finally say. "For earlier and that whole . . . thing."

His head cocks to the side slightly. "The kissing thing or the boyfriend thing?"

It's so blunt that I can't help but let out a soft laugh. I'm not sorry about the kiss, even though that feels like the most obvious thing to apologize for so we can move on. I'm not even sure I want to move on.

"I don't know," I say. "It's just . . . you're my friend. That means a lot to me, and I don't want to mess that up."

He leans a shoulder against his doorframe, his expression pensive. "You could never mess it up, Marnie."

Even though I've spent the past two hours thinking about the taste of your tongue?

The thought warms my cheeks even as I push it away.

"What if I had a secret husband in the attic?"

The corner of his mouth twitches in that way I know is a smile. "Not even then."

I smile, too. "Okay. So . . . still friends?"

"If that's what you want."

Is it? I don't even know anymore.

"What do you want?" I whisper.

He stares at me like he's taking his time weighing every possible response. Then he takes a step forward. And another. He's standing so close, I can feel the warmth radiating off him, smell the sawdust and sandalwood from his skin. It sends a low hum through my bloodstream.

"I want to kiss you again."

His voice is so deep, so matter-of-fact. As if his words haven't just set off a thousand small explosions in my chest.

"Oh," I say, my mouth gaping open for another moment before I think of what to say. "Then I think you should do that."

A moment passes before his hand comes up to delicately cradle my jaw, like I'm breakable. And I suppose I am. A broken person trying desperately to put herself back together. Except I feel more put together, more myself, than I ever have. And that's largely because of him.

If magic were real, Ben Morgan would be magic.

With that thought, his lips meet mine. The kiss is soft, gentle, like he's working in slow motion, like he knows he only has this one moment and he has to savor it. Commit it to memory. It sends a sharp ache through my chest, because if that's true, I need to savor this, too.

I open my mouth to his, letting his tongue caress mine as he uses his hand to angle me just so, a motion so small but so self-assured I can't help but moan.

He swallows up the sound as he takes another step forward, and suddenly I feel myself pressed against the hallway wall, the plaster cold even through my sweater. It only highlights how warm his skin is, his breath and his tongue.

I wrap my arms around his neck, pulling that warmth to me so tightly that I swear I hear him groan. I know he's holding back, I can feel the tension in his shoulders, in how he's positioned his body around mine. And as much as I want him to know he doesn't have to, I also feel the low simmer of anticipation in my blood. Because if this is Ben holding back, I can't even begin to imagine what it's like when he lets go.

"Do you know how long I've wanted to kiss you?" he murmurs against my lips.

"But you don't do relationships," I reply, so breathless I should feel embarrassed. But I really, really don't.

"It's a good thing you're not looking for one, then."

I laugh against his lips, but he devours it with another kiss.

His hand is still on my jaw, while the other travels down, those rough fingers gripping my hip through my jeans and pulling me closer. And . . . oh, at that angle I can feel everything. All of him. I don't care if he wants a relationship or not, if this will mean anything in the morning. I just want—

The harsh blare of the buzzer for the front door downstairs reverberates out of Ben's apartment.

We both freeze, our breath intermingling as we stare at one another, like we've both been shaken violently awake.

The buzzer sounds again, followed by the sound of a cell phone ringing nearby.

"Shit," Ben murmurs, resting his forehead against mine, catching his breath. Then he pulls his phone from his pocket. Pete's name is on the screen.

"What the hell do you want, Pete?" Ben answers, eyes squeezed shut.

Even with the phone to his ear, I can hear Pete's reply. "I FORGOT I NEED TO TAKE A PISS."

"Can't that wait until you get home?"

"I DON'T THINK I'LL MAKE IT PAST CHARLESTOWN."

The buzzer rings out again.

"Pete—"

"COME ON, MAN! EVERYWHERE ELSE IS CLOSED! I CAN'T—"

Ben hangs up and lets out a long breath. "I'm sorry. I need to go deal with . . . whatever the hell he's about to do to my bathroom."

"Right. Okay," I reply. My smile feels wobbly, like it's being jostled by my racing pulse.

He straightens, the serious line of his brow returning as he takes one last survey of my face. If he sees how fragile my smile is, he doesn't let on. He just steps backward into his apartment and presses the buzzer button beside his door.

I turn and will my hands to stop shaking long enough to unlock my dead bolt so I can retreat inside. I manage it just as I hear Pete's feet bounding up the stairwell.

I don't look back at Ben as I slide into my apartment. But as I get into my pajamas, wash my face, and brush my teeth, my attention stays on my door, listening to hear if he knocks.

He doesn't.

CHAPTER 22

"So you kissed your ex-boyfriend," Bobbi says. His brow is pinched and I know he's been working hard to follow along as I've recounted the latest series of events during the first lull in the Friday morning rush at Strange Brew. On the other side of the counter, Claire listens intently, lips pursed.

"No, I kissed Ben," I clarify.

"Who's Ben?"

"Her neighbor," Claire replies.

Bobbi turns to her. "But I thought she went out with her ex?"

"No, that's tomorrow night," she answers.

"But it's not a date. It's just a dinner thing with friends," I add, as if that clarifies things.

Claire's eyebrows knit together. "Does he know that?"

"Who, Ben?" I ask.

"No, your ex."

I blink. Oh, right. That would be the obvious question, wouldn't it? Except for the fact that I've barely thought about Matt over the past few weeks, let alone my feelings for him.

"We broke up," I say. "I think he might even be seeing someone else."

"But he still agreed to have dinner with you," Claire says, as if the implication is obvious.

Bobbi's eyes are wide, enraptured. "Oh my God, this is better than the last five seasons of *Love Island*."

I wish that was a compliment. Instead, it sounds like my life has careened so far off course that I've managed to reach reality TV levels of dysfunction. But I haven't spent the past twenty minutes detailing the baseball game, the bar, the *kiss*, to impress my coworkers. I need advice. I'm desperate for it. Sara is too close to the situation to be objective, and Ben is . . . well, even closer. So my sanity barometer is the staff at Strange Brew.

"You know, you're really glossing over the most important detail here," Claire says to me as Bobbi takes the order of a couple who just walked in.

I turn to her from where I'm practicing steaming oat milk. "Which is . . . ?"

"How was the kiss?" she asks, one eyebrow arched up.

Heat suddenly rushes through my veins, settling low in my belly.

I haven't had too many first kisses, and none of them were particularly thrilling. My first one ever was in third grade, when Dylan Fisher sat down next to me on the school bus and, after a few minutes of silence, asked if he could kiss me. I don't remember if I even answered or not, but he went for it anyway. The tight seam of his lips planted against mine for a few moments, and then he pulled back, an expression on his face that told me he wasn't impressed. And, to be fair, neither was I. We just looked at each other as if to say, *that's what all the fuss is about?*

Then there was Scott Dillard in seventh grade, who kissed me on a field trip to the aquarium. And Paul Meyers, who kissed me after prom my junior year of high school. A few others in my twenties, but none of them were particularly special.

I always told myself that Matt made up for it. We could never agree whether our first date was the night Sara and Garrett not-so-subtly had us all show up at the same sushi restaurant in Santa Monica, or the official double date two weeks later, but there was no question about our first kiss. Matt met me at the Santa Monica Pier and we got ice cream at Scoops before wandering down the boardwalk. We eventually found an empty bench and sat down, eating our ice cream for a few minutes before he turned and asked if he could kiss me. I remember it being messy, a sticky mix of mint chocolate chip and fudge swirl, but when I recounted the story to Sara later, I told her it was perfect.

Still, no matter what I told Sara, Matt and I were never what you would call "hot and heavy." Tender, yes, but passionate? I try to make the word fit, force its shape into a hole in my memory. It refuses to budge.

But Ben . . . kissing him was like being plugged into a socket. Even the memory sends a pulse of electricity running through my veins. It was everything my grandmother had always promised the universe had waiting for me: excitement and passion. Divine energy and cosmic vibrations. Magic.

But the memory dampens when I remember that Ben hadn't knocked after Pete left last night. All I got was a text.

BEN

Good night, Marnie. Let's talk tomorrow.

I had tried to stop myself from overanalyzing it—I already knew Ben texted like a serial killer, so that part wasn't exactly new—but there was still an odd foreboding about it, like I would be spending the entire day waiting for the other shoe to drop.

Which is exactly what I've done.

"The kiss was . . ." My words falter as adjectives flood my brain. *Amazing. Addictive. Life-altering.* But I push them away as I dump my latest failed attempt at steamed oat milk into the nearby sink. "It was just a kiss. It didn't mean anything."

Bobbi finishes ringing up an order, then turns to me. "Why not?"

"Because we're friends."

"And?"

"And he's my neighbor, I just got out of a long-term relationship, I'm recovering from a traumatic brain injury," I reply. "The list is long. Besides, I know for a fact that he doesn't do relationships."

Claire shrugs. "Then just do sex."

My pulse spikes as my mouth falls open.

She looks utterly unbothered. "What?"

"Maybe I don't want to sleep with him," I reply.

"That's exactly what a person who wants to sleep with someone would say," Bobbi interjects.

I turn and throw him a scowl.

"And what did Ben say?" Claire asks.

My eyebrows pinch together. "What do you mean?"

"You've talked to him since, right?"

The way she says it makes me think that I should have, but it only happened last night. When would we have had the chance?

Well, that's not entirely true. I heard him leave his apartment this morning, locking his dead bolt and testing it, like he usually does. Except I could have sworn he paused this time, like he took a moment to consider my door before heading down the hall to the stairwell. Or had it been my imagination?

Either way, he hadn't knocked, and he hadn't texted again.

You haven't, either, I remind myself.

It's true, but only because I don't know what to say, how to broach not only the kiss, but these feelings that have been growing in my chest for weeks. Or how I'll deal with the very real possibility that he might not feel the same way. So instead, I focus on pouring another serving of oat milk into my stainless-steel jug.

"Not yet," I answer.

Claire cringes.

"What?" I ask.

"It's nothing," Bobbi inserts, hands splayed like he's brokering peace. "I'm sure he's just giving you space. I mean, you don't even remember breaking up with your ex, right? Ben probably assumes you feel like you cheated or something."

I pause when I realize he's right. This does feel like cheating, but not on Matt. It feels like I'm cheating on Sara. She's the one who always envisioned Matt and me getting married, living next door so our future children could grow up together. Even now, when I'm on the phone with her, I feel like I have to withhold details of my life, prop up her expectations so I don't break her heart. Maybe that's why she doesn't know that many details about the breakup to begin with—I was censoring them to spare her feelings back then, too.

Unfortunately, it's backfired spectacularly. Sara is more intent than ever on getting Matt and me back together. Meanwhile, I've spent weeks following clues scattered around my apartment to try to remember the past year, and it's only brought me closer to Ben.

I shake my head and pray to the universe that my cheeks aren't too red. "It's not cheating. Ben and I are friends. That's it."

Claire snorts. "Yeah. Friends who have tasted each other's tonsils."

I cringe even as a laugh bubbles out of me. "That's so gross."

She shrugs as if that minor detail doesn't change the facts.

There's a steady stream of customers for the next few hours. When it finally slows down again at two, Claire goes on break and Bobbi disappears into the back to take a delivery, leaving me to watch the counter. A couple of weeks ago, the responsibility would have triggered an existential crisis, but after successfully making two skim lattes this morning, I feel like I can conquer the world.

I decide to take advantage of the lull and reach down to where my tote bag is stashed under the counter to grab Ben's copy of *The*

Count of Monte Cristo. I open to my bookmark and start reading where I left off yesterday, the moment Edmund reveals his identity to Caderousse. I'm so engrossed in the story that I barely hear the bell above the coffee shop's front door ring. A moment later, I see a customer approach in my periphery. I tear myself away from the book, donning a warm smile.

"Hi, welcome to Strange Brew," I say to the woman standing at the counter. "What can I get started for you?"

The woman is smiling, too, but it fades the moment she makes eye contact with me.

"Marnie?"

My heart drops. She knows me. That must mean that I know her. Somewhere in my brain, I know I do. But it's ephemeral, like a dream you try to remember after you wake up. Every time I try to focus on it, the details slip further away.

"Hi," I say, trying to mask my confusion.

"Hi," she replies, shaking her head slightly. "Sorry, I didn't know you worked here or I wouldn't have . . ."

She tries on her smile again, but it looks fragile. She's shorter than me, though her hair is longer—beautiful, wavy chestnut-brown locks that fall over the shoulders of her black wool coat. She has caramel boots up to her knees and a black velvet headband that ties the outfit together in a way that I didn't think was possible in real life. It's effortless in a way that I envy. Something I would have remembered, if I could.

"I'm not usually in this neighborhood," she continues after another moment. "I just had a meeting with a client."

"That's okay," I reply, even though I have no idea if that's true or not.

Either way, the woman looks relieved.

"I kept hoping I'd run into you at some point," she says. "I didn't know if any of my calls or texts were going through."

My mind flits back to those seventeen missed calls waiting when I finally got my phone back at the hospital. "I've been locked out of my phone for a while."

"Oh." She forces a short laugh. "I thought you might have blocked me. Not that I would blame you."

My eyebrows knit together. I almost ask why I would do that, but that would mean revealing that I don't remember. We'd waste so much time rehashing everything I've been through over the past few weeks instead of focusing on her and whatever happened between us. Suddenly, Bobbi reemerges from the back.

"Hello, welcome to Strange Brew," he says to the woman. Then he clocks how I'm staring at her, eyes narrowed, and he jumps into action, the same way he has whenever I've been confused by an order over the past two weeks. "What was that order? I can get it started for you."

"Just a latte to go, thanks," the woman says. She looks almost thankful for the distraction.

"Sure thing," Bobbi replies. "And what's the name for that order?"

"April."

The name catches on something in the back of my mind.

"April," Bobbi repeats as he writes it on the side of a paper cup. "Got it."

The silence is painful as Bobbi turns to the espresso machine, expertly working its knobs to brew her drink. I know I should say something else to this woman, ask her how I know her, or why, but before my broken brain can come up with the right question, Bobbi hands her the drink. "Here you go."

"Thanks," she says, tapping her card to pay. Then she pauses before turning to me again. "It was good to see you, Marnie. For what it's worth, I'm really happy for you two."

For a moment, it looks like she might cry, but instead, she forces another smile and turns to leave.

Bobbi watches her disappear through the front door, then whips around to me. "What was that all about?"

I stare back, dumbfounded. "I have no idea."

Because despite how hard I try to recall it, I can't. But something tells me I really should.

CHAPTER 23

I leave work at three for my cognitive therapy appointment. The bell above the door at Strange Brew jingles as I leave, but I barely hear it, and I don't look back as Bobbi shouts goodbye. I just tug my scarf tighter around my neck and wait on the sidewalk for my car to arrive. Capobianco's doors are open and the smell of roasted garlic and olive oil wafts out, intermingling with the stubborn sweetness from the bakery two doors down. If it were a normal day, I would relish it. Instead, all I can think about is the woman who came in an hour before.

April.

The name tugs at a memory, but the details disappear as soon as I get close enough to grab them.

I hate this. I hate not recognizing my life, or the people in it. How, even though I understand some of the choices I made over the last year, from quitting Probus to signing up for a photography course, I still don't remember actually making them. It's like my life is happening to me rather than vice versa, and I can't do anything about it except burst into tears.

Thankfully, a blue Nissan Altima pulls up to the curb before I can start. I slide into the back seat, offering the driver the meekest of smiles, and try to focus on the view out my window when my phone starts to ring deep in my bag. I see Sara's name on the caller ID.

"Are you packed?" I ask, forcing levity into my voice.

"Packed and ready to go!" she practically squeals. "We have a car coming to pick us up at seven a.m. sharp."

I hear a deep voice murmur something—probably Garrett—and she scoffs.

"You're ridiculous," she says to him. "You know traffic always doubles the travel time!"

I smile. I know exactly what Garrett probably said—how getting a car so early when their flight doesn't leave until two is ridiculous—and I know exactly the look Sara threw at him, how he probably laughed as she did. It makes me miss them both so much it hurts.

"All right, so here's what's happening," Sara continues. "We land at about four, then we're going to head to our hotel, shower, and get ready. We'll meet you and Matt at the restaurant at seven."

I nod even though she can't see me. "Got it."

"What time is Matt picking you up?"

"He's not. I'm going to grab a taxi," I reply, tempering the annoyance in my tone.

She sighs at this obvious wrench in her plans. "Okay, fine. More importantly, what are you wearing to the restaurant?"

"I'm not sure."

"You still haven't decided?"

I slide my teeth over my bottom lip as I think back to the dresses I had laid out on my bed earlier this morning. "I have options, don't worry."

"Good. Okay, I have to run. I'll have Matt text you about that ride, okay?"

I frown. "Sara—"

"Can't wait to see you tomorrow! Bye!"

And then she hangs up.

I'm still bubbling with anger when I arrive at the hospital and head up to the fifth floor. The call with Sara plays on repeat in my head as I hone in on every moment I should have stopped her, when I should have finally been honest. By the time I'm shown into an exam room, I know I need to call her back, set boundaries before tomorrow night. But as I reach into my bag for my phone, there's a knock on the door and Janine appears, a warm smile on her lips.

"Hello, Marnie," she says. "Ready to run a few tests?"

I offer her a smile, even though I can't think of anything I'd rather do less.

We spend the next hour going over the same litany of evaluations and exercises I did a few weeks before. It agitates my already-growing frustration, so by the time we sit down in the exam room again to discuss how I'm feeling, all I want to do is leave.

"And you're feeling okay? No new headaches or issues with coordination?" she asks, noting it on her tablet.

I shake my head.

"Anything from your box of mementos looking familiar yet?"

"No."

"How about—"

"Can I ask you a question?" I blurt out.

She looks up from her tablet. "Sure."

"When will I get better?"

"Like we discussed before, recovery isn't linear, Marnie. Yes, physiologically your brain has healed. But the brain is also a complicated place. Certain parts can recover at a predictable trajectory, while others will have starts and stops. Periods where it feels like things are moving forward and others where it plateaus."

"Okay, but can't we at least estimate how long it will take for me to get back to normal?"

"That depends on how you define normal."

"Back to how I was *before*," I plead.

She stares at me for a long moment, then pushes her reading glasses to the top of her head so she can meet my gaze directly. "There might not be a way back to the way you were before."

The words land with a heavy thud in my chest, stealing my breath. "What do you mean?"

"You're doing phenomenally well. And I'm confident your memories will start returning soon. But while we continue to work on resolving your cognitive issues, we need to also acknowledge that some may not resolve completely."

I blink, shock rippling through my body. "Are you saying . . . some of this might be permanent?"

"The data is on your side, Marnie. You'll likely get your memories back, but there could be gaps. Moments that are still hazy.

Directions could still be a struggle, too. Your emotions might still feel hard to manage. There's no way to tell right now. But what we *can* do is give you the tools to be ready for whatever your new normal looks like."

But I don't want a new normal, I want to scream. *I don't want every day to be a challenge anymore.*

I've spent weeks retracing my steps, following a shoebox full of clues in the hopes of remembering the past year, believing that if I just found the right place, the right memory, my brain would magically fix itself. And what do I have to show for it? Nothing. I'm in the same exact place as when I left this hospital.

Sara was right. Hope is not a strategy.

Janine watches my expression, then leans forward, offering me a supportive smile. "It's okay to miss that version of you from before. But you'll be proud of this new one, too. I promise."

I know she's trying to make me feel better, but I want to tell her that I don't want a new version of me. I only want to remember the old one. And I thought I would. I honestly thought, somehow, the stars would align and the universe would give me this one thing.

I suddenly feel so stupid. How could I have thought it would be so easy? How had I let my grandmother's promises of magic and destiny trick me again?

How am I still here, right where I started?

CHAPTER 24

When I leave my appointment, there's a line of cabs parked outside the hospital, but I walk past them, straight down to Cambridge Street.

A cold gust hits me on the corner. I hug my coat closed and turn right, letting my feet choose the direction, toward Carmen Park, past the brown awnings of the Union Oyster House and the wooden statue of a British soldier on the corner of Creek Square, while my mind replays Janine's words over and over in my head.

There might not be a way back to the way you were before.

It feels like my heart is splintering apart. All these weeks I've been chasing the old me, trying to pin her down, when really, she was already gone. My brain is broken, *I'm* broken, and no amount of hard work or items checked off a list will change that.

I turn onto Hanover Street and walk past the rows of vendors at Haymarket until the neighborhood begins to narrow in a way that's become familiar. Voices spill out of restaurants, laughter and conversation over the clinking of glasses and silverware.

I walk another block before I see the neon sign for Modern Pastry just ahead. It's still fairly early, so it's not lit up, but their sandwich board is set up on the sidewalk, advertising cannoli and biscotti.

Today was a bad day. Maybe the worst one since the accident. And the only person I want to talk to about it is Ben. I want to call him and let all the fears and frustrations spill out, because right now it feels like they're taking up too much space inside me.

But I stop myself before I reach for my phone. After his text last night, I'm terrified of what he might say, how he might break my heart even more by reminding me what I already know: He doesn't do relationships. So I just peer into the window of the bakery, watching a group of tourists place their cannoli order.

After they leave, I go in and order a lobster tail from the older woman behind the counter. She barely takes a break in her conversation with her coworker as she places the pastry in a small white box and ties it up neatly with twine.

I take my lobster tail and continue down Hanover Street, past the signs to Italian cities thousands of miles away, past the playground at St. Leonard's, then turn left at the statue of Paul Revere, walking past Old North Church to Copp's Hill Terrace.

The leaves on the trees are now an explosion of yellows and red, and someone has put a couple of jack-o-lanterns along the wall looking over the harbor. I find the same bench where Ben and I sat, empty as if it was waiting for me, and land heavily on its wood-slatted seat. The autumn sun gleams off the water ahead, and for a few minutes, I watch the boats glide back and forth from the river. Then I look down at the pastry box on my lap.

Yes, today was a bad day. And despite how much I want to call Ben, he can't fix it any more than the universe can. I have to figure it out on my own.

But first, I need to wallow.

The wind picks up, sending my hair up and out in every direction, as I carefully untie the box's red-and-white string, then lift the lid. A lone lobster tail sits in the center. There's a dusting of powdered sugar across the top, a hint of its cream filling peeking out from its golden pastry. A promise that, while it might not make things better, it could help. Just a smidge.

So I pick it up and shove as much of it as I can into my mouth.

I make it back to my building just as the sun dips below the roofline, sending muted streaks of pink and yellow across the sky. The tip of my nose is cold, and I can still taste powdered sugar at the corners of my mouth. I'm sure it's visible, too, but I don't care. All I can think about is getting into my pajamas, making myself a cup of tea, and continuing my wallow in silence.

Except there is no silence. As I ascend the stairs, "Dancing Queen" starts blaring from the second floor.

I don't know if it's sadness or frustration or sheer rage at the universe. But I don't keep going upstairs. I turn onto the second floor and march down the hall to the apartment directly below mine.

My knock isn't polite this time, and to his credit, my nemesis—Brian, if I recall his name correctly—opens the door as if he's expecting me, wearing spandex pants and an oversized T-shirt. His smirk disappears when he sees my face. Or maybe it's my hair. I have no idea what state it's in, I haven't looked in a mirror for hours.

"No ABBA," I say through gritted teeth.

"I'm not listening to ABBA," he replies flatly.

I squeeze my eyes shut, like it might keep the tears at bay. "I know you're rehearsing for a tour of *Mamma Mia!*, and that's really impressive, but I'm having a *really* bad day."

"Yeah? Join the club," he says. "You promised to take my head-shots a *month* ago. I ended up having to have one of the under-studies take them on his phone behind the theater and they look like mugshots."

My eyes snap open as something stirs awake in the back of my mind. Not a memory, but the shadow of a memory. A moment of recognition.

"I said I would take your headshots?"

Brian rolls his eyes. "For the record, don't volunteer to do something for someone if you're just going to ghost them when it comes time to deliver."

"Why didn't you say something?"

His eyes narrow on me. "What, you want me to *beg*?"

"No, I just . . ." My words falter as I try to grab more of the memory, but it slips back into the corner of my mind.

"You just, what?"

"I don't remember, okay?" I blurt out, throwing my arms out at my sides. "I don't remember anything! I fell and hit my head and now the past year is just *gone.* I don't know what I'm doing here or why I stayed in Boston all this time, or why my grandmother told me to trust the universe and fate, because it's all bullshit. But I can't even get mad at her, because she's dead! It's just me, on my own, with a missing year's worth of memories that, it turns out, I might never get back. So all I ask is one night without ABBA. Just one. Okay?"

He stares at me, stunned. "Okay."

"Okay," I say with a nod.

Then I turn around and head back into the stairwell, my steps echoing against the cement walls until I reach the third floor. I ignore Ben's door, which is easier since I know he's not home yet. He has a class on Fridays. Suddenly, I'm so mad that I know that, how that fact is taking up space in my brain when so many other things aren't, that my rage is renewed all over again. I unlock my door, then slam it shut behind me. My coat and bag are abandoned on the floor as I walk to my bed and land face-first into my duvet.

"Dancing Queen" is still playing downstairs, but after a moment, it abruptly stops. I listen to the silence, bracing myself. Then, ever so faintly, I hear the opening chords of "Gypsy" by Fleetwood Mac float up from the floorboards.

Had I told Brian that this was my grandmother's favorite song? I don't know. And for the first time in weeks, I don't try to remember. I close my eyes and listen, pretending it's a bit of magic, *her* magic, and for a moment, I let myself believe.

CHAPTER 25

Brian gets through most of Fleetwood Mac's greatest hits before I finally get up. I wash my face and get into my pajamas—along with a sweatshirt for extra warmth—then shuffle to the kitchen and fill up the kettle, putting it on the stovetop and grabbing my Paradise Cove Beach Café mug from the shelf.

I stare down at the faded words on the porcelain while I wait for the water to boil.

It's just you and me, mug, I think. *We've stuck together this long, we can do this.*

The kettle whistles and I pour the steaming water over a waiting chamomile tea bag. A moment later, my phone dings with a text message. My heart stumbles, and I pick up my tote from where I dropped it on the floor and dig through it for my phone, hoping to see Ben's name on the screen. Instead, I see a text from Matt.

MATT

Hey, did you need a ride to dinner tomorrow night?

Sara mentioned I should swing by and get you

Let me know

I snap my phone closed, leaving it on the counter as I start toward the sofa, my mug cradled in my hands.

Maybe this is my life now. My destiny is to wallow. That's not *so* bad, I think, letting my slippers drag on the hardwood. That is, until I get my first rent bill and don't have enough money to pay it. Or I never find a way into my old phone. Or—

The thought is cut short by a blur of motion, furry and gray, running across the floor and over my foot to disappear under the sofa.

I scream, jumping up and sending my mug into the air. Tea splatters in every direction, flying across the floor, the sofa, the rug, as the mug hits the hardwood floor once, twice, then shatters into a dozen pieces.

I squeeze my eyes shut. I can feel the tears coming. I had been so good for so long keeping them at bay, but messy, emotional Marnie is back. There is no way to stop her, so I give in, letting my head fall back as the sobs overwhelm me. I'm hiccupping to take in air, my whole body heaving with each breath.

I'm done. So completely done that I barely hear the door across the hall open, followed by a knock on mine.

"What?" I bellow, my voice wobbly.

There's a deep, rumbly sigh that sounds suspiciously like Ben's. "Are you okay?"

I walk over and open the door. He's standing in the hallway, wearing those worn jeans he had on when we went to the grocery store for the first time, along with a pair of work boots and a thick wool sweater. His messenger bag is still over his shoulder, as if he only just got home from work. He looks so perfect that I want to start crying all over again because I know I'm definitely falling in love with him and I have no idea what to do about it.

"I'm spiraling," I cry.

He considers for a moment, his expression thoughtful. "Do you want company?"

I throw my arms out at my sides because why not? Let's finish this day off properly by giving the man I'm falling in love with, who has been ghosting me all day, a front row seat to watch me hit rock bottom. I turn around and head back into my apartment. He follows, shutting the door behind him.

"What happened?" he asks.

"I broke my mug, and now it's everywhere," I say, waving at the scene of the crime: the handle by the kitchen, what looks like part of the rim by the TV.

He blinks, and the tension that had been keeping his entire body taut falters. "Your mug?"

I nod.

"We can glue it, or get you another one—"

"We can't get another one!" I sob. "It's *my* mug! The one I've used since I started drinking tea back in middle school. The one I packed to bring to Boston."

He crosses his arms over his chest, and it looks like he's trying very hard to follow what's happening here.

"It was something I remembered, okay?" I say, my voice pleading. "Nothing in my life looked familiar, and then I saw this mug and I thought it meant *something*, like all I had to do was follow the trail of all those other objects and I'd remember them, too. And I've been trying so hard. So so hard, Ben! Because I believed my doctors when they said I would remember. And I believed the mug was a sign. But it turns out there are no signs or magic. I don't even have my mug. And it's all that mouse's fault!"

"The mouse?"

I wipe my nose with the sleeve of my sweatshirt. "I just made some tea and was walking over to the sofa when I felt something on my foot, and he was *there*. That's why I screamed and I dropped the mug. Now it's broken into a million pieces, and I'll never get it back because . . . because . . ."

"Because of the mouse," he finishes for me.

I scrunch my eyes closed and nod.

"Do you want me to take care of it?" he asks.

"You can't glue it, Ben! It's destroyed!"

"Not the mug. The mouse."

"Oh." I shake my head. "No. You'll just kill it."

"Well, you can't—"

"Let him wander around my apartment, giving me the plague? I know that! But that's not his fault! He's just a mouse, doing mouse things and trying to survive! Just because he's an inconvenience and annoying doesn't mean he doesn't have a right to exist!"

He pauses, the hard line of his brow softening. "Talk to me, Marnie."

I throw my arms out at my sides again, so overwhelmed with everything I want to say, I don't know where to start.

"My mug is gone," I reply. "And none of my memories have come back. And I have short hair!"

The corner of his mouth ticks up. "It's not that short."

"It's *so* short, Ben," I say, sending him my most stern expression. "These could have been micro bangs. I don't know!"

"Marnie—"

"And everybody thinks I'm a ditz!"

He pauses. "Nobody thinks you're a ditz."

"Of course they do! I'm a blonde from Southern California! The stereotype is ubiquitous!" I shake my head. "And they're right. I threw away my career. I have no idea what I'm doing with my life. I can't even steam oat milk!"

Somewhere in my mind, I hear my grandmother's voice: *Don't hold on to anger, Marnie. Let it flow* through *you.* But I need to hold on to it right now. I deserve to.

"And you didn't talk to me!" I blurt out. "You kissed me like that, what was probably the best kiss of my life, and then poof, nothing!"

His head cocks to the side. "The best kiss of your life?"

"Don't change the subject!" I exclaim. "You texted to say we should talk, and I spent so much time wondering what you were going to say, how you would break my heart, and then you didn't say anything!"

"I stopped by earlier," he says, his voice a bit softer.

I blink, his words taking a second to land in my brain and stick there. "You did?"

He nods. "I thought you'd be back from your doctor's appointment, but you weren't home yet, so I slipped a note under the door that said I'd try again when I got home from work."

As much as I'd love to challenge him on it, I barely remember coming home today, let alone if there was a note there waiting for me. I was too hurt, too broken, and suddenly my anger crumbles under a fresh wave of grief in my chest.

"I might not get my memories back." My voice suddenly sounds small, like the weight of the admission is crushing me. And in a way, it is. I feel like this diminished version of myself, vulnerable and weak and more alone than I've ever felt in my entire life. "I might never know why I stayed in Boston after Matt and I broke up. Or why I got this haircut. I might never be able to follow directions again or keep track of instructions. Even if I do, my brain will never go back to normal. All this work and focus meant nothing, because I'll never be *me* again."

He takes a cautious step toward me. "You're still you, Marnie. Even if parts of you feel different, they're still you."

"But what if I don't know who that is?" I ask. "I used to have so many dreams, Ben. I wanted to do so many things. But then life got hard and they disappeared, one by one. Now all I have left is me. But I don't even know who that is anymore. And I have to figure it out all on my own. That's so terrifying, I don't think I can . . . I don't know how to . . ."

There are too many words, and I can't catch my breath fast enough to say them. It's just too much, the reality of everything I have to face now on my own. I don't know if I can keep from buckling any longer.

Then Ben's arms are around me, pulling me into a warm embrace. My face digs into his sweater, breathing in the smell of sandalwood and sawdust as his chin rests on the top of my head. The weight inside me dissolves, and it suddenly feels like this embrace is the most important thing that has ever happened in the history of the whole world.

"You're not on your own, Marnie," he murmurs. "I'm right here. But you don't need me to do this. Because you don't need to do anything. You're Marnie Stephens, the woman who was raised to believe in magic. The one who stepped in to take care of her grandmother when that magic disappeared. The person who woke up in a strange city, with no idea how she got there, and faced it head-on. The one with a heart so big she won't even consider hurting something as small as a mouse. You're you without even trying."

I pull back enough to stare up at him. "But what comes next? How do I decide what to do when I don't even know how I got here?"

He leans down, meeting my eyes with a gaze so intense, my breath catches. "Be brave and do it anyway."

So simple. So matter-of-fact. As if he believes it. Like he thinks I actually could. Maybe that's why the words feel like they've suddenly filled the hollow bits in my chest with something glowing. Warm and electric and alive.

Be brave, I think.

So I lean up and kiss him.

It's not like the kiss in the bar, or the one from the hallway. This one seems to catch him off guard. The seam of his mouth remains sealed, and all I can think is, *Please don't pull away.*

Then, a moment later, something miraculous happens. He doesn't. He kisses me back, devouring my gasp as his arms pull me against his body again.

"Marnie . . ." he murmurs. It sounds like a plea, like he knows we should stop, but I honestly can't think why. This is all I've wanted for weeks. I could even outline every single moment I've thought about it, tell him how I've weighed all the pros and cons, but this isn't the time for a Marnie diatribe. So I deepen the kiss, rake my hands through his hair, and let him know that whatever he needs to say, it can wait. Right now, I just want him.

He groans, sending a heady mix of adrenaline and warmth running to my core. Relief and excitement and want meld together as my arms wrap around his shoulders, trying to get him closer, to feel his body against mine. But I can barely coordinate my movements. Each limb is vibrating on its own frequency, operating independently, so all I can do is give myself over to it as my fingers pull at his shirt.

The last thread of his restraint seems to snap as his hands grab my hips, holding me in a vise grip. Then he's lifting me up and I'm vaguely aware that I'm on the kitchen countertop now. I can feel the cold Formica through my pajama pants, but that's secondary to his mouth, how he nips and licks down my neck, holding my legs apart so he can position himself right there between them.

My head falls back against the cabinet with a thud as I close my eyes. Every worry and stress seems to have disappeared under the wet slide of his tongue. My brain has given up on trying to think anything other than the demand more, more, *more*. I want more of him. I need it.

I open my eyes when I feel his hand tugging at my sweatshirt. He pulls it up, then lets out a frustrated groan when he sees a T-shirt underneath.

"Why do you have so many layers on?" he admonishes as he comes back in for another kiss.

I let out a breathy laugh against his lips. "Why aren't you faster at getting them off?"

His low chuckle vibrates through my body. Then he ducks his head down and begins nipping and sucking at my breast through the cotton fabric. I lean into it, so fervently that I wobble on the edge of the counter. But then his hands are there, bracketing my hips, steadying me.

"I've got you," he murmurs.

And he does. Every single part of me, even the bits I don't remember. Ben has me and it's the only thing that's felt right in ages.

I try to say this, to respond with words, but it's just a mumble. I'm too lost in the feel of him, how his one hand is still gripping my hips, while the other is slowly working its way up my leg, closer and closer and . . .

His fingers graze the apex of my thighs through my pajama pants. Once. Twice. Then his fingers press ever so delicately on that perfect little spot.

My hands tangle in his hair as I gasp, but he leans in to swallow it up with a kiss. Then his lips travel down my neck, his stubble rough even as his tongue feels soft and delicate, while his fingers keep a steady pressure between my legs, thrumming in time with my pulse.

Oh God. I'm already close. So close . . .

Ding.

My phone is sitting right next to me on the counter, so the sound of the text message echoes around us.

"Ignore it," I whisper.

The phone dings again.

"Are you sure?" he murmurs.

Before I can tell him to throw the phone in the trash and focus, it dings again and Ben glances down at its small screen. Then he stills.

I pull back enough to look at him. "What?"

"It's Matt," he replies.

"I know," I say, reaching out to pull his weight against me. "He just wants to know if he should pick me up for dinner tomorrow night or if we're meeting at the restaurant."

Ben's eyebrows draw together, and I think I actually see the burning embers there suddenly cool.

"You're having dinner with Matt tomorrow night?" he asks.

I pause, trying to read his expression, to understand how this has changed the entire evening in just a few seconds. "Yes, along with Sara and Garrett. They're flying in for the weekend. I thought I told you."

"You did. I just . . . I didn't connect the dots," he replies, his tone so flat that my heart trips.

"It's not a date, Ben."

"But Sara set you two up, right?" he replies plainly.

"Yes, but that doesn't mean anything *now*." It's not a lie, but I hate how it's not exactly the truth, either. "The four of us have always been close. She just misses that."

"And what about Matt?" he asks, his expression unreadable. "Does he miss that, too?"

It feels ridiculous to be having this conversation while I'm sitting on the kitchen counter with my sweatshirt halfway off and a huge wet spot over my breast, but then, his reaction feels a bit ridiculous, too.

"That's not fair, Ben," I say. "After my grandmother died, Sara, Garrett, and Matt were the only family I had left. And even though I'm glad Matt and I aren't together anymore, our breakup affected all of us. That's half the reason I've spent so much time chasing these clues all over the city. If one of these mementos is from my relationship with Matt, then it might remind me why we broke up. Then maybe I could start to understand everything else."

Something shifts in Ben's expression. He's usually so in control of his emotions, but right now it seems like he's battling to keep them at bay while not revealing a single one to me. Still, something bleeds through the cracks. A bit of hurt and surprise.

"Mementos from your relationship with Matt," he repeats, almost to himself. Then he shakes his head. "We were revisiting things you thought you did with your ex."

"I don't even know if that's what they are," I say quickly. "My doctor just told me to revisit places I might remember, and I thought . . . I kept these things for a reason, Ben. It doesn't matter if they mean something to me now, they meant something to me then. So if I could go to those places, see if anything looked familiar, I could . . . maybe I would . . ."

"I get it, Marnie," he says, his voice low. "I get it."

It's silent for a long moment, and for the first time since I've met him, it feels awkward, like there's more to say but I have no idea what. Then another text message arrives on my phone with a loud *ding*. This time, neither of us looks down at the screen.

"I should go," he finally says, taking a step back.

I slide off the counter, fresh panic blossoming in my chest. "Ben, stop. I didn't mean—"

"You didn't do anything wrong, Marnie."

"Then why are you leaving?"

The heavy line of his brow adds a new sadness to his eyes, shadows over the small explosions of yellows and browns. "Because you deserve to figure out what you need without weighing it against what everyone else wants. Especially me."

But that's what you do when you love someone, I want to say.

Then I remember that night at the bar, my conversation with Lauren. This is what she had warned me about, isn't it? The reason why Ben doesn't do relationships. He'd rather be alone than have his heart broken. Or break anyone else's.

He doesn't realize he's about to break mine anyway.

Hurt and embarrassment and shame heat my cheeks as he turns toward the door but stops, looking back to meet my eyes. "Good night, Marnie."

And then he's gone, leaving me staring at the empty space he had filled so perfectly only a minute before.

CHAPTER 26

The muffled chorus of "Fernando" is playing somewhere in the background when I wake up the next morning. I pull my duvet up around my chin and turn over, trying to hold on to the last vestiges of sleep, but it disappears as a car horn blares outside. I open my eyes, staring across my bedroom to the window, the gray skies above, the roofline of the building across the way.

And then I remember: *Oh, right. I'm in my bed. Alone.*

I squeeze my eyes shut, as if that might erase the last twelve hours from reality, or at least from my brain. But it's no use; the memory only becomes more crystalline. The feel of Ben's fingers on my body, the smell of his skin against my own. And then the rough edge to his voice as he pulled himself away.

I should go.

The memory sends another hairline fracture down my heart.

I force myself out of bed and make my way to the kitchen. I fill the kettle and place it on the burner before I remember that I broke my favorite mug, so I use a boring white one that I don't remember instead.

As I shuffle to the sofa, tea in hand, something blue catches my eye. Right there, on the floor by the front door. I walk over and pick it up, only realizing what it is when I flip it over:

Marnie,

Stopped by before my workshop.

Will try again tonight.

Missed you today.

—Ben

He did stop by. Despite all my anxiety and stress yesterday, he had wanted to talk. He even sat here and listened as I spiraled after breaking my mug. But instead of appreciating that, I told him, point-blank, there's a chance he'd spent weeks helping me re-create memories I originally made with my ex. Can I really blame him for walking out? Getting involved with me would be the worst kind of emotional roller coaster. Sure, he never expected me to be perfect, but my mess is still substantial. It isn't Ben's responsibility to clean it up. That's on me.

I hold the note to my chest as I turn toward the living room, letting my gaze slide over the sofa, the low bookcase, the books and the pictures. Things I chose just for me. Proof that, at some point over the past year, I had found the courage to trust myself. I had survived the breakup with Matt, found this apartment. I had started to build a life. I might not remember it, but the evidence was all around me.

Then my eyes find the memory box sitting on the sofa. I study its angles for a few minutes, the carefully written list on top. It has been a crutch these last few weeks, bearing the weight of all my hopes and fears and worries. But in the end, it was just a box of junk. It wasn't going to save me. Holding on to it any longer makes me feel like I might actually drown.

So I pick it up, walk it to the kitchen, and drop it in the trash, watching as the black garbage bag swallows it up and the metal lid slowly closes over the top.

~

By the time my Uber pulls up in front of the Fig and Vine, I'm ten minutes late.

The exterior of the restaurant is soulless, a new development in an area apparently called the Seaport, even though it appears to be purely a shopping destination on the waterfront. My mind wanders to Capobianco's and the smell of fresh bread and fried garlic that wafts from its doors every day when I'm leaving my shift at Strange Brew. How good it looks through its tall front window, how much I think Sara would love it.

Maybe next time.

I step out of the car and take a deep breath of the cool night air. It fills my lungs and clears my head. At least, that's what I'm telling myself.

An attendant opens the restaurant's doors as I approach, and a vast space opens up in front of me, its cement walls and steel beams dimly lit by a huge chandelier, all metal and angles, hanging in the middle of the crowded room. The hum of conversation is just loud enough that I can barely hear the hostess as I approach her podium.

"I'm sorry?" I say, leaning in.

"Do you have a reservation?" she repeats.

"Yes. It's under Sara Barnett?"

She scans her computer screen just as I hear a loud, familiar voice somewhere across the room.

"Marnie!"

I look up and immediately see Sara. She's standing beside a table along the far wall, waving her arms as she practically jumps into the air. I smile, and a bit of the tension in my shoulders releases.

Then I see Matt sitting beside her, and I stiffen again.

"I see them, thank you," I tell the hostess.

I work to keep smiling as I navigate the dining room toward their table, hoping it doesn't look too forced. It must work, because Sara is so excited she meets me halfway, embracing me in a warm hug.

"I've missed you so much!" she squeals.

"Me, too," I say into her hair. Her smell is familiar. I hadn't considered that it might not be, that over the past year I might have forgotten that particular mix of vanilla and freesia in her perfume. But I know, I *know* it, and for that I squeeze her a bit tighter.

She pulls back and gives me a quick once-over. "God, you look so good. And your hair is so *short*."

"Yours is so long!" I gawk at her black hair that's at least six inches longer than I remember. I'm instantly jealous.

"Prenatal vitamins are amazing," she says with a smug sigh. "Come on, let's go see the boys."

We wind our way around the crowded room until we arrive at our table. It's situated in front of a large window overlooking the city skyline, which I can only assume Sara secured through sheer force of will.

"Marnie!" Garrett calls out, his booming voice loud enough to make a few nearby tables turn. He looks every bit the former college hockey player, though his previously long brown hair is now cut short to fit his corporate job.

He stands up and gives me a big hug. Over his shoulder I see Matt stand, too. He looks less tired than when I saw him a few weeks ago, but still weary. It reminds me a lot of how we both felt before we left for Boston—worn down but putting on a brave face.

Garrett releases me and Matt steps forward, giving me the lightest of kisses on my cheek.

"You look great," he says, and offers me a meek smile.

"You, too," I say.

Both statements sound obligatory, but Sara doesn't notice. She's watching the two of us from the other side of the table like she used to watch episodes of *Maxton Hall*: biting her lip and barely stifling a squeal.

"Should we sit down?" Matt offers when the moment borders on awkward.

"Yes! Yes, let's sit. I'm starving," Sara says, taking her own seat and looking across the room. "Our waiter was just here. I'll wave him down so we can put in our order. You can pick something on the fly, right, Marnie?"

I nod and sit down next to her, with Garrett to my left and Matt across from me. It's the exact same seating arrangement we've always had, ever since our first double date three years ago. I don't know if it was ever discussed, just a tradition we maintained during every Saturday night out together, something we fell into so easily that I've never realized it before.

"So, Marnie," Garrett says, leaning back in his chair. "How are you? Sucks about the head."

Sara rolls her eyes. "*Jesus.*"

"What? It does suck. Did you know traumatic brain injury is the leading cause of death for adults under the age of forty-five?" He stares at me, waiting for the information to sink in. "And you're eighty percent more likely to have another one now. That's just math."

"You've always had a way with words, man," Matt says, shaking his head.

"It's fine," I assure them, then turn to Garrett. "I'm good. Better than I was a few weeks ago."

"But you still can't remember anything."

Sara lets out a labored sigh.

"What?" Garrett looks genuinely surprised by her reaction.

Thankfully the waiter arrives and goes over the specials, which I don't pay close attention to, and everyone gives their orders to him, but I don't listen. I'm too busy trying to remember how I usually got through these dinners. If Sara monopolized the conversation, things were fine, but whenever Garrett decided he wanted to attempt small talk with me, I struggled to feign interest for however long it took for Matt to realize I needed saving. And I can't expect Matt to save me tonight. I'm on my own.

The waiter finally gets to me and I look down at the menu, picking the first thing I see with the vegetarian symbol next to it. As soon as he leaves, Garrett turns back to me.

"So what else have you been up to, Marn?" he asks.

I don't think I can muster the usual "nothing much, how about you?" so I opt for honesty.

"Other than recovering from a traumatic brain injury and trying to remember the past year of my life? Nothing much," I say, punctuating it with a sharp smile.

From the corner of my eye, I see Matt's eyes widen, while Garrett chuckles. "Right."

"What about you two?" I nod to Sara, hoping to loop her into the conversation. "What have you been up to this year?"

"Working. And trying to get you two back together," Garrett replies, motioning between Matt and me. Then he laughs again.

"Subtle, Garrett," Sara says, shaking her head. But she doesn't look embarrassed. It feels almost choreographed. Like the time she invited me to tour her gym a few years ago, knowing the exact times Matt worked out so we could "accidentally" run into him.

I dare a quick glance to Matt. He looks as awkward as I feel.

"Isn't this great?" Sara continues, oblivious. "All my favorite people together. When was the last time we did this?"

Two months ago, I almost say. The night before Matt left for Boston. He and I had fought in the car on the way to the restaurant about the move—how much he was leaving for me to do, how I didn't appreciate the pressure he was under at work—but Sara had been planning his goodbye dinner for weeks, so when we walked in, we smiled and gushed and pretended like everything was okay. We were always good at that.

Before I can answer, Matt says, "New Year's. We flew out for your party, remember?"

"Oh my God, that's right. What an insane night!" Sara exclaims. When she sees my blank expression, she leans forward. "It was such chaos, Marn. We started at Tito's—it was Tito's, right?"

"I thought it was Juan John's," Garrett says.

"We started at Tito's, then we went to Juan John's," Matt clarifies.

"And then Garrett got a call about this private party at some art gallery, but he thought they said Westlake Village when it was actually in Westlake, near MacArthur Park!" Her head falls back as she laughs, and even Matt breaks into a smile.

"Hey, the bar was really loud, okay?" Garrett replies.

I have no idea what they're talking about, and I should probably be asking questions, striving to catch up. But I also realize this could be any of the past moments we all spent together, whether I remembered them or not.

Conversation moves on, a whirlwind of updates about friends and mutual acquaintances, work issues and upcoming vacations. I have nothing to add and don't feel the need to try, so I just listen intently until our drinks arrive. It's only then that I realize I'm not the only one abstaining from alcohol tonight. Sara has ordered a sparkling water as well.

A moment later, she stands up and taps her knife against her glass.

"Announcement time!" she sings. "Now, I know it might seem crazy to tag along on Garrett's work trip just to spend twenty-four hours in Boston, but I have a good excuse!"

Beside me, Garrett is barely biting back a smile. Meanwhile, Matt looks as clueless as I am.

"Well," Sara says coyly. "After a year of long hours and hard work and just so many tears, we have some big news."

I straighten in my chair. "You got the promotion?"

"Of *course* I got the promotion," she replies. "But that's not the good news . . . We're pregnant!"

I gasp as a swell of happiness and relief and sheer joy rush through my body. I'm on my feet in a heartbeat, wrapping Sara up in another hug. I don't care that everyone in the restaurant is staring at us, this moment is too important.

"You're having a baby!" I cry.

"I know," she says, laughing as she pulls back to look at me, tears in her eyes. "It's so wild."

Matt stands and gives her a hug, too, and suddenly Garrett has wrapped me up in his arms, sniffing back his own tears.

"It's the best news, Marn," he says gruffly. "She's amazing."

I nod. "Yeah. I know."

"When are you due?" Matt asks as we all sit back down.

"May 16. Which is the perfect birthday, really. You never want to be too close to Christmas, for obvious reasons, and you don't want it during the summer because they won't be in school with their friends, and that makes the entire birthday party planning process so difficult," she says, as if we have any experience with this. "I'm thinking of a baby shower in March, before Garrett gets too busy at work. Do you think you'll be back by then, Marn?"

I pause, replaying the last few minutes in my head to find where I missed a step. "Back where?"

"In California," she replies. "You said you were going to move back."

"I said I would consider it," I say carefully. "But my doctors are here, my apartment, my job."

She laughs. "I'm sure there are barista jobs in California, Marn."

The table falls into an awkward silence.

"You know I'll be there for the shower, and when the baby comes. But I'm not moving back. Not right now," I say, making sure my voice is even.

"But why stay?" she asks, looking truly confused. "Now that Matt's moving back—"

"You're moving back?" I cut her off as I look over at him.

Matt looks between Sara and me, like he's been ambushed.

Sara's eyes go wide. "You didn't tell her about the job?"

"We haven't really talked much, Sara," Matt replies, shifting in his seat.

She rolls her eyes and turns back to me. "Matt was offered a VP job in San Diego. He starts next month. Isn't that great?"

I blink. Is it great? I don't know enough about Matt's life now to comment, even though the moment clearly calls for it.

"Is it with the same firm you're with now?" I ask him.

"No. It's a new company, pretty small. But lots of potential," he replies.

Another one of Matt's signature nonanswers. Information that doesn't provide any information at all.

"So you get it now, right?" Sara leans toward me, smiling again. "If you move back, we'll all be on the West Coast again, and—"

"Matt and I broke up, Sara," I say. The words land like a lead weight in the center of the table. "I might not remember the details, but we did. Then I moved out and built a life on my own. And, yes, my memory of it might still be missing, but that doesn't mean I didn't make that choice."

"It also doesn't mean it was the right choice," she replies sharply. "You can't throw away your relationship, your career, your whole *life*, just because the move stressed you out."

Somewhere deep in my brain, I know that's not what happened, at least not all of it, but her words snag on that jagged bit of my heart that's still confused, still vulnerable and raw.

"I'm sure it was more complicated than that," I say.

"Not *too* complicated, since you two met up to talk about getting back together. That's the whole reason Matt broke up with April."

April. My mind flickers back to the woman who came into Strange Brew just a few days before. April is Matt's ex-girlfriend. It's like a puzzle piece slides into place in my brain. I can't quite see the full picture, but I know it fits.

"That's not true, Sara," Matt says. "April and I had been having issues for a while."

I look over and catch his expression, how he's staring over at Sara with exasperation. It suddenly occurs to me that while I've been fielding her attempts to get us back together over the past month, Matt has, too.

Garrett leans toward her, lowering his voice. "Let it alone, babe."

"I just don't get it," Sara continues, as if she didn't hear him. "Your whole life is in California, Marnie. Now that Matt is coming back—"

"Sara. Stop!" I cut her off. "This is why I can't tell you anything. You only hear what you want to, and then, once you have your mind set, no one can change it. Yes, you would probably do a better job of running my life than I can, but it's still *my* life. So please listen to me when I say that Matt and I are not getting back together, and I'm not moving back to California."

She stares at me, slack-jawed, and it suddenly feels like we've tipped the scales into something awful, an argument you don't come back from.

Our waiter appears with our entrées, smiling and blissfully unaware of the conversation he has just interrupted.

"Pesto ravioli," he says, then carefully sets the dish in front of me, complete with a full stem of basil for garnish.

"And here are those steamed Maine lobsters."

He floats around the table, placing bright red lobsters, their little claws perfectly placed on beds of kale, in front of Matt, Sara, and Garrett. Three of them. Does that mean there's one left alone in a tank somewhere? One lobster sat and watched as their soulmate was snatched up along with two of their friends?

"Marnie?" Matt murmurs. "Are you okay?"

Lobsters mate for life, I want to remind him. But then I remember that I shouldn't have to.

CHAPTER 27

We leave the restaurant an hour later. Sara barely says a word to me as she gets into an Uber, and Garrett gives me a meek smile as if apologizing before he shakes Matt's hand, then follows her. We wave goodbye, but the car has tinted windows, so I have no idea if they wave back. It leaves a sinking feeling in my chest.

Matt sighs, watching them go, then turns back to me, a weary smile on his face. "Well, that was a clusterfuck."

I smile, letting out a breath that feels like it's been stuck in my throat all night. "It wasn't that bad."

"Says the girl with a head injury," he murmurs wryly.

I let out a dry laugh.

"She'll be okay," he continues, motioning down the street where Sara and Garrett's Uber turned and drove out of view. "Just give her some time."

I don't know if he's right, but I still nod, pulling my coat tighter against the evening chill.

A moment passes before he continues.

"I didn't break up with April just to get back together with you."

I turn to look at him. Under the streetlamp, I can see the bags under his eyes, the weariness in every crease of his forehead.

"Then why did we meet up?" I ask.

"I needed to see a friendly face," he says with a shrug. "April and I had just broken up, and I was feeling lost. And, yeah, maybe I thought we could give it another shot, but that's just because I was so fucking lonely."

I consider, piecing the information into the puzzle in my brain. "Is that why you were so cagey with me when we met up for coffee? Because you were embarrassed?"

"Of course I was embarrassed. You shot me down," he says, then throws me a rueful smile.

My brow furrows. "I did?"

"Yeah." He rakes a hand through his hair, mussing it into something I recognize. "It hurt, but I also get it. I haven't been happy for a while, and you saw that. Even when we were in California, I was struggling."

It's true, I had seen it, just like I can see it now in the lines on his forehead, the shadows under his eyes.

"I thought Boston would fix it," he continues. "Then I thought the problem was us. But after we broke up, I still felt lost. I had this great job, great life, but I just felt . . . empty. I think when I started dating April, I expected her to fix that. When she didn't . . ."

"Collateral damage?"

He lets out a long breath. "Yeah."

Another moment passes before I say, "She came into the café, you know."

His gaze snaps back to me. "She did?"

I nod. "I had no idea who she was, but she acted like we knew each other. Like she needed to apologize, even though she was the one who was sad."

"She and I worked together," he replies. "You two met a few times. For a while, I thought you two would be friends, and then . . ."

I cock my head to the side as I listen, and just like that, facts slide into place in my brain. The details are missing, but I suddenly know the truth, and it fits exactly how I know it should.

"You cheated on me with her," I say. It almost sounds like a whisper.

His head falls to meet his chest.

I wait for the anger to flare up in my chest, the hurt and betrayal, but there's just . . . nothing. Like my heart already knew, it just needed my head to catch up.

"What happened?" I ask.

His gaze slides across the sidewalk. "April and I started our jobs the same week and spent most of our time together, but it was only at work. I even told her about you, and she was excited for all of us to hang out. Then you arrived, and it was okay for a while . . . but then my hours got longer. You weren't happy at Probus. It felt like we were both lost. Living separate lives. It was like, without Sara and Garrett, we didn't know how to play the part. Does that make sense?"

An odd relief settles over my body. The knowledge that I wasn't alone in this.

"Yeah," I reply. "It does."

Matt sighs. "It only happened once. I told you the next day. And we decided to break up. We both moved out of the apartment a couple of weeks later."

I let the words sink in, flow through my brain, connecting to facts I hadn't considered before. "Does Sara know?"

"God no." He shakes his head.

I know what he means. I had kept so much from her, too.

"We were really good at pretending, weren't we?" I say.

"Yeah. We were." He looks over at me, his eyes kind. "Maybe that was our problem. We were so good at pretending, we never really stopped long enough to become friends."

I hadn't considered that before, but it fits. I loved Matt. In a way, I still do. But he was never my friend. Not really. I would never pull him to a street market on a random Saturday morning. Or look forward to spending my day off exploring a museum with him. I never confided in him, or let him see me at my worst. None of the things you build a relationship on.

"Full disclosure?" I say. "I was scared to move out here with you. I had no idea what I was doing with my life and I was worried I would get swallowed up by yours."

He smiles, small and sad. "Full disclosure? I still don't know what I'm doing with my life."

I laugh.

He turns back to the street. "I'm so sorry I cheated on you, Marnie."

The words feel substantial, fitting into that space in my heart that had felt empty for so long.

"I think we were over long before you cheated, Matt."

"Yeah, maybe. But it hurt you. And I never wanted to do that."

I nod, letting another moment pass before I say, "I'm sorry for tonight. I didn't mean to go off on Sara like that."

"It'll be okay. At the end of the day, she just wants us to be happy."

Ben's words from weeks earlier come back to me and I sigh, sending white tendrils through the air in front of me. "You can't fake happiness."

Matt smiles. "Yeah. You've said that before."

I blink. "I have?"

"The night we met up. After I made a fool of myself and asked if you wanted to get back together." He chuckles to himself. "I said I thought we could make each other happy. And you said 'you can't fake happiness.' Then you gave me a hug and left, said you had to get home."

My pulse starts to thunder in my ears. I had repeated Ben's words to Matt before. Which means I knew them before the accident. Which means . . .

"Matt, did I ever give you a copy of *Jane Eyre*?"

"I don't think so. Why?"

"Did we visit the Isabella Stewart Gardner Museum?"

He shakes his head.

"What about Monopoly?" I ask, working hard to keep my voice from shaking. "Did we ever play?"

He smiles again even as his eyebrows stitch together. "Why would we play Monopoly?"

My heart is beating so fast it feels like it's trying to escape from my chest. For weeks I've been chasing clues from my apartment, moments that Sara was so sure tied back to Matt, but he has absolutely no idea what any of it means. But I think I do.

"Matt, I have to go."

"Okay," he says, but I've already turned and started down the road, my eyes scanning for a cab.

I need to get home. I need to talk to Ben.

CHAPTER 28

My body is vibrating as I climb the stairs up to the third floor of my building. I don't even know which emotion comes from where. It's just a mess of confusion, hurt, and an absurd, embarrassing hope, all swirling into a perfect storm inside my rib cage.

Rationality tries to step in—excuse after flimsy excuse about how I could be wrong, how my broken brain has mixed up the facts—but as I arrive at my welcome mat, my heart isn't buying it. My pulse still hammers in my chest, making it almost impossible to fit my key in the dead bolt.

When I finally do, I throw open the front door. I didn't close the curtains before I left, so the streetlamp outside sends long shadows across the room, half illuminating the Persian rug and worn blue sofa. It's familiar, but now it has a completely different feel, like the space has finally removed its disguise.

I don't bother taking off my coat as I turn on the lights and walk over to the trash can. The memory box is still sitting there at the bottom. I reach in to extract it, careful that nothing falls out, then bring it to the sofa. The bottom left corner is marked by an oblong wet patch from where it had been resting against an old tea bag, and I know it will probably stain my dress, but I don't care. I sit down and place the box in my lap, trying to ignore the sound of my pulse in my ears as I lift the lid and drop it to the floor.

Inside are all the items I've been poring over for weeks. The Monopoly dog. The museum map. The movie tickets and the bookstore receipt. And there, underneath all of them, the piece of red-and-white string.

My heart stumbles again.

I know that string. The fact that I didn't recognize it before is almost as startling as where I know it from: Modern Pastry. It's the same string that tied up the box for my lobster tail yesterday. The same one from when Ben bought me a pastry all those weeks ago.

I push the box onto the cushion beside me, as if I just discovered a bomb inside.

This isn't full of memories with Matt. It's full of memories with Ben.

Anger and pain flare together in my chest. How had I missed this? And how could he stand by and watch as my broken brain tried to figure it out, and not say a word?

What would you have done if he had told you? a voice whispers in my head, and I can't help but pause. What if he'd told me the truth that first day I met him? Or when I first revealed all the items in the memory box? He had been a veritable stranger then. Would I have believed it if he told me all these items were from memories with him? Even if I had, I still wouldn't remember him, or whatever it was that had been going on between us.

But I deserved to know, I remind myself. I still do.

So I pick up the shoebox and walk back through my front door to stand in front of Ben's. And then I knock.

Silence.

Then I hear footsteps from inside his apartment. A moment later, the door opens and Ben stands on the threshold. The view reminds me a lot of that first time I knocked, when I was positive I'd woken him up. This time his sweatpants have been replaced by a pair of jeans, and he has on a dark navy sweater. But his expression . . . he looks awful. Bags under his eyes, his mouth slack. Like he hasn't slept in a year.

My heart constricts as I hold the box close to my chest and say, "I need to talk to you."

He stares down at me, the fluorescent light in the hall making the line of his brow look that much more stern. But I can still make out how his eyes are slightly more amber than brown tonight.

He opens the door a bit wider and steps back, giving me space to enter.

I walk into an apartment similar in shape to my own, but slightly bigger, more lived-in. There is a kitchen to the left, small and neatly organized, with a small coffeemaker in the center of the turquoise linoleum counter.

In the living room, there are bookcases along each wall, surrounding the space with a haphazard collection of books stuffed into every available crevice. A dark green sofa sits in the center of the room, its deep cushions worn and uneven, as if they remember the weight of each person who's ever relaxed there. Near the window is a wide armchair with faded plaid upholstery and a book tented over one arm.

There are a couple of lamps on, drenching the space in warm light. It pulls the edges of the room closer, a place carved out for the person who lived there.

I walk to the rows and rows of books along the wall. Ben remains near the door, watching me closely as I scan each title, like he knows exactly what I'm doing. Which is good because I have no idea. I'm just waiting for something to register with my brain. A clue that will tell me I'm not crazy. That everything I've connected in my head is real.

Then I get to the corner. There, behind the armchair, low to the ground, is a pile of old board games. Battleship. Yahtzee. And, at the bottom, a long-faded red box with *Monopoly* printed on the side.

I bend down and put my shoebox on the floor so I can pull the game from the pile, careful so the others don't topple over. When it's free, I place the box in front of me, slowly lift off the top, and remove the board. There's the pile of money, the property cards, the dice, and a small divot that keeps all the metal game pieces together: a top hat, a cat, and a battleship. A penguin and a thimble. But there's no dog.

I turn to where Ben still stands a few feet away in the doorway. He's waiting, and his expression, a mix of anxiety and sorrow, makes my heart lurch.

"The dog is missing," I say. It's impossible to mask the hurt and anger in my voice.

The soft line of his mouth is straight as he nods once. "Yeah. It is."

I knew it would be. Even if my brain didn't remember, my heart knew. That only makes the ache in my chest worse.

"You didn't tell me," I whisper.

"I didn't know it was missing. Not until you told me you found it in your apartment." The corner of his mouth twitches, but it's not the same as I've seen before. He's not holding back a smile, he's forcing one. An apology.

My chest tightens, and I suddenly feel like I can't get enough air. There are too many emotions in there, taking up too much space.

"This whole time, you knew." My voice sounds harsh, but I can't bring myself to care. "Why didn't you tell me?"

He lets out a deep sigh, like the words he's about to say will hurt. "Because you didn't know who I was."

"So you just followed me as I went to every place you and I had been before and you didn't say one word?"

"Marnie—"

"What was going on between us? Were we sleeping together?"

He reels back, like I've hit him. "Jesus, Marnie—"

"Were we?"

His jaw ticks. "No."

"Then what?"

"You were my friend."

"No." I shake my head. "If we were friends, you would have told me the truth!"

"What was there to tell?" he asks, unfamiliar urgency in his deep tone. "That we've lived across the hall from each other for months? That somewhere along the way we became friends? That you were the person I looked forward to seeing the most every day and never had the courage to tell you?" He runs a hand through his dark hair. "Even if I thought that was a good idea, I wasn't sure you wanted to know."

"Why not?"

"Because you had Matt," he says, like he hates having to admit it. "I thought you had gotten back together with Matt."

My brows stitch together. "Why would you think that?"

"A couple of days before the accident, you told me he had reached out about grabbing drinks. I knew he would want you back because he'd be insane not to. That's the night I found you downstairs. You must have come back from meeting him and collapsed. I took you to the hospital and stayed to make sure you were okay. Then they told me I could go home because they'd been in contact with your boyfriend. Matt Amos." He shakes his head. "I thought you had gotten back together. And yeah, that hurt like hell, but I just wanted you to be happy, Marn. Even if it wasn't with me."

My mind flits back to last night and his reaction to seeing Matt's name on my phone, the pain and hurt that ultimately became resignation. Strong, infallible Ben, still believing he isn't good enough. That in the end, he isn't worth choosing.

"But why didn't you tell me once you realized he and I weren't together?" I ask.

"Because at that point, I thought you were remembering. You told me about your mementos, the places you wanted to visit. I thought it was coming back to you. That if I let you go at your own pace . . ."

"And if I never figured it out?" My voice is barely above a whisper.

He's quiet for a minute, his expression stricken. "Then I was happy just to be used by you, Marn."

There it is, the truth I've been searching so long for, and he'd been by my side the entire time.

I look back down into the box, at the items that meant so much to me that I kept them to remember forever. Suddenly, anger gives way to guilt, which is compounded by something tender and frightening.

I'm mad at Ben, yes. But I'm in love with him, too. It's ridiculous that I didn't notice before, because now I can't feel anything else. It's overwhelming, a love that's so big and unwieldy it feels like it could swallow all my other emotions whole.

Ben sits down on the sofa across from me, his face looking tired and hurt. And terrified. Almost as terrified as I feel. But I'm also ready to be brave.

I reach into the shoebox and pull out the Strange Brew napkin, holding it up for Ben to see.

"What's this from?" I ask.

He lets out a sigh. "You had only been living here for a couple of weeks when you started working at Strange Brew. I ran into you in the hall as you were leaving for your first day. You were so nervous, so I decided to stop by after work. You gave me a coffee on the house, and I wrote my classroom number there on the back, just in case you were ever nearby and wanted to stop in."

My heart is tripping over itself now. *Yes, you remember this*, I think. This is one of those things that I know, even though it's like I'm feeling my way in the dark.

"You knew I worked there," I say.

He nods. "I called after the accident to let them know what happened. To make sure they kept you on staff until you were ready to come back."

That's right, Bobbi had said someone had called. It had been Ben all along.

I put the napkin back in the box and hold up the map for the Isabella Stewart Gardner Museum.

"One of my former students was involved with the renovation of one of their galleries," Ben says. "He was really proud, got me a couple of tickets so I could see. You mentioned you hadn't been there before, so I waited until your day off and asked if you wanted to go. We both agreed it wasn't a date, since neither of us was looking for a relationship, but . . ." He cuts himself off, then sighs, like whatever he wanted to say doesn't matter. "We spent hours there, just wandering."

My mind drifts back to the labyrinthine galleries of the museum, how Ben had studied my reaction to each room almost as much as he had studied the art. I had thought he had been trying to understand the motivation behind the trip, but now . . . I let out a shaky breath, putting the map back in the box.

I pull out the movie tickets next.

"You told me how much you loved Grace Kelly," he says. "And how you hadn't been to a movie that wasn't an action film in years. So I slid those two tickets under your door. There wasn't any expectation for you to take me. I knew you had just gone through a breakup and I . . ." He lets out a shuddered breath. "I was hoping it might make you smile. You didn't do a lot of smiling in those first months after you moved in."

Tears burn at the corners of my eyes as his words tug at a memory, something familiar trying desperately to break through.

I put the tickets back and pick up the Brattle Book Shop receipt.

The corner of his mouth ticks up. "I finished some work renovating the research wing at the Boston Public Library and you wanted to see. While we were there, we started talking about our favorite books. I hadn't read *Jane Eyre*, and you hadn't read *The Count of Monte Cristo*, so we decided to trade. Except you didn't trust me not to dog-ear the pages in your copy of *Jane Eyre*, so you bought me my own."

I smile, even as my heart lurches toward him, as if it might escape from my chest. "You read *Jane Eyre* for me?"

He barely nods.

A sob catches in my throat as I put the receipt back. Then I pick up the small metal Monopoly dog, holding it out in the palm of my hand.

He stares at it for a long moment, his eyes softening like he's replaying the memory in his mind.

"That was from the week before the accident. We had tickets to a game at Fenway, but it got rained out before we even left. So you came over and we ordered food. Then you pulled out Monopoly. I had forgotten I even owned it, but you insisted we play. By the time we finished, you had completely wiped me out, but I didn't care. You were smiling and laughing and . . . you looked so beautiful, I couldn't stop thinking about you after you left."

Sara's theory suddenly floats to the top of my mind: If you feel like you're falling in love with someone, play a game of Monopoly together. If you come out the other side still liking the other person, then it was meant to be.

That's why I had pulled out the game. Why I had saved each one of these items.

"I think I was falling in love with you," I say, my voice barely above a whisper.

His throat bobs, as if he's swallowing some emotion down, and he nods slowly. "I think I was falling in love with you, too."

I look back at the contents of my memory box. This road map of a relationship that hadn't even started yet. Memories that meant so much, I had tried my best to hold on to them. And, I realize now, Ben had been helping me to hold on to them, too.

I slowly walk to the sofa and kneel in front of him.

"Sara and I got into a fight at dinner tonight," I say. "Matt is moving back to California, and she expects me to move, too. When I told her no, she pushed back and now I don't even know if we're talking."

Ben doesn't move, though I can see a muscle in his jaw tick amid his stubble.

"But afterward, I did talk to Matt. He told me about what happened the night of my fall. How he invited me to drinks because he wanted to get back together. He also told me that I turned him down. I was never going to get back together with him. I was coming home to you," I say, looking up and forcing him to meet my gaze. "I chose you, Ben. I chose you *twice*. I saved all these memories because they meant something to me. And when I lost all those memories, I still found my way back to you."

I carefully edge my way into his lap. His arms move to make space, hovering around my body. He's so warm, and the smell of sawdust envelops me as I nestle my face in the crook of his neck.

A moment passes before his arms tighten around me, cradling my body against his chest, while my hair absorbs his shuddering breath. Then he turns his head slightly, just enough for our lips to meet.

This kiss is delicate, like he isn't sure if I've forgiven him, if this is okay. So I turn my body to face him, straddling his hips as I deepen it, letting our tongues intertwine as I cradle his face close to mine.

I love him. Of course I love him. I have always known that, haven't I? Despite how much I ignored it, dismissed it as attraction or lust, somewhere in a hidden corner of my heart, I knew. I'd become an expert at pretending away fundamental truths about myself, so good that I still might have missed this. I could have let him slip away and never really known.

He suddenly groans, the sound sending a thrum through my veins. His hands are holding me so tightly I can feel my pulse thrumming where each fingertip digs into my back. It's like a frenetic metronome, keeping steady time while we kiss and nip and sigh. As if making up for lost time is something we can measure.

Suddenly, he shifts, my legs still wrapped around his hips, and it takes me a moment to realize that he's stood up. That he's clutching me tight to his chest as he walks through the nearby doorway to the bedroom.

He kisses my neck as he leans down to place me on top of his sheets. It's like falling into a pool of him—warm flannel and the smell of sandalwood and soap. I close my eyes and let it envelop me as his lips journey to my collarbone, as his hands find their way to the hem of my dress. I can feel the calluses on his fingers as they skirt along my legs until he finally pulls the hem up over my head, throwing it to the floor. A moment later, his fingers tug at my tights, but they don't budge.

"Never thought I'd say this, but I miss the pajama pants," he murmurs.

"I can go grab them if you want," I whisper. "They're on the floor of my bedroom right now."

A low chuckle as he pulls at the tights again, finally bringing them down and off my legs. Then he moves up my body to unclasp my bra. The air is cool against my skin, and I reach for him, desperate to feel his weight against me again, but he pulls back just enough to stare down the length of me. His broad hand slowly spreads out against my sternum, those callused fingers spanning my rib cage. My pulse is thundering in my ears, but I don't move until his gaze comes back up to meet mine. His eyes are hungry, like he's already worked out exactly what he's going to do to me, step by step. By the time he leans down to kiss me again, I'm panting, fingers in his hair and my legs around his hips, demanding more.

He nips and sucks on my lips, then works his way down my neck to my chest, speaking words into my skin that I can't make out. I try to respond, but all that comes out is a mumble, then a gasp as his free hand slowly works its way up my thighs, closer and closer until his fingers graze my underwear, barely ghosting over the spot he had teased before. I think he's going to tease me again, keep me pinned here until I'm begging, but when he leans back, I can see the same desperation in his eyes. Like he needs this just as much as I do.

Then he pushes my underwear aside and sinks his finger inside me.

I gasp, nails digging into his shoulders as he brings his lips to my ear, whispering all the things he wants to do to me as he slips in and out.

At some point I'm not hearing words anymore. His voice is only a deep vibration hitting my core, reverberating out to every inch of my body. Each nerve is independent, humming at its own pitch while my body is left with only pure instinct—fingers raking his hair, gasps and groans escaping from my throat. I'm so disconnected I can't even remember to be embarrassed. All that matters is his lips traveling down my jaw as his fingers work deeper, faster, bringing me to the edge, so close I could fall.

And oh, I think I might. I can feel it there on the horizon, blossoming into my field of vision like a solar flare. Ben must see it, too, how my limbs tense, my breath hitches, because his eyes flare with something hot and alive. Then he bends down between my legs, licking and sucking, and I don't care if the neighbors hear, I cry out. There's nothing I can do about it—every nerve ending is being pulled to that place where his lips are, tightening and tightening while my eyes squeeze shut and my hands grip his hair, grounding myself as it all finally releases, a perfect explosion in Technicolor as I come.

The vibrations are still humming beneath my skin as he kisses along the inside of my thigh, up my stomach, to my neck. When I open my eyes, he's standing at the end of the bed, gaze locked on me as he peels off his T-shirt, as he unbuttons his jeans and lets them fall to the floor. Then he reaches into his nightstand and pulls out a foil wrapper, taking his time as he rolls the condom down his length.

When he's done, I look down at his body and my breath catches. It's like my brain is so hyper-focused on the intricate way his muscles come together, the dusting of hair along his chest, the hard length between his legs, that it forgets my lungs need air. I crawl toward the edge of the mattress, then move to kneel in front of him, so hungry for his kiss that when I lean forward, I almost fall off the bed. Luckily, he catches my shoulders and pulls me close to his chest.

"Where do you think you're going?" he murmurs.

"Nowhere," I whisper. "I'm not going anywhere."

He bends forward so we fall into the bed, and our kiss becomes hungry and deep, teeth and tongue, as our limbs tangle together in the sheets. A moment later, he turns us both and I'm straddling his hips. I can feel him there, hard between my legs. A slight shift of my hips, a rock forward then down, and he slips inside me. He hisses against my mouth, then licks down my neck as my head falls back, relishing the feel of him.

When I finally begin to move, it's slow. Languid strokes that are both torture and ecstasy. I close my eyes as his arms wrap around me, his forehead resting between my breasts, and I know his eyes are closed, too. It's too much, the relief and joy melding together, the insatiable hunger that slowly builds until it takes over again. My fingers disappear into his dark hair. I moan, a strangled sound, and his lips find mine, like he wants that sound for himself. To share every sensation, every ache and throb.

The thought sends me over the edge again, wave after wave of electricity surging through my veins, making my body taut.

"Oh my God, Ben," I cry out.

He groans at the sound of his name. Then he flips us again, his body now over mine as his thrusts become frantic and hard, until finally he shudders, his head against my collarbone as he comes.

For a long moment, all I can hear is the sound of our breathing. My legs are still wrapped around his hips, and his arms are around my back, holding me close.

"I'm still really mad at you," I whisper into his hair.

He nods against my shoulder. "I know."

"But I love you more."

His body shifts enough for him to meet my gaze. His gorgeous face is flushed, his expression sated and tired, and his eyes have that soft edge to them, framing the browns and golds that suddenly look so vibrant. "I love you, too."

"Good." I smile, pushing a few dark strands away from his forehead. "Then you can spend the next fifty or so years making it up to me."

The corner of his mouth twitches as he releases a breath. "I can do that."

CHAPTER 29

There's no ABBA when I wake up the next morning. In fact, as I slowly open my eyes, I realize that it's completely quiet. There's no music, no noise from the street. All I can hear is steady breathing behind me, so close I can feel it warm against my ear.

I ignore how my bangs stick out at odd angles as I turn to see Ben over the edge of the flannel sheets. The sun is only just coming up, casting his bedroom in watery gray light. He's lying next to me, this hulking thing who, even while asleep, manages to know how to arrange himself around my smaller frame. His eyes are closed, and I let myself study the slope of his nose down to his full lips, the stubble covering his chin and jaw.

Then the corner of his mouth twitches with a smile.

"Good morning," I whisper.

"It's not morning until my alarm goes off." His eyes are still closed, and his voice has that rough quality that I first noticed a few weeks ago when he answered the door. I feel it run down the entire length of my body.

"What time is your alarm set for?" I ask.

His arm wraps around me, pulling me closer to his chest. "It's Sunday, so I didn't set one."

"Then what time do you get out of bed?"

His lips move a touch closer to my ear as he murmurs, "Exactly."

I laugh softly, letting my legs intertwine with his as he kisses along my shoulder.

This doesn't feel familiar, but it also doesn't feel brand-new. It's like I was always supposed to end up right here, that I knew it deep down even if the rest of my brain hadn't caught up yet.

For the first time in weeks, maybe even years, everything just feels . . . right. Not the normal I expected, but a new version that I get to define. Maybe that's why I love it all so much.

"Can I ask you a weird question?"

Ben doesn't reply, just peeks through one eye, waiting for me to continue.

"When did I cut my hair?"

"A few weeks before the accident."

"Do you know why?"

He reaches up, smoothing away a few stray strands from my cheek. "Because you wanted a change. And you wanted to make that decision without anyone else's approval."

My heart swells a bit, proud of the past version of myself. "Did I like it?"

"No. You wore a hat every day for two weeks."

I laugh, loud enough that I should be embarrassed, but I'm not in the slightest. "Okay, *that* sounds familiar."

"I had to speed through the end of *Jane Eyre* just to get you out of the apartment to talk to me."

A warm glow fills my chest with the reminder. "That's right. You read *Jane Eyre* for me. What did you think?"

He lets out a heavy sigh. "It's so bad, Marnie."

I reel back. "What?"

"He kept his wife in the attic. The poor woman's only escape was to burn the entire place to the ground—"

"Okay, but—"

"And then he starts pursuing Jane, who is his employee—"

"Fine, but—"

"Then he asks her to marry him, as if—"

I kiss him before he can finish. His mouth opens for mine, slow and languid, as his arms tighten around my body.

"We've already had this argument, haven't we?" I whisper against his lips.

"Yeah," he murmurs. "We have."

"I'm still right, though."

"If you say so."

I lean in to kiss him again, but stop. "Wait, if you read *Jane Eyre*, does that mean this is the second time I've read *The Count of Monte Cristo*?"

He nods. "You borrowed that same copy a few months ago."

"Did I like it?"

"Well, there aren't any wives in the attic or carpenters in sleeveless T-shirts, but you seemed to muddle through."

I smile again, feeling tears forming in the corners of my eyes.

Ben's brow furrows. "What's wrong?"

I know I'm about to start crying, but for the first time in weeks, I don't care. This man read *Jane Eyre* for me. He loved me and he helped me, without expecting anything in return. And on top of all of that, he remembers Kurt Russell's wardrobe from *Overboard*.

"Nothing," I say. "I just really love you, that's all."

I text Sara on my way to work a few hours later.

MARNIE

Hey you. I'm sorry about last night. I never meant to hurt you. Think we can talk before you leave? I'm working today but I'd love it if you could stop by xo

I add a link to Strange Brew's address and press send.

She doesn't reply, but I keep checking my phone, keeping it in the pocket of my apron as I clear tables, restock the sugars and creams, and even manage to help Bobbi make a cappuccino without going through an entire gallon of milk.

At two o'clock, the dining room has thinned out, and I'm checking my phone again when the bell above the door rings out.

"Hello, welcome to Strange Brew," I call out.

"Hi," Sara's voice replies.

I look up and there she is, standing in the doorway. Her dark hair is pulled back in a ponytail, her clothes—a black turtleneck and skirt with a camel-colored coat—are immaculate. But her eyes are puffy and she's not wearing any makeup. In fact, it doesn't look like she slept at all last night.

"Hi," I say.

"I got your text," she says, lifting her chin a little. "Do you have a second to talk?"

"I'd like that," I say, walking out from behind the counter and motioning to a table near the window.

"Do you want a coffee or tea or something?" I ask as we sit down.

"I'm fine," she says stiffly.

I nod. "Listen, I'm sorry about last night."

She rolls her eyes as she looks down at her lap. "No, you're not."

My brow furrows. "Of course I am, Sara. I never—"

"You never wanted to get back together with Matt," she cuts me off, finally meeting my gaze. Except she doesn't look angry or hurt. She looks remorseful.

"No, I don't," I reply.

She nods, not because she agrees, but because it looks like it might ward off her tears. "I think I knew that," she says. "But I convinced myself that if I could just get you two together—if I could make you both see how well it all works when you're together—"

"The four of us worked," I gently cut her off. "But Matt and I couldn't build a relationship around you and Garrett. Especially not on the other side of the country."

"I know. I just miss you so much, Marn. I miss us."

I can feel my own tears start to burn my eyes, too. "I know."

"And I'm having a baby!" she exclaims, her tone suddenly indignant. "How am I supposed to have a baby without you?"

"With lots and lots of drugs," I say.

She laughs, though it sends a few tears down her cheeks.

I reach across the table and squeeze her hand.

"You're my best friend, Sara," I say.

"But best friends are supposed to tell each other everything," she mumbles. "Even the embarrassing stuff. They don't keep secrets because the other one is a control freak who judges everybody."

"You don't judge *everybody*."

"But I *am* a control freak."

"Yeah, but ninety percent of the time, we're grateful for it." I shrug. "You planned my grandmother's funeral when I could barely get out of bed. And helped coordinate my transfer to Boston. You keep us all going, Sara. Without you, we'd be lost. I'd be lost."

"I feel lost without you now," she says, her face finally crumpling with tears.

"I'm right here," I say, offering her a smile.

"Okay." She sniffles. "But no more secrets."

I bring my hand to my heart. "No more secrets."

She nods, then turns to look out the window. "You know, I thought if you and Matt got back together, you'd move back to California with him. You'd be close by when the baby came. It would be so perfect."

"Maybe. It's just not what I want," I say.

"So what do you want?" she asks, offering me a small smile.

I sigh. "I don't know."

"No, really, I promise not to give advice or hijack your plan or—"

"I'm serious, Sara. I don't know. I still don't have my memories back, or any idea what I was doing in Boston besides making coffee," I cut her off, barely curbing a smile. "But I'm enjoying figuring it out."

"Good," she replies. I can tell it's taking all her willpower not to offer her two cents, and my smile broadens.

"But one thing I can tell you," I say, "is that even though I'm not moving back to California, I promise I'll be there for every milestone with this baby."

Her bottom lip begins to wobble. "Really?"

"We're family, Sara. You're never getting rid of me."

She nods, using a nearby napkin to wipe away her tears. "You know, it's really annoying to have this conversation when I look like my face has been stung by a hundred bees and you're glowing like you just had about a hundred orgasms."

I laugh nervously. "Well . . ."

Her tears instantly stop as she perks up. "What?"

"I shouldn't—"

She holds up her hand to shut me up. "No more secrets, remember?"

I smile. "Yes, I remember."

"Good," she says, leaning forward and arching an eyebrow at me. "Now shut up and tell me *everything*."

CHAPTER 30

I leave work an hour later feeling wrung out, emotionally and physically. Sara had stayed for another hour, and I filled her in on Ben and all the details I had withheld over the past few weeks to spare her feelings while she was hyper-focused on Matt. She even listened intently when I told her about my upcoming photography class, and demanded that I fly out to LA to take her baby's first professional portrait.

Still, by the time I unlock the front door of my apartment building in the North End, exhaustion has pooled behind my eyes. The lobby smells faintly of that familiar lemon cleaner, and I actually find myself taking in a deep breath. Enjoying it.

Home, I think. This is home.

I pull off my knit cap, sending my hair out and up and in every direction, then start forward toward the stairwell. I almost miss a glance at the mailboxes, my body already planning the route upstairs, the knock on Ben's door, the feel of his arms around me as he pulls me into a hug. But then something catches my eye—one of the mailboxes is close to overflowing.

Mailbox 3A.

Oh my God. When was the last time I checked my mail?

I scramble over, picking through my key ring until I find the smallest one and slip it into the lock. As soon as I turn it, a pile of envelopes pours out—only about half of which I manage to catch—while even more remain stuck inside, their corners jutting out like they've been trying to escape for weeks. They probably have.

Most of it is exactly what you'd expect. Grocery store flyers. Credit card offers with my name printed optimistically across the front, like they have more faith in me regaining access to my bank accounts than I do. It all feels impersonal, proof that life keeps advertising itself even when you're not paying attention.

Then I see another envelope.

It's thicker than the rest, cream-colored, with my name typed neatly across the front. The return address reads: PHOTO-RAMA.

My heart gives a small, surprised kick. It's the pictures from my 35 mm camera.

I shove the other mail back in the mailbox, then rip open the envelope. The photos are neatly stacked in a paper sleeve and I pull them out, careful not to get my fingerprints on them.

The first one is of Salem Street at dusk. Bova's Bakery glows against the evening light, illuminating the line of people waiting to get inside.

The next photo is of the dining room at Strange Brew, then the next is of Bobbi, eyes crossed as he makes a face for the camera. There's one of Claire, too, then a few of them together.

Then I flip to the next photo and my breath falters.

It's Ben. He's relaxed, his reading glasses tucked into the collar of his sweater as he glances over to someone off camera. As I look closer, I realize I recognize the room. This was taken in the gallery with the missing paintings at the Isabella Stewart Gardner Museum.

Did he know I took this photo? Or the next one, of him sitting on his sofa, reading *Jane Eyre*. Or the next, of him at Haymarket, surveying a selection of produce. Or the next, of him in Harvard Yard, looking up at the gnarled branches of the trees.

These are my memories. The moments I had been chasing for weeks. The fall might have stolen the negatives, but here are the prints. This is the proof.

I rush upstairs, past the second floor and the echoing notes of "Fernando," to the third floor. Ben's door is locked but I pound on it until I hear his footsteps. He pulls it open, wearing that pair of sweatpants I love and a hoodie, and offers me that rare smile, warm and intense and just for me.

"You okay?" he asks.

"Look," I say, handing him the pile of photographs.

He takes it, flipping through them one by one, brow furrowed. By the time he gets to the bottom, his expression is awestruck.

"These are incredible. I didn't even know you took these," he says.

"I know," I say, my smile returning. "I'm a really good photographer."

"Yeah, you are." His voice is soft, a mix of astonishment and pride.

Somehow, my smile broadens even more as he wraps his arms around me, lifting me up and walking slowly back into his apartment as he murmurs words of praise into my ear. How he's proud of me. How he never doubted me for a minute.

Something warm and glowing and alive hums in my chest. It takes me a moment to recognize what it is: happiness.

I'm happy, I think, as Ben lays me down on his bed and whispers how much he loves me. As I curl into his body and bury my face in his neck. *Right now, in this perfect moment, I'm happy.*

Then Ben leans back and pushes my errant bangs away from my face, only to have a few strands bounce back out and poke him in the eye.

I smile and arch up to kiss him. And he kisses me back.

This is happiness.

How many mistakes did I have to make to get here? There were so many wrong turns, so much doubt and second-guessing, but somehow, it still led me to this. Is that destiny? I don't know. But right now, it feels pretty damn close.

EPILOGUE

Eight Months Later

"Do you want the good news or the bad news?" Ben asks, his voice low and serious despite the fact that he's wearing his favorite sweatpants and a navy blue Paradise Cove Beach Café hoodie while sitting just a few yards from the Pacific Ocean. It's too dark to see the water's full expanse, but the steady roar of the waves has been the soundtrack to the past few hours as we set up our campsite on the beach.

I turn to where he's sitting next to me in a low beach chair, his reading glasses perched on his nose as he studies his glowing phone screen. If the hard line his brow makes across his face is any indication, I'd almost think he was deciphering some sort of sacred ancient text and not the rules and regulations for Point Mugu State Park's beach campgrounds.

"Let's go with the good news," I reply.

"Well, we're in compliance," Ben says, motioning to the campfire crackling in front of us. "Designated metal fire ring, clear perimeter, water on hand. We're good."

I nod like I had any part in helping with that. Instead, I've been organizing, then reorganizing our snack cooler since we arrived on the beach that afternoon. "So what's the bad news?"

"Apparently we have to be on the lookout for mountain lions," he replies grimly.

I shrug one shoulder, pulling my hair up in a ponytail. I might still be chasing the perfect shade of blond, but at least it's long enough now that I can pull it back away from my face. "Okay."

He barely moves except to look at me over the rim of his glasses. "Okay?"

I wave indiscriminately at the beach ahead and the rolling mountains that rise up in the darkness behind us. "We're in *nature*, Ben. This is their habitat. Technically, we're infringing on their territory, so the least we can do is stay out of their way like you would do for a deer or . . . I don't know, what's a dangerous animal in Boston that you should avoid at all costs?"

"Bruins fans," he murmurs.

I laugh and, despite the stern line of his brow, the corner of Ben's mouth ticks up, too.

As soon as Sara scheduled her C-section—she refused to wait for nature to take its course—Ben and I booked tickets to Los Angeles. It wasn't until I started planning our itinerary, a long list of all the places back home that meant something to me and which I wanted to share with him, that I realized the last few days of our trip corresponded with something else: my grandmother's birthday. And not just any birthday, her eighty-fourth. Her Jupiter return.

It was Ben's idea to book a campsite right on the beach so we could light a small campfire (current fire level permitting, of course) and celebrate her birthday at the stroke of midnight, just like she had done for my first Jupiter return all those years ago. Cynthia Aldridge may not be here to set her intentions, but I want to share my intentions with her. The first is to be a good godmother to the newest member of our found family unit.

Sara and Garrett welcomed Meadow Elizabeth, the most perfect seven-pound, three-ounce human being to ever be born, on May 16, right on schedule. Ben and I were there to meet her, along with Matt, who drove up from San Diego for the weekend.

I was surprised how much it felt like old times. The four of us fell into a familiar rhythm, one that seamlessly expanded to include Ben. Somehow, even the addition of things like diaper shopping and troubleshooting issues with Sara's new breast pump felt natural. And I guess it was. We were growing and evolving just as we were supposed to.

Once Sara and Meadow arrived home from the hospital five days later, and I had triple-checked the nursery for the second time, Ben and I loaded our rented truck with Garrett's camping gear and drove up the Pacific Coast Highway to Point Mugu.

As much as I would have loved to reenact the moment from my twelfth birthday exactly as I remembered, rules and regulations meant that if we wanted an open fire, we had to move to where there were designated fire rings available. But that also meant camping on the beach, so after a quick detour to the Paradise Cove Beach Café for lunch, we drove up and claimed the perfect spot, just a few yards from the water. Now we had a Nordisk Oppland 3.0—"the Cadillac of tents," as Garrett described it—set up beside us and a fire roaring at our feet. All that's left to do is wait for midnight.

I reach into the pocket of my hoodie and pull out my new iPhone, the one I bought two months after the accident when it was clear that I couldn't sit around and wait to remember my passcode before moving on with my life. If my memories ever come back, my old phone is waiting in the drawer of my desk, holding steady at seven failed passcode attempts. In the meantime, it's time to move forward.

I press the side button and the screen illuminates.

11:59 p.m.

"One more minute," I say.

Ben looks over, giving me that almost-smile I love so much.

I'm glad I get to show him this version of California. Not just the glossy neighborhood in Burbank where Sara and Garrett live, or the areas usually visited by tourists, like Hollywood and Santa Monica, but the wild and reckless bit that defined my childhood. Wind that smells like kelp, sand that sneaks into the cuffs of your jeans and follows you home, the jagged edge of the land where it falls away into the ocean. Where my grandmother taught me the names of constellations, most of which I don't remember, but it doesn't matter. I remember her.

The fire pops, sending a brief spray of sparks upward. Ben's attention snaps to it, his eyes tracking their glowing arc to make sure they die before they travel further away. When they land safely in the sand, he exhales, even as I smile. I'm not worried about the fire. To be honest, I'm not worried about much of anything, which might be a first.

Suddenly, my phone lights up and the soft, trilling sound of my alarm rings out.

It's midnight.

Ben stands up, then offers me his hand as I do the same. He doesn't let go once I'm on my feet, just intertwines his fingers with mine and gives a soft squeeze as he looks up into the darkness.

"Happy birthday, Cynthia," he says.

I look up, too. The night sky is a mess of stars the way I always loved when I was growing up. A giant glowing clump here, a scattering there. It's like the universe accidentally spilled them out over the darkness and is just too lazy to pick them all up. But there's still order to it, a rhythm that I can't see but know is there.

Jupiter has returned to the exact same spot in the sky as when you were born, my grandmother's voice whispers in my head. *That deserves a celebration.*

"Happy birthday, Grandma," I whisper.

We stand there for a long moment, listening to the waves as they roar up the beach in a steady pulse. Then Ben turns to me again.

"So how does this work?"

I smile. "You just tell the universe what you want to manifest this year. What's important to you. What you want to welcome into your life."

His brow furrows, as if he's still not completely clear on the goal.

"Here, I'll go first," I say, then I turn my head back up to the stars. "I will travel to Japan!"

When I turn back to Ben, he's watching me, the corner of his mouth slightly ticked up again.

"Your turn," I say.

He sighs, and I almost think he's going to come up with some excuse, but instead, he seems to consider, then tilts his head back to shout, "I'm going to go with her to Japan!"

"And Spain!"

"And Spain, too!"

I laugh, turning to him again. "You have to come up with your *own* intentions."

"And what if I intend to be with you?" he asks, his deep voice becoming almost a whisper.

I squeeze his hand. "You can multitask."

He chuckles to himself, then looks up again as he seems to consider.

"I'm going to play pickleball with my mom!" he finally yells.

I laugh. Joyce Martin has been trying to convince him to come up to Rockport and sit in on her pickleball team for months now. Ben had used every excuse under the sun to avoid it, even tried to pawn the responsibility off on Lauren, but since she found out she was pregnant in February, she had the perfect excuse. Now it was all on Ben.

"I'm going to make a photography portfolio. And sign up for that pottery class in Cambridge!" I shout upward.

"You want to try pottery?" Ben asks.

I roll my eyes. "You can't talk about your intentions."

"Why not?"

"It dilutes the energy needed for manifestation," I say, even putting on my grandmother's dreamy voice as I recite her words.

"Of course," he deadpans. Then he tilts his head upward again. "I'm going to try pottery with her!"

I can't help but laugh again.

My grandmother would have loved him, I think. Sure, she would have teased him relentlessly about the campfire permit, then asked what his sign was (Virgo), and nodded knowingly like that explained everything. But she would have smiled, too, because she would see me smiling. She would know how happy I was with him because I would have told her all the memories we've made together. How he walked me to the grocery store that first day I was home from the hospital. How he bought me a burner phone and invited me to a Red Sox game. Showed me his favorite painting and told me all his stories, even the most painful ones. How we ordered takeout on our first date and I forced him to play Monopoly, even though he hated it. How he had laughed when I finally had enough money to build hotels on Park Place and Boardwalk, so touched by my excitement he didn't even care that it meant he would lose. How—

Wait.

I blink, forcing my brain to return to the memory. Yes, it's there, as if it has always been. It's like someone's adjusted the focus, making the details sharp and clear. Ben and I are sitting on the floor of his apartment, a Monopoly board between us. I'm the top hat and he's the little dog. The TV is on but muted, playing scenes of the rain delay at Fenway, but the two of us barely notice. In that moment, all I know is that I don't want it to ever stop raining, just like I never want to leave that apartment. I was already falling in love with him then.

I'm starting to remember.

Tears prick the backs of my eyes as I turn to Ben. It takes him a moment to notice. When he does, his eyebrows draw together.

"You okay?"

"Yeah," I whisper. "I'm just really happy."

His eyes take on a soft edge, and he squeezes my hand again. A long moment passes, then he turns his face back to the sky.

"I'm going to ask this woman to marry me!" he bellows.

I still, my tears halting as my heart explodes into a hundred points of light in my chest. "What did you say?"

"Sorry, I can't talk about my intentions," he says with a heavy sigh. "It dilutes the energy needed for manifestation."

Then he smiles and pulls me into his arms, drawing me up and placing a soft kiss on my lips.

I melt into him as my grandmother's voice fills my head: *Just be still and let the magic find you.*

But this doesn't feel like magic. It feels earned. More than a dozen doctors' appointments, endless tests. A hundred small choices that never feel like destiny, but like effort.

There is nothing mystical about that. And yet, this feels miraculous.

Maybe that was the secret all along. Destiny is real—we just build it ourselves. And in that way, my grandmother was right after all. The magic isn't what happens to us. It's that we keep going anyway.

ACKNOWLEDGMENTS

Full disclosure: I am very bad at asking for help. This comes as a shock to literally no one who knows me, but still somehow catches me off guard at the worst moments, such as when several life events pop up in the middle of writing a book. Luckily, I have an incredible group of people supporting me, without whom this story would never have made it into your hands.

First and foremost, thank you to my editor, Molly Gregory, whose guidance, patience, and support kept me going more than she will ever know. You not only made this a better book, Molly, you made me a better writer. And to the entire team at Gallery: Jennifer Bergstrom, Sally Marvin, Carrie Feron, Jessica Roth, Fallon McKnight, Matt Attanasio, Christine Masters, Danielle Mazzella di Bosco, Julia Jacintho, and Stacey Sakal—thank you for your endless support and enthusiasm.

To my agent, Joëlle Delbourgo, your faith in me is boundless and I can only hope to live up to it. Seriously, where would I be without you? Thank you. And to Dr. Erin Reynolds, for sharing your knowledge with me and making sure Marnie's journey was as authentic as possible—I appreciate it so much.

To my husband, Tom—the Wendy to my Jack. Thank you for your endless patience, your well-timed hugs, and for understanding the signs of a dysregulated nervous system and never holding it against me. I love you. And to Poppy and Henry, the two most incredible human beings I have ever met, thank you for showing me how to face life with confidence and humor. I'm so honored to be your mom. Love you forever and ever, and then some.

To Audrey, for not only inspiring this story but showing me every day what it means to advocate for yourself, to fight for change, and to never stop laughing. You really are magic. And to our entire crew: Jenna, Jessica, Nicole, and Zoran, for offering laughs, pep talks, and well-timed memes no matter the continent, thank you.

To my mom and dad, Joan and Kevin, as well as Conor, Joowon, and Harper, for the love and support even when I was holed up from the outside world. And to my UK family, who are the best cheerleaders in the world—thank you.

And finally, to you. Thank you for reading, for sharing, or for just picking up this book and flipping to the acknowledgments. Never forget that you're magic, too.

ABOUT THE AUTHOR

Emily Harding is the author of *How Freaking Romantic* and one-half of the writing duo behind the For the Love of Austen series, including *Emma of 83rd Street*, *Elizabeth of East Hampton*, and *Anne of Avenue A*. She is a graduate of Emerson College with degrees in both creative writing and film. After working over fifteen years in television development and production, she found her way back to writing.